MW00399291

THE GUARDIANS

THE BEAUDREAU SERIES BOOK ONE

J.A.M. CORMIER

The Terra Alliance - The Guardians - The Beaudreau Series (Book One)

Copyright © 2024 J.A.M. Cormier

Published by Magic Judy Publishing

Editors and Proofreaders: Anna Lisa Vitale and Ashleigh Voros of Split Leaf Saturdays

Cover Design: Mayhem Cover Creations

This is an original publication of Magic Judy Publishing

Authored by J.A.M. Cormier

ISBN: 978-1-7382371-2-8

TRIGGER WARNINGS
RECOMMENDED FOR 18+

The topic of slavery and abduction, including with children, comes up and is ongoing, although it is not violent in nature. However, it could upset anyone sensitive to the topic. There are suggestions of abuse, however nothing overt. There is light violence and weapons use. Military situations are part of the main storyline and there is some death, albeit only with background characters.

And there is sex ... yes clear and explicit sex.
The scenes are obvious, but the book is not all sex *(sorry)*!

I've tried to keep the story a fun read, even with the sometimes serious topics. Each book will centre around a different couple, but the sci-fi plot will continue through each couple's journey. I'll apologise ahead for the cliffhanger; well ... **not really** ... it's necessary as each ending leads into the next story and couple. At least you get an HEA for Jesse and Zersus (but who knows how things will go!!!)

I hope you enjoy The Terra Alliance
The Beaudreau Series | The Guardians | Book One

MUSIC PLAYLISTS

JESSE'S PHYSICAL TRAINING PLAYLIST

Pull Up to the Bumper - *Grace Jones*
How Deep Is Your Love - *Calvin Harris, Disciples*
Play That Funky Music - *Wild Cherry*
Escape (feat. Hayla) - *Kx5, deadmaus5 & Kaskade*
Doing It To Death - *Fred Wesley and the J.B's (James Brown)*
I Feel Good (feat. Anthony Watts & DJWS) - *Pitbull*
Magic Carpet Ride (Steir's Mix) (feat. Philip Steir) - *Steppenwolf*
Lose My Breath - *Destiny's Child*
Chase Me - *Con Funk Shun*

SPAR TS-5 BAND PERFORMANCES

Drive (feat. Delilah Montagu) - *Black Coffee & David Guetta*
Trouble with My Lover - *Robert Plant & Alison Krauss*
Drink You Away - *Justin Timberlake*

PROLOGUE
JESSE (AGE 6 - YEAR 2036)

Not now, Dad, let me sleep.

Huh? Who stole my pillow? And blanket? Had to be one of my brothers.

Wait, what? Where did my bed go? How did I get on the floor?

It's so cold.

I shiver, rubbing my eyes and realising this isn't the floor in my room.

If I wasn't awake before, I am now.

I look down; I'm still wearing my pink jammies, but why am I not in my bed?

I try harder to focus. I rub my eyes again to get rid of the sleepies. Everything seems so dark. I look around. I'm alone in a strange place.

Okay, I'm scared.

I sit up, grip my knees and try not to cry.

Where is my Dad? And my brothers, where are they?

I don't like this place.

I try to remember last night. When I went to bed, my Dad tucked me in. A little later than usual because I tricked him into a few extra stories before I agreed to sleep. That's the last thing I remember.

My eyes adjust a bit more to the dark, and that's when I see I'm not alone. Beside me is another girl. I think she's six, like me. Gee, I don't know.

How did we both get here? I'm kinda glad I'm not alone.

I look past the strange girl and see them; BARS. This is bad. This is really, really bad. I think we're in a cage. Who would put us in a cage? That's just wrong.

I was getting more scared.

"Psst, honey, are you okay?"

I look over my shoulder and see a pretty blonde lady with a baby in her arms. But behind her were tons—and tons—and tons of other people.

Oh boy, this is SUPER bad.

I nod. "I'm okay."

I'm sure I sound like I'm going to cry. I can't help it. I'm trying hard not to. I have to be tough like my brothers.

"What about your friend?" She nods to the other girl beside me.

"She's not my friend. I've never seen her before." I crawl to her. I shake her a bit to see if she will wake up. She moans a little and opens her eyes. She blinks at me. I can tell she is confused like I was when I woke up. Oh no! She's gonna cry. If she does I'm gonna too. She looks at me again, down at her PJs, and I know she figured out she isn't home.

"Don't cry, you're not alone, I'm here and so are they." I point over my shoulder. The girl looks to where I'm pointing, and her eyes widen. Like me, she's surprised by the people in cages. She has to be really scared. She grabs me, hugging me so tight. She is crying crazy hard. I'm trying not to.

I'm really not much of a hugger. Who would be as the only girl with five brothers? They're such a pain. Okay, Dad hugged me all the time for all the "mom hugs" I was missing, but I never took to them. Too girlie. But this is different. She's a girl. I let her hug me. She needs it and, if I'm being honest, I do too.

She starts to calm down a bit and relaxes with her hug. Thank goodness, because it was really hard to breathe.

"Do you know where we are?" I ask the lady in the cage beside us.

"We are on a Nomad ship but where we are exactly, I have no idea."

Oh boy, super bad. I want to cry more now.

Nope, no crying. *You must be tough for you and your new friend.*

"How did we get here?"

The lady looks sad. "I don't know, hon. Everyone came in at different times. I was just before you with this little guy. You two were just a few hours ago. Everyone, including me, was unconscious when we got here. That's all I know."

I take a deep breath. I hate being scared. I whisper to the girl with me, "What's your name?"

"Katie," her voice trembles and she rubs the side of her face. *Please don't cry anymore.*

"I'm Jesse. I'm six," I said, holding three fingers on each hand. It was what I did with my brothers. Gosh, I miss them. I hope they are okay. "How old are you?" I try not to show her how scared I am.

She raises one hand, indicating five fingers. I'm older and, even though I'm a girl, I'll protect her. That's what my brothers would expect me to do.

"How are we going to get out of this?" she asks me.

I just shake my head and shrug. I'm smart, but not *that* smart.

I'm about to ask the lady with the baby what her name is when I hear a noise coming from the door to this awful place. Everyone in the cages backs up, so Katie and I copy them and move back, towards the lady's side of our cage.

The weirdest-looking people I've ever seen walk through the door. I look at Katie and she shrugs, wrinkling her nose as if she's had a whiff of something terrible. I'm sure she is thinking what I am—gross.

The two *things* stand right in front of our cage. The bigger one of the two looks at me really weird. He is super creepy. He has blue skin. Instead of clothes, his body is covered in scales going up and down. Wait, I think those *are* clothes. Yikes, is he wearing a person? No, that can't be right, but his clothes match his skin. It looks like a coat with a bunch of scaly swirls that look like his skin. His head has those weird swirls, too. Even has them around his yellow eyes and it makes them really creepy. His skin colour is different shades of blue. Not a pretty blue like the sky, it reminds me of a dirty pair of old grubby blue jeans. Boy, he gives me the shivers. Creepy Blue Guy, that is what I'm going to call him.

He won't stop looking weird at me like he wants to eat me. Yikes, I think the hair on my arms is standing up. I'm probably just imagining it cause he kinda scares me. But then he looks at Katie for just a second. Okay, so yeah, it is just me he is creeping on—yikesaroni!

The two weirdos move to the other side of the cargo bay, and the lady beside us whispers, "He has a particular interest in you." She looks sad.

"Why me?" I don't get it. I'm nothing special out of what had to be a gazillion people in cages.

The lady asks us to move closer to her, so we slide over. Katie is still hanging onto my arm super tight. We don't want to get caught moving by the creepy blue guys.

"You don't understand him?" the lady asks. Both me and Katie shake our heads.

"I guess you weren't given translators like the rest of us. It helps in understanding them. I don't know if that's actually a good thing though," she says. She's humming to the baby in between talking to us."We've been here for longer. He told his companion that you two girls were chosen and put aside for him, but he is only looking to take you with him." She looks at me with concern.

That isn't good. I might only be six, but my dad always told me about evil people.

"He's Nomad, right?" I ask.

The lady nods.

He can think what he wants, but I won't go. I will do what my dad says. Anyone tries to take you, fight back. I am not going anywhere.

Katie and I watch them as they walk around the cages. The creep is giving orders to the other guy, pointing at people and probably telling him what to do with them.

We are all in trouble. And really, what could I do? Nothing, I'm a little girl with a tiny bit of Judo training. I'm scared. I don't want anything to happen to me. I don't want anything to happen to my new friend, Katie. And the lady with the baby. She's so nice.

I softly ask, "Is the baby yours?"

She replies, "No, he was here when I arrived. No one else could get him to stop crying. I recently lost my newborn daughter and husband, so I guess he naturally took to me." That made the lady cry a little, and when I glance at Katie, I can see she is wiping away a tear, too.

"Does he have a name?"

She shakes her head.

I look at Katie, turn back to the lady and say, "Let's give him a name."

The lady smiles while she closely watches the two creepy blue guys. "I think that's a great idea. My name is Alice, by the way. What do you think is a good name?"

Katie says her three brothers are Zane, Samuel, and Jackson. What great names. Alice turns to me and asks, "What about you, Jesse? Do you have any brothers or sisters?"

I nod. "I have five brothers. Cain's the oldest, then Nate, then Alex and Adam are identical twins, and then Danny—he's my twin. My mom died when I was two in a car accident. So I'm the only girl with a bunch of boys. My dad says I look like her."

Katie looks to make sure the two creepies are not too close. She has a tiny smile on her face. "Wow. I thought I had a lot of brothers." She looks like she is going to cry again. I know why; like me, she doesn't know where her brothers are.

I look at the small bundle and approach the cage to see him. Katie follows behind me. I reach out, and he grabs my finger in a tight grip.

"He's so cute. And strong." I stroke his hand.

Alice looks at us both. "He likes you. He didn't like being touched by anyone else."

I smile at that thought and suddenly, a name pops into my head.

"Maverick," I say. "My brothers Cain and Nate love this one movie with a character using that name. They said they wanted to be Mavericks." I sadly smile, thinking about them and that stupid movie.

Alice nods. We look at Katie, and she nods. Alice smiles and looks down at the little bundle. "I think that's a perfect name."

We continue to watch the creepy blue guys move towards the end of the cages, and I can't help but think I want my brothers to meet this little guy. That might never happen. Would I even see them again?

As if Alice can read my thoughts, she says, "Remember, they're losing the war. It's over. Someone will come for us."

She sounds so sure; gosh I hope she's right.

And what about the rest of my family? I can't stop thinking about them. I hope they aren't on a ship like this one. That would be awful.

I watch the two creepy blue guys start to make their way back to us when the door opens. A whole boatload of the blue guys come running inside. They're ranting and raving. I hear screaming and yelling outside the door. And wait, is that gunfire? I look over at Katie, and we both look at Alice. She smirks and says, "I think the cavalry has arrived."

Huh? I have no clue what she means, but I'm hoping it's a good thing.

The Nomad disappear quickly through the door. It shuts, and we hear it lock. "Do you think they locked us in? They wouldn't drop us in space or something, would they?" I say the first thing that comes to my mind, and I can see it freaks everyone out. Whoops! I hope they only locked the door.

We can faintly hear the noise out there. I hold my breath.

Then, we hear knocking on the door. It can't be the Nomad because why would they bother knocking? It's their place; wouldn't they just walk right in? Yep, they would just walk right in. So nope, they wouldn't knock. I do the only thing I can think of … I yell, "We're in here!!"

Everyone else starts yelling, too. The knocking continues. It's like they are letting us know they hear us.

What is only minutes seems like forever, and eventually, the door opens. In comes a group of men. I think they are here to help us.

They rush over and start opening the cages. Katie is crying beside me. She isn't much of a talker, but she can squeeze hard when she hugs, like right now. I let her and tell her it will be okay. While we might be in space somewhere, at least we are with regular people like us.

A young guy comes over to our cage. I'm pretty sure he's one of those other people that dad says has been helping us with the creepy blue guys. His uniform is different from most of the others he's with. He smiles at us. He's kinda cute. I've never seen any of those people before, but I heard they were tall. Boy, is he ever. He has long dark hair, black eyes and lashes, and his skin looks tan. Weird when you think about it cause they're from space. Uh, no sun there, right?

He tries to speak to us, but we can't understand. He calls over to another man. He reminds me of my dad. He looks friendly and smiles. He crouches down at the entrance of the cage, which they managed to open, and says, "Hello ladies, my name is Matt Williams and this is my young friend, Danlon. You can't understand him?" He asks.

"No, we don't have what that lady calls translators," I answer and point to Alice.

Mr. Williams looks over at her and smiles. "What's your name?" he asks her.

"I'm Alice, and the girls are Jesse and Katie," she indicates to us," and this little guy, the girls named Maverick. He looks to be about six months."

Oh boy, the look on Mr. Williams's face. He looks upset. His expression reminds me of my dad when my brothers did something super dumb, which was pretty much all the time.

Danlon indicates with his hands that he's coming in. Katie and I nod. She's still crying, but not as much. I think she realises they are saving us. Danlon goes to her and picks her up in his arms. He extends his other hand to me. He slowly leads us out of the cage. He's too tall to stand up in the cage. As soon as we were outside of it, he stands up straight and lifts Katie up high into his arms. He puts his other arm around my shoulder. I look up at him and smile. I like him and Mr. Williams a lot.

I look over my shoulder and see the friendly Mr. Williams leading Alice, the baby, and several boys out of their cage. Others let everyone else out. Gosh, there are so many and most are kids like Katie and me.

Danlon calls out to Mr. Williams and says something to him that we can't understand but Alice does and stops walking. At first, I'm not sure why. Then, it occurs to me that they probably don't want us to see what happened outside this room. I don't know about Katie or Alice, but I never want to see another creepy blue guy again.

They lead us to sit along a wall, as far away from the cages as we can. They give us water and some food. It tastes like a protein bar. It's not bad, and I am so hungry.

While we wait, I watch Mr. Williams going back and forth, in and out of the room. He is a very tall man with thick brown hair and a full beard. A few people call him Lieutenant. I guess he's important. What I like best about him is his eyes. They are a nice, warm brown and crinkle like my dad's on the sides when he smiles.

Another older man comes in as we sit here. Mr. Williams introduces him, "Everyone, this is Colonel Cummings. He's going to let you know what will happen from here."

Oh boy, one look at the Colonel's face and it gives me a bad feeling. Something is wrong but none of them look like they want to tell us. Sometimes, I hate being six. I bet my brothers would know. They knew everything. Well, maybe not Danny because he was the same age as me, but Cain would know for sure.

The Colonel guy clears his throat. "There is no easy way to say this. Home as you knew it — well, it's a bit different."

He's having a tough time continuing when Alice asks, "How long were we gone?"

Easy question, right, but the Colonel doesn't look like he wants to answer.

Mr. Williams answers, "You were gone varying times. Some of you have been missing for weeks, and some only a few days. It appears it went in the order you were in the cages, with these two young ladies being the last two taken." He glances over at Katie and me.

Yep, that's what we were, taken! Mean creepy blue guys.

"How far from Earth are we?" Alice asks again.

"This ship only made it to Jupiter, so not too far, but far enough not to be affected — umm, Colonel, do you want to explain?"

The Colonel stands there for a minute, runs his hand over his face, shakes his head and leaves. "You tell them, I just can't."

Mr. Williams looks at us. He doesn't want to tell us either but got stuck doing it. What could be so bad?

"I don't know how to explain this," he pauses, "Earth is not the same as it was when you were taken."

I don't understand that. What does he mean?

Alice asks, "What?"

I think I got it, maybe? I tilt my head and look up at him. "It's because of them, isn't it?"

Mr. William looks at me with surprise. "Yes, it is — sort of." He hesitates again but then takes a deep breath and begins. "I'll try and explain the best I can. Our Krean friends," he indicates Danlon and a couple of other Kreans I hadn't noticed until now, "showed up to help us fight the Nomad about six months ago. Does everyone follow so far?"

We nod, and there are many yeses.

"Okay, well," another sigh, "the Nomad realised with the combined forces of us and the Kreans, they would lose the war against us. As they had done to the Krean's home planet when they were losing, they planned to destroy Earth. The Krean's would not let them do that and developed a way to stop them.

"Without getting overly technical, the Kreans designed a weapon to counter the effect of the Nomad's explosive device." He glances at us, and everyone nods.

I notice Danlon looks uncomfortable, so I walk over and grab one hand; Katie grabs the other, and we drag him over to sit with us. He's a big guy, but still young. He looks like he was in pain. I feel awful for him and can tell it bothers Katie, too. She snuggles up next to him.

Mr. Williams continues, "Well, there was an unfortunate side effect to the combination of the Nomad's weapon that they planted at Earth's core and the Krean's weapon that was designed to counter it."

Everyone is silent. I have a feeling what happened is just more bad news. I don't even have to look at Mr. Williams's face.

"The result of the combination of the two weapons is we now have four planets; well, five if you include the moon as the magnetic centre that holds them all in place. What we technically describe as a divergence of Earth occurred. Earth disappeared and then instantly reappeared in four different formations."

He stops, takes a deep breath, and gathers himself. "We have no idea what ended up where. It's all a mess right now."

Alice speaks up again, "So, does that mean our homes are gone?"

Mr. Williams winces. "Honestly, we don't know. We have no idea who ended up where. What survived and what didn't. The extent of what is left is ..." He hangs his head, and everyone sits silent.

I glance around. Almost everyone is young, right down to little Maverick. And we don't have homes anymore. I can't help it; I could feel the tears coming. All I can think about is my dad, my brothers; especially my twin brother, Danny. They can't all be completely gone ... can they?

CHAPTER
ONE
JESSE (AGE 34 - YEAR 2064)

I TAPPED MY COMMUNICATOR. "Report positions, Katie."

She and Harley, from my team, and Suzy, from TS-4, were running last-minute scans to ensure we're not going to be walking into any surprises.

"Everyone is in position, and your entry points are clear. The bad guys are maintaining their positions. No indication they know we are here, Sis," Katie reported.

I shook my head at her and laughed. She hadn't picked up on the standard lingo and never would. I admired her like hell for doing her own thing and loved her as my sister, but she's a royal pain in the ass. Sid and John joined in with a chuckle. They were thinking the same thing.

John commented, "You two couldn't be more different as sisters."

"Hey," I said. I could hear the others on the comms snickering.

Katie piped up, "Aren't you guys supposed to be undetected? The entire planet will know we're here at the rate you're going."

"Aye Aye, Sis," I said. She huffed on the other end of the comms.

I motioned to Sid King, my second in command of TS-5, and John Carruthers, lead for SPAR TS-4, to move to the final position with me. John and I commanded our dogs to prepare with a few hand signals. King, my German Shepherd, and Brutus, John's Belgian Malinois, were our trained K-9s. At the other entry points were Joe and Steel to the east while Lucy and Mo were staying well-hidden and ready to go on the roof. In sniper positions, which they would maintain on the outer perimeter, are Neil and Carlos. We were preparing to infiltrate a building carved out of the rocky mountain in a hard-to-hide portion of the desert on Terra Four.

We dropped a distance away yesterday and had been observing the comings and goings for 24 hours. Keeping our presence unknown had been a challenge but that's why we are the best.

We had the three entry points covered — front, east and roof — the back of the building was built into the rock. Unfortunately, that left us no way of knowing how far back the building went past the portion outside the rockface, and the scans could only penetrate inside an additional 500 feet, making the operation blind once we got further inside.

Sid gave a thumbs-up. All three entry points were covered and ready on the mark. The team was GO at 2400 hours when we observed fewer guards were present. Not that we would have difficulty dealing with more, but why make our job harder if it wasn't necessary?

"Katie, we go in fifteen. Can you give me your final scan of our primary mission targets?" We needed to have a clear idea of where the captives were being held. The last thing we needed was for one of them to get caught in the crossfire. Our primary reason for being here was to rescue and take them home.

"From what we can tell, they are dead centre in the building, but it looks like there are way more than we initially thought."

Just what we don't need right now. "How many more?"

"I can't be sure. That's too deep into the rock, and the scans can't get a clear reading but it looks to be at least 50. Maybe more. It's hard to tell with all the body masses jammed together, but I'm going based on weight averages."

Katie was the best, so I trusted her calculations.

Harley piped in right after her. "Suzy and I concur. And that's a rough estimate based on them being adults. Could be a lot more if…" He left off there and we all knew why.

No one wanted to consider how many children could be in the group. And we knew they targeted them as easy prey. Bastards.

I could see the guys' faces and almost read their minds. We'd all hoped this mission would be a small operation. Based on everything we had dealt with over the last year — with people going missing — and our informant's details, we'd expected around 20 people. But things had been getting increasingly worse, especially in the last few months.

While I'd have liked to say I was surprised, I wasn't, and I didn't think anyone else on the team was either. This was, by far, the largest group of people abducted for off-world slave trading that we had come across. Tonight, our mission targets were going home, and we were stopping this shit.

"Sixty seconds, and we go," I commanded. "Everyone stay sharp and don't let any of those bastards get away. Katie, Harley, and Suzy — you three will follow behind us after we have secured the location. Be ready to get in there and download their systems. Priority is to get their data. Activate your biosuits upon entry and closely monitor the readouts."

We were operating with new cloaking systems on our biosuits. We could see each other, but no one else could see us. Even the dogs had their own versions. Katie and Harley had designed the concept when I suggested it, but we hadn't had a lot of time to test the suits outside of our training environment. We were on a desert planet and had no idea how the suits would do in this hot, dry climate.

Tonight, we were hoping they would give us an advantage. If

not, it didn't matter. This operation on Terra Four was done. We were here to make sure that happened.

We all reached our breach points, activated our biosuits, and at precisely 2400 hours, we entered.

I was the only one carrying a Krean pulse weapon, so I took the lead with King beside me. Sid and John had our traditional laser weapons. They entered after me, side by side, with Brutus between them. We moved through the main entrance right after the security rotation passed. Joe and Steel entered simultaneously from the east while Lucy and Mo moved in from the roof.

Once inside, we had three hallways. John, the two dogs, and I took the hall directly before us, which we knew led to the main holding area. Joe and Steel followed down the left corridor to clear it while Sid took the right to meet up with Lucy and Mo.

Katie reported, "A few bad guys have broken off from the main group and are heading your way."

"Confirmed."

"You're going to find two small alcoves about a metre ahead. It should be large enough for you and the dogs on each side. You need to move to reach it before they reach the small curve ahead of the alcove."

"Roger. John, let's move."

I looked down at King and commanded him to move with me. Both dogs didn't miss a beat.

I also double-checked the reading on my communicator to see if our cloaks were holding. John checked his and nodded. Hopefully they would hold, and we would be untraceable to these assholes heading our way.

I could see King quivering at attention beside me. He was ready to pounce at my command. I'm sure it was the same for Brutus. They both moved alongside us without a whisper.

We found the alcoves. I tucked in on one side with King, John and Brutus on the other. We waited. Weapons ready. Dogs on command to stay. We could hear the enemy approaching and chatting. I looked over at John and knew he was ready. We would wait for them to pass our hiding spot. After what seemed like forever, the three guys walked past us. We struck them quickly together with our weapons from behind, while the dogs caught them entirely by surprise from the front. The idiot in the middle froze, making him an easy target.

I grinned at John, who just shook his head at how easy that was. "Let's get them secured," I said, turning and using my pulse weapon, set to stun, to immobilise them. What pissed me off was that these guys were not Terra Four locals. Because the climates were so different for each Terra, what a person wore was a good indicator of what planet they were from. These guy's clothing had Terra Two styling.

John finished securing them. "Who the hell are these guys?"

"No idea. Let's get some photos and send them over to Katie. She can transmit them back to TechStar base."

John took out his mini-tablet, took the shots and sent them.

"Wow, those guys don't look like they belong on Terra Four," said Katie over the comm.

"We agree. Send those off to the chief immediately. We need to figure out who they are," I ordered.

"Roger Dodger." I rolled my eyes, and John just chuckled a bit. That girl!

"Let's move," I said.

We heard Joe over our communicators, "We are in position and waiting for you two slackers."

"Same. What is keeping you two?" said Sid.

"Brutal," Mo laughed.

"Okay, okay, we're coming. We had a little something to take care of. Enough chit-chat."

"Katie? Still have no movement?" I asked.

"Confirm no movement."

John and I got back into formation, weapons ready and hand-signalled to the dogs to follow.

As we moved further forward, I watched King's ears perk up. I gave the sign to hold. We could hear a commotion ahead of us. Harley let us know that he clocked several biosigns heading towards us. I checked the status of the suits and noticed we were losing cloak integrity so they could potentially see us.

Thank god Joe, Sid, and Steel were coming up behind them. Right then, my suit glitched, and I appeared right in front of the assholes. The group of them froze. King and Brutus jumped on a couple of them, and they let out a girlie screech. Not dog lovers, I guess.

I chuckled because the look on their faces was priceless. We got ourselves four Nomad. John and I hit the two that the dogs distracted from the front, and the others nailed the remaining two from behind. They went down like bowling pins. While they were still conscious, they weren't going anywhere. My guys stood with their rifles trained on them, and I could hear King and Brutus let out heavy, deep growls. Our captives were scared shitless. God, I love those dogs.

I communicated to Katie that we had come across four Nomad. I could hear her gasp. The last thing we had expected to find was the species that almost ruined our world, on Terra Four. It's been 28 years, and we thought they were gone for good. This was bad. I felt it in my bones. The only news of Nomad was from Krean warships deep in space. Shit!

The guys started prepping them for transport with the humans we downed previously. Now, more than ever, the priority was gathering intel.

"Lucy and Mo, report," I said into my communicator.

"We're heading towards the area where the captives are being held. We haven't encountered any other guards," said Mo.

"Boss lady?" That was meant for me.

God, he's as bad as Katie. "Harley?"

"We noted a large group heading past the holding area ahead of Lucy and Mo. We can't scan that far into the rock."

"Got it. Guys, let's go. Steel, you okay finishing up with these guys?"

He snickered a bit. "Seriously? Hell yes, that should be fun. I'll follow as soon as I'm done."

I indicated to the others that we needed to move. We motioned for the dogs to follow. We spread out once we reached the first open area.

We found cages full of people. I stopped in my tracks and took a quick breath. There were so many of them. The team looked at me for instructions. I headed over to the cages while they followed.

I approached the first cage and saw a dark-skinned man looking at us. Our cloaks had completely failed at this point.

"Two of us came through here. Did you see them?" I asked. I wasn't sure if Lucy and Mo's suits were still working.

The man came to the edge of the cage and indicated the direction moving away, further into the tunnel and rock. "They headed that way. The aliens took several young woman and small children from our group." You could see the intense hate combined with sadness on his face. He spat, "You guys need to get them back. That man right there," he indicated a man huddled in the corner crying, "one of those little girls is his daughter." I felt that right in my heart.

"We are heading that way. Some people will come along shortly to get you out of here," I reassured them. As we moved out, I wanted to ensure Katie, Suzy, and Harley got those people out of there before anything else. "You guys need to get in here now. We need assistance. There are approximately 100 prisoners. Call the chief and let him know we will need additional transport. And we have approximately seven prisoners as of right now."

"Confirmed," was the only response I got back. We formed a line and headed in the direction indicated. I was so angry. All I could think about was Katie and me in that cage 28 years ago. I had no idea exactly how young these kids were, but I knew what the lasting effect of this ordeal would have on them.

We moved along the carved-out corridor. The only plus was

that there were no other routes they could have taken. Suddenly, we heard laser fire ahead. We had little protection, so we had to move in hot and not miss our targets. John and I signalled the dogs to stay, they wouldn't be protected, while we lined up side-by-side and ran in fast like warriors on the field. Thank god we're all expert shots and incredibly quick, plus we had the element of surprise on our side.

Lucy and Mo had found a small outcrop that provided some protection from the aliens and were returning fire, but there wasn't enough room for us, so we hammered out our shots. The Nomad were dropping like flies. Nomad were not known for being quick or accurate shots, which was probably why they eventually lost the war. Right now, that was working to our advantage.

As I moved closer, I saw some young girls had dropped to the floor. Damn, that was smart. By the time we were done, several Nomad were dead. As we walked closer, one of the little girls got up to say something just as my communicator went off. It was our two snipers, Neil and Carlos.

Neil reported, "We caught a couple of them trying to escape. They sure as hell aren't going anywhere now."

Carlos snickered, but then I heard chaotic shouting, "Fucking hell, something is taking off."

And then I heard it from our location. The sound of an engine. It was coming from further down the corridor. We took off running but were too late.

I felt a little hand tug on mine and looked down to find a little girl who couldn't have been older than five. I knelt to her level, and she said, "They took them."

I asked, "Who took them?"

"Those ugly blue guys. Their skin is super creepy; kinda like snakes all over. They took a whole bunch of ladies and kids. They didn't get me," she announced proudly. "I bit one of them super hard. He dropped me, so I ran and hid." She had this determined look on her tiny face. Tricky little thing, I thought. I heard snickers behind me. My team probably thought the same thing. The guy deserved it.

And here we thought we were rid of them. God, were we wrong.

"Can you help me with the others?" I asked her. She nodded and placed her hand in mine as we returned to where we had ambushed the Nomad.

As we got closer, the other kids came running. I noticed that King and Brutus were following the kids, and a few of them had attached themselves to the dogs. John, Joe, Sid, Lucy, and Mo just smiled as I was swarmed.

I had one little girl in each hand and turned to see Lucy with a couple while the rest of the kids walked with us, keeping the dogs close. The rest of the team followed closely behind.

Just then, Katie came walking up to us. She looked like she would cry when she saw the little girls attached to me. "They are so young," she whispered. I knew exactly what she was thinking and why. And as she had when we were kids, she hugged me. That was still Katie's way of expressing herself.

I could see the kids looking at us. I knelt and brought them all close. Katie joined me. "See my friend here?" I said, indicating Katie. I watched all the little heads nod up and down. "Well, she and I met in a similar situation."

"You did?" asked one little girl to my right.

"Yes, we were taken by a creepy blue guy long ago. I was six, and Katie was five. We were on a ship out in space." I heard them all gasp and could feel all their wide eyes on me, waiting for the rest of the story.

"We thought we would never see home again, but you know what?" They all nodded and waited for me to continue. "We were saved. A wonderful group of men found the ship and saved us." All those little faces flashed us smiles. "Now Katie is my sister, the best thing that ever happened to me," I said.

All of them clapped, jumping up and down. Katie tearily smiled and mouthed to me, *same.*

"Okay, now let's get you back to your families, shall we?" I stood, and we continued to the main chamber. "Did you find their systems?" I asked Katie as we reached the cages.

She nodded. "Harley and Suzy found their tech. I'm headed over there now. I just wanted to make sure everyone was okay."

I watched her head off to join them.

As we gathered everyone, it took several hours to get the people out of the cages, place the families back with each other, and then lead them to the front of the building where the chief had arranged for transport. All of them would be taken to Tech-Star's base in Lazarus, the largest city on Terra Four. From there, they would return to their homes after they gave statements.

In a separate transport, the seven prisoners would also return to the same base, but their stay would be much less pleasant. I knew they would be questioned, but I'd be surprised if the Kreans wouldn't get involved because four of the prisoners were Nomad. God, what a mess this was going to be.

I stood and watched the rescued people being given provisions, especially water. The dark-skinned man I met earlier came up to me. He put out his hand and I shook it while he gushed, "Thank you. Not just for rescuing us but also for reminding us that people like yourself are willing to help. All those kids you brought back won't stop talking about you."

I smiled at him, but I sighed to myself because we didn't save them all. One taken is one too many.

He kept shaking my hand, almost as if trying to comfort me. Just then, the other man from the cage, who had been crying about his daughter, was about to get onto the transport when his daughter broke free and ran to me.

It was the tiny, tough little girl that bit the Nomad. She slammed her tiny body into me, hugged my legs, smiled up at me, and ran back to her dad. He looked at me and mouthed, "Thank you." I just nodded. Seeing a family not torn apart by this bullshit was the best feeling in the world.

The situation for Katie and me was far more complicated

when we returned from being kidnapped. Earth was a mess. We got lucky, ended up with a great family, and grew up in a beautiful home on Terra One. Even so, it never negated the fact that both of us lost our families, and I felt a tiny twinge of jealousy that these people were going back to theirs.

Once everyone was on the transports and gone, both teams headed back inside to find Katie, Suzy, and Harley. The three were tapping into the left-behind systems.

We found them arguing.

"What the hell are you guys arguing over?"

Harley looked at me, and his face was bleak. "We found something that you're not going to like. Nobody is going to like it. It's bad." Harley was the most easygoing of us all, so it had to be bad for him to look grim.

I turned to the ladies, and their expressions were no different.

"What's going on? Why do you all look so upset?" I asked them. They slowly moved out of the way so we could see the screen.

It was one of those large screens full of random star charts. There were so many marked spots. I wasn't familiar with these places as they were not in our solar system. Then I moved to the other screen, and that was when I realised why they were upset. There were lists. A lot of lists. There were no names, but "HUMAN" or "KREAN" indicated and then age, male or female. There had to be hundreds.

"Fucking hell," Sid grimaced.

I sat on a chair, leaned forward, and sank my fingers into King's coat. I needed that comfort. I could see the look on the teams' faces. Nobody said anything. Nobody had to; it was obvious what we thought would be an easy operation to end … had been going on for much longer than we imagined. We needed to get this information to TechStar.

I knew what we were looking at. It was a shopping list of people, and the marks on the star charts may be where they had been taken. There was no way to know who these people were without names.

We were aware of many people still listed as missing, but could we match some up to the list? Maybe. Plenty of people went missing at the beginning of the divergence. So many people seemed to disappear into thin air. I know the consensus is they never reappeared, like my family, but what if their disappearance had nothing to do with the divergence? I sat up and stared at that damn list.

"We're going to need the Krean's help," I told the team. There was no way this was something we could do on our own. The Kreans had been dealing with the Nomad for much longer than we had, and they had the starships to travel through space. They likely even knew the star systems on the map.

"Question." Sid asked, "How did we miss the back tunnel during our surveillance, never mind that they had a ship?"

I could see everyone nodding, and I agreed, "Yep ... and how did that ship get onto this planet in the first place? With the Kreans' surveillance from the moon, no random ship should be able to land on one of the Terras." As I looked around at everyone, I could see that they were disturbed by the thoughts that formed with that question.

Katie responded, "We aren't entirely sure. We may find the answer in their security system. Which reminds me, we found something else you need to see."

She grabbed me and pulled me over to another separate monitor. She pulled up what looked like security footage of the location. There were a lot of recordings of the Nomad, damn those creepy blue guys. With great satisfaction, I was happy to see they forgot to purge their data.

Towards the end of the video surveillance recording, you could see them scattering when they realised we were there. And right in the middle of the group was *him*.

I looked at Katie; she was chewing on her bottom lip and rubbing the side of her face. Her nervous ticks. She knew him just as well as I did. That rat bastard, that creepy blue guy that had smirked at us when we were in that cage 28 years ago.

As I glanced back at the screen, it was as if he knew we were looking at him. He stopped, looked at the camera and made that signature smirk. I wanted to wipe that look off his face. I was pissed. I looked around at everyone from both teams and, while they may not understand who he was, there was no mistaking the smug look he gave us, and they didn't like it either.

I knew this was the beginning, and I would see him again. Only this time, I wasn't a six-year-old. This time, I would make him regret messing with Katie and me.

"Gather up everything," I directed Katie, Harley, and Suzy. "We need to get that back to the Snowden Valley base. The chief will want to see all of this, and I am sure he will have to pass this along to the Magistrates and the Kreans."

Katie looked at me. "You don't think we will have to go on a warship, do you?"

Warships were a bit of a phobia for her and, to be frank, I wasn't fond of the idea either. The only time you'd catch us flying through space were short SPAR transports. I had no more desire than her to fly around space on a warship. Shit. I nodded at her, and she started rubbing again. I had a bad feeling about this.

I spun on my heel and headed to our transport pickup, followed by the team. All I could think was how much this was going to suck, but whatever it took to bring home our people and maybe eliminate one creepy blue guy, I know we'd do.

CHAPTER
TWO
ZERSUS

I MOVED through the corridors of my warship. My second-in-command found something as we were coming up on Jupiter. It's been a while since we've seen the Terras, having been exploring other solar systems for almost a year.

I'm not fond of the fact that we'd been called back to Terra Moonbase. However, several of my warriors were looking forward to it. Most had family on one of the Terras since we settled there, including my brother and me, so I understood everyone's excitement. Of course, my brother and I would take the opportunity to visit our parents, but I barely tolerated leaving the Aries. I preferred to be out in space, not stuck on Terra Two. I was a Prime and belonged on the Aries. Terra Two never felt like home.

Putting my feelings aside, I couldn't ignore Supreme Commander Danlon's request. Something was happening back on the Terras. My quick conversation with Danlon lacked details, but I knew the man well enough to know he was worried. What about? I had no idea, but it was urgent. I avoided heading back to Moonbase unless the ship needed updates or supplies.

As I reached the entrance to the ship's bridge, I heard my

second, my brother Issbeck, let out a string of curse words he had picked up from our time on Terra Two.

"We have a problem?" I asked him as I walked through the doors.

"A problem? Maybe. Best? Something odd." Issbeck turned to me and shifted his chin towards several screens running standard space scans. What had him worked up was an indicator alert. The location was the lower left portion of what appeared to be Jupiter's upper atmosphere. Now I understood his agitation; we had detected a ship. One that should not be there.

"Have they spotted us? Is the cloak keeping us hidden?" I asked Simal, our bridge navigator. I wanted to be sure the cloak was working. It had been installed with our last maintenance check-in at Moonbase and had been experiencing some technical issues. This was another good reason to return to Moonbase and get the latest update on that tech. Danlon mentioned that the cloak system's designer made significant improvements.

"It would appear to be," Simal said. "I am confident they cannot detect us."

Issbeck sat in front of another set of screens and fine-tuned the scans. I walked up behind him and bent over, watching his progress.

Looking at the two of us together, you could tell we were brothers. Even though we wore our hair differently and I was several inches taller, we could pass for twins. The most significant difference was our eye colour. I didn't have a Kindred yet, so my eyes were black. Once a Kindred connection was made, they changed to amber. With the death of a Kindred, the eyes of the survivor became blue. Issbeck lost his Kindred at the young age of 20, causing his eyes to turn blue. I irrationally worried about him all the time. Sure, it was ridiculous. Even though he was younger than me, he was our strongest warrior. He would make an incredible prime one day. Just not anytime soon, I hoped.

Looking down at the monitor, I saw it the same time he did.

"Fuck," we said together. "How the hell is that possible? A Nomad freighter?" Issbeck began narrowing the scan's capabilities, and we were getting a full read on the ship.

I looked over to Simal at the other screen. "Confirm they can't see us," I commanded.

He turned to me and confirmed, "Our cloak is holding."

I moved over to the empty seat on the other side of Issbeck. Both of us worked on further improving the scans. We needed to get as much information as we could from the freighter. Issbeck stopped and looked at me, "How is this possible?"

"What have you got?" I asked.

"Looks like there are multiple crew members on the bridge, maybe a half dozen, but it's the cargo bays. Is that what I think it is? I can't get a clear read, but it looks like a large set of bio scans?"

I looked carefully at his screen, bent down and made a few more adjustments, and sure enough, "Yes. People. A lot of them. They are all crammed into a small space, making it look like one large bio reading." That was the only description I could come up with. There was no space in between the single, large bio reading. This wasn't good.

I straightened up and looked at the warriors on the bridge, "Looks like we stumbled onto a Nomad freighter circling Jupiter. And the freight they are carrying is humanoid." I was trying to keep it together. I had heard from Supreme Commander Danlon that they had been having problems with missing people on the Terras for quite some time, but I would never have considered that the Nomad were behind it. Everyone thought they were long gone from Terra space. "Okay, warriors, listen up. The ship, I'm guessing, is a slave trade freighter."

They absorbed that information, and I watched the look change on their faces. Simal especially. Next to Issbeck, he was one of our strongest, but he lost his father a while back and, to this day, he has not been found. I felt his anger rolling off in waves. I also doubted he was the only one in our crew that had experienced family trauma. You don't go to war against a species like the Nomad and come out unscathed.

"We need to come up with a plan. Not just to take the freighter but also to ensure that none of the people in that cargo bay get hurt. They need to be returned to Terra and their families. War Room," I commanded. I didn't need to turn around to know the key warriors were following behind me, leaving behind a few to continue monitoring the situation.

I sat at the head of our gathering with Issbeck and Simal on either side. The rest of our bridge warriors, six in all, sat down. Issbeck keyed in a few commands, and the large screens at the far end of the table came down from the ceiling. We could see all the freighter details from our scans.

The freighter had minimal weapons. We would typically categorise it as a supply ship, which was odd. Nomad supply ships travelled in groups and were escorted by their fighter ships. Finding one alone was highly unusual. It appeared to be hanging around, waiting for something. But "what" was the question. We discussed possibilities and felt they may be meeting another ship. I sent a command to the bridge to expand our outward scans to keep an eye open for other ships.

After much back and forth, we decided the best way forward would be to send a set of cloaked larger Wraith transports. They could attach to a ship and drill through while using a force field to protect the passage and ships from space. It's a unique piece of technology we had used quite a bit to rescue our people from the hands of the Nomad in the past, and we had perfected the process. We also had the added benefit of our large Wraiths being cloaked. The cloak worked much better on the transports since the tech was designed for that use.

After we have completed the rescue, we would use the Aries' magnetic pull weapon to capture the freighter. It wouldn't be safe to use the pull before ensuring the safety of the captives; the Nomad could try to dump them in space, or worse. We were not going to let that happen.

Issbeck would lead the Wraith crews. With my approval, he headed to the launch bay. Simal and I went back to the bridge to monitor the progress. "Will the cloaks hold on the transports?" Simal asked. "We haven't had to use them on a mission like this."

"That's why I've stayed behind, as much as I wanted to be part of the rescue team." It was the best plan. I had the most knowledge of the cloaking system. The mission depended on the cloaks not failing. From the Aries, I could coach the crews on adjusting for any fluctuations, if necessary.

Simal and I watched the eight Wraith transports move towards the freighter. I still couldn't help but admire the cloak designer's forethought in making it so we could continue to see our ships when running the cloak.

When we discussed this, we decided to send more Wraiths than we might need. We had no way of knowing how many people were in the cargo bay considering the scans couldn't separate the bio signs. Even that tiny detail pissed me off; they were jammed in tight.

The best guess we could make, based on the square metre measurement of the holding area, was 30 people. We didn't think the bay held more than that but it could be more if they had smaller people or children. The Wraith transports comfortably held 20 adult-sized people. We sent out 10 crew per ship, so each trip back would have room for a minimum of 10 additional adults.

I could see the first Wraith approach the freighter. We would not take the chance of trying to connect more than one at a time. Once the Wraith latched on, it would create the pass-through tunnel. I had targeted a specific location for them to connect closest to the cargo area. It was a reasonable distance away from their bridge. We were also keeping a close eye on the other bio signs. If they stayed on the bridge, this would all go smoothly.

Time ticked by. Both Simal and I were on the edge of our seats. We watched the first Wraith leave, head back to the Aries, and the second ship latched on. We must have estimated correctly as there were three attachments before all the ships headed back.

"All clear, Prime. We have all of them," Issbeck reported back.

"How many?"

"Ten adults, all women and thirty small children."

If we hadn't come along they would have been gone.

I heard Issbeck clear his throat. "Prime, they weren't just human. Several were Krean."

Simal and I sat there silently with the others on the bridge. It took me a minute to get my emotions back under control.

"Simal, get that damn freighter in our bay," I ordered.

He nodded and began the sequence to pull the freighter into the bay. We were taking these Nomad back to Terra Moonbase. They would regret taking these people.

As Simal took care of the final details of rounding up these monsters, I told him that I was heading to the War Room to converse with Moonbase. I sat down and sent an urgent message to Supreme Commander Danlon.

While I waited, it was a challenge not to let my anger get the better of me. I found it difficult at my age to control my temper more and more, not having found my Kindred. Our Kindred soothed our inner souls. In older times, when our planet Allora still existed, I likely would have met mine 10 years ago. As each year passed without Kindred, I had to focus on controlling my emotions. I had no idea how Danlon did it, as he was older than me and didn't have his.

Could we survive without? Yes, but it made controlling emotions more challenging. And eventually, I'd have to give up my position as prime. I wouldn't be able to continue to put myself in situations where I might lose control or hurt someone. I hoped that was a long way off.

"We have an incoming message from Terra Moonbase," Simal notified me. I was surprised at the fast response.

"Put it through."

Supreme Commander Danlon appeared on my screen. His expression said everything. He was not happy and I couldn't blame him. I hadn't left out any details in my transmission.

"Prime Zersus," he greeted me.

"Supreme Commander Danlon, you received my message quickly."

"Enough with the Supreme Commander, my friend. It's just the two of us here; Danlon will do. I was hoping to speak with you once you entered the Terra system but getting this communication was not what I expected," he said.

I nodded, "We were shocked to come across the freighter, but I'm glad we did. We would have lost those people, mostly children, forever."

Danlon nodded, rubbed his hand over his face and across the back of his neck, and then dropped a bomb. "That's the reason I called you back."

For a moment, I was speechless. Well, shit!

I watched him sigh and sit back. "We recently had an incident on Terra Four. A couple of SPAR teams rescued over 100 people, but that wasn't the worst of it—they were able to infiltrate the tech systems at the location. The perpetrators didn't have time to erase it before they ran. The information download led us to find out the Nomad are behind the abductions that have been occurring on the Terras for years."

I sat there silently for a minute. I frowned at the thought that we will face these monsters again.

Danlon paused, and my instincts screamed that I wouldn't like what was coming. "They were able to get footage from a security camera of the group of slave traders as they were leaving."

Okay, I thought, *that's good.*

"One of the Nomad is someone we know very well."

I couldn't be sure if I heard him right, but there would be

only one reason he would look as angry as he did. "Are you telling me that Curalim was there?"

Danlon nodded.

"Motherfucker!" I stood up quickly, pacing.

Simal and my brother walked in at that point and heard. They were watching me closely. Both knew that I had a short fuse. I closed my eyes and concentrated on my breathing. I could feel myself getting my control back. I was still madder than hell and felt for my friend, Danlon, who had suffered a great loss at the hands of Curalim. I returned to the screen once I was calmer. "Sorry about that. How the hell are you so calm?"

"Because I know he's still alive. We will capture him, and he will be punished for his crimes against Kreans and humans," Danlon said with determination. He meant every word. "The other thing I haven't mentioned — the SPAR teams captured several Nomad and humans that appeared to be helping them. They were initially taken to TechStar's Lazarus base to be held until they could be transferred here for interrogation. The morning of their transfer, they were all found dead."

I sat my ass down and let that sink in. The meaning was clear. There were traitors.

"Prime," said my brother. "We have the freighter inside Bay Three and all Nomad have been taken to the cell chambers. I have Captain Beaudreau and Kiv arranging rooms for the women and children."

I turned back to the screen, and Danlon told me we needed to get back to Terra Moonbase as quickly as possible and to keep a close eye on our prisoners. They wanted them in one piece and available for interrogation. I asked him if he wanted me to chat with them, but Danlon wanted to deal with it himself. I promised him that getting to Moonbase was our priority. I gave a nod to Simal and my brother. They both headed back to the bridge to get us on our way.

After I was done with my conversation with Danlon, I went

to see how things were going with the people we had rescued and how Captain Beaudreau and Kiv were managing.

As I entered the bay, I stopped in my tracks. In front of me were eight Krean children. Kiv was kneeling with them in a group while Cain had the human children with him.

I was completely overwhelmed and could feel my emotions getting out of control. I couldn't stay here. I left and headed to the training arena. I needed to let off some steam.

The damn Nomad. This time, they had made a mistake. They would regret their continued determination to mess with us, Kreans and humans, and I would be a part of their takedown.

CHAPTER
THREE
ZERSUS

"Aries warship to Terra Moonbase. We request permission to dock." I watched Issbeck and Simal guide the Aries closer.

"This is Terra Moonbase. Permission granted to dock at maintenance bay 32," control responded.

Danlon wanted the Aries in tip-top shape, based on the bay we had been assigned. All bays floated in space above the Moonbase's main structure. At any given time, fifty ships could be docked, but I did note that there were a number of the outer bays with ships that looked partially built.

It was exciting to dock and see warships being built. I knew they were getting ready to launch the next version. The Aries is a Phantom II. The new Phantom IIIs are the updated design. We could see one was nearly finished from our docked position.

I hadn't discussed the details of our return with anyone other than Issbeck and Simal. Everyone on the ship would be given a choice on whether or not they wanted to be a part of whatever mission Danlon had in mind. The Krean Space Corp was a volunteer organisation. While one trained very hard to be a warrior in the program, you still had a choice on what assignment you took. The Techstar military had adopted this practice as well. Loyalty and trust were something I had to earn from my crew, and I took great pride in being able to do that. I'd be surprised if anyone wouldn't join us on the mission, but the option to leave the ship was there every time we came back to Moonbase. I was sure we would be going out after the Nomad, and was one hundred percent on board with that, but I wouldn't put my crew in danger. It had to be their choice.

I watched Simal slowly ease the Aries into the docking clamps. We moved between the two hanging bays on either side. The clamps would activate to hold us in place while machines would work outside the Aries and ensure damaged areas were repaired. We always ended up with some impact from debris as we travelled through space and Moonbase did a much better job with repairs than any method we tried while on a mission.

In the meantime, Issbeck took care of the crew.

"Issbeck, ready everyone for departure. Will Captain Beaudreau and Kiv be taking care of our guests?"

He turned to me and smiled, "Yes, they will be getting them to base. Captain Beaudreau found all their families, so they will go home after they've provided their statements."

"Good. I am sure their families will be relieved to get them home." I was happy we could report something positive from this mess and return these individuals to their loved ones.

"Incoming message, Prime." Simal indicated the main screen.

I nodded, and Danlon appeared.

"Welcome back, Prime Zersus, Issbeck and Simal, Aries crew," he indicated to everyone who respectfully lowered their heads to acknowledge his position. "Magistrate Eton joins me." He moved aside and the magistrate appeared on the screen.

I watched everyone on the bridge snap to attention. I knew of the magistrate but had never met him. From everything I heard, he's a good man. He'd been chosen to represent the Kreans in the Coalition alliance with the voted leaders from the Terra planets. His fairness and kindness were two of his many positive qualities.

"Relax, everyone," he smiled. "Prime Zersus, it would appear that we have a problem that needs to be resolved. How long before the Aries is docked and unloaded?"

"Yes, Magistrate, we do." I looked at my brother. "Where are we in the process, Issbeck?"

"We have about 30 minutes to complete the docking sequence," he indicated.

"I'd say that it'll be about two hours, and we should have everything completed. What are my orders?"

Danlon responded, "Head over to central command when you're done. Bring Issbeck and Simal. Let me know when you are on your way. I know you want to ensure your guests are well cared for."

I nodded. "Affirmative."

They signed off.

I couldn't shake the feeling that change was coming.

◆

It took us longer than planned to get everyone cleared off the ship, including getting the Nomad prisoners secured on Moonbase. I didn't feel right leaving without ensuring all the rescued people were properly cared for.

While I might be the Prime of the Aries, I was also just a Krean man, and I could feel the tension pouring off the crew. They needed me to be visible so, without question, I was. The whole process took us three hours.

Once we were sure everything was completed, Issbeck, Simal, and I were finally ready to head to central command to meet with Supreme Commander Danlon and Magistrate Eton. We informed them we were on the way. I still couldn't shake this sense of foreboding.

I wasn't usually like this. I knew what was happening but there were details we hadn't been told. I felt we were in for a few surprises.

As the three of us made our way through the moonbase, I

couldn't help but reluctantly admire the base's construction. The first and most important thing we did when developing the base was create an atmosphere on the moon. It hadn't had one, but the humans and Kreans had agreed that the moon would be a good planet to use as an intelligence and military base.

After the divergence, the moon became the magnetic centre holding all five planets. The moon's position made it ideal to build our communication technology on it which could then be fed to all of the planets. Even the easily generated Etion power created with Krean engineering was also provided to the Terras from the moon. The Terras would never suffer from a power shortage or be without a method of communication.

I had to admit, it was all ingenious and I couldn't help but be proud that we had managed to rebuild our species and help the humans rebuild theirs. After the divergence 28 years ago, there were a few years where survival and rebuilding seemed near impossible; nobody knew if Earth's humans would survive the split of their planet which is probably why we never left. We stayed to help them and it resulted in a new home for us. After years of living in space, many Kreans welcomed having a home planet, my parents included.

The central command structure was a large, round building with multiple levels. We moved along one of the outer arms towards the circular structure. Once there, we had a perfect view of the Aries. Below us, we could see multiple arms coming out from the centre. They went all around the building like a spider.

The arms held many of the training and supply sections, and you could see people moving in and out on foot and in vehicles designed for the Moon's rough terrain. The Moonbase is indeed an architectural wonder. And then, as if that wasn't enough, it blends into the moon's environment. If you didn't know it was there, you might miss it.

Two men approached us as we reached the central command section. Danlon, one of my best friends, was one and it was great seeing him. While he was a bit older than me, he had been a mentor at first and then a friend second. I'd do anything for him. The other male was Magistrate Eton. He introduced himself to the three of us.

I could tell that Danlon was anxious. He was fidgeting with his stripes. My eyes went to them. I remembered well when he got those. He had no one else because his family had died during the war on Allora, so my parents, Issbeck and I attended the ceremony. We were all proud. He's like a third son to my parents.

We followed the two of them into a room to our right. One of the many command rooms that made up the inner section of the building.

I turned to Danlon as soon as we were seated. "So, spill it. I can see you fidgeting with your stripes. A dead giveaway that you're either dreading what you have to tell me or ..."

"Yeah, I'm dreading it. You are not going to like it," he said while Magistrate Eton wore a grin.

"Well, this is going to be good," Issbeck responded. He was trying not to laugh.

Simal raised his hands as if to say, "Keep me out of it."

What the hell, why was this so bad? It's not like they knew anything more than I did. Seriously, sometimes these guys' maturity level was questionable.

The comm signalled an incoming call. Magistrate Eton said, "That would be the other person joining our meeting." A man appeared on-screen — a human. I assumed it was someone from TechStar based on the uniform he was wearing. "Gentlemen, I assume you all know what a SPAR team is?" The magistrate looked at us with his question.

Issbeck and I nodded, but Simal answered, "No, sir, I'm not entirely familiar with them."

The magistrate turned to the screen and said, "Do you want to do the honours?"

"Sure," our guest said. "Let me start by introducing myself. I'm Chief Frank Cole of TechStar. I head up the SPAR program.

SPAR stands for Security, Protection and Reconnaissance. The teams are our 'special forces,' a term originally from Earth. They are heavily trained in forms of intelligence, fighting, weapons, warfare; you name it. There are five teams of six, all operating at different levels. The top two teams are TS-4 and TS-5, with five being our best. Any questions before I continue?"

We shook our heads.

"I'm here to talk to you about a recent mission. SPAR teams four and five returned a week ago from what should have been a simple mission on Terra Four. It turned out to be a far cry from simple. That is why Supreme Commander Danlon requested your return.

"I'm going to play the footage of what happened when we infiltrated. We were there based on intel we received about a slave-trading operation. Our operators have body cameras, so we've married together all of their footage so you'll get a view from all the body cams in sequence."

The video started rolling and I felt like something hit me. The first person to appear was a woman. She was obviously leading the infiltration. Watching her took my breath away. Christ she was gorgeous! I noted everything about her; the short burgundy hair, unusual for females; her height, taller than most human females. Her smooth and well trained movements. She had a large dog with her, commanding it with hand signals. Neither she nor the team member beside her spoke. Her confidence practically screamed at me through the video. I was trying hard to concentrate on the action happening, my attention was solely focused on her.

Suddenly the video shifted to the other guy. I realised he had a dog, as well. I don't know why, but knowing she wasn't alone made me breathe a bit easier. But I was still tense as we watched.

It took a while to make it through the footage. We watched the SPAR teams quickly take down the perpetrators, human and Nomad. I assumed they were the ones assassinated in their cells, based on what Danlon told me.

It was heart-wrenching to watch all those people in cages. I noticed my brother watching me. That was when I realised I was digging my hands into the arms of my chair. I had to relax. My emotions were simmering on the surface. Every time I watched this woman in danger, I wanted to yell at the damn screen. At the point in the video when they ran straight into a group of firing Nomad, I felt sick. Even though I knew she was okay and she could take care of herself. I tried not to look over at my brother because I knew he was paying attention to my reactions. I could only hope he would chalk it up to me being upset about the people being taken. I needed to get a handle on my shit.

I had always mistakenly viewed humans as being on the weaker side. This video was proving that theory wrong. I was impressed with the skills of the SPAR teams. They were as well trained as any of our warriors.

Towards the end of the video, we watched the security footage they had retrieved. I glanced over at Danlon and noted the tension in his body. It couldn't have been easy to watch them miss Curalim. They had been so close.

As the video ended, Chief Cole appeared back on screen.

"Lieutenant Commander Jesse Williams, the first person you saw on the video, was in charge of the operation along with the other team lead, John Carruthers. She was the one who identified the Nomad, Curalim. She didn't know his name at the time, but she recognized him from a previous incident."

We all looked at each other. How could she have known him? The last time he was seen, she would have been relatively young.

"Did you say her name was Jesse?" asked Danlon.

"Yes, that's right."

"Damn, I know how she knows him," he whispered so low we almost missed it. I could see many emotions pass over the man's face. At first I saw anger, but then I could swear I saw pride, which I thought was odd.

He clenched his fists and, like me, I knew he had a bit of a control issue. It was strange that he would react like that over someone he couldn't know well. However, being older than me and still having no Kindred would be a constant challenge for him. "She was on that damn ship 28 years ago. She and another little girl named Katie."

I could see Chief Cole look down and rub his brow and frown. When he looked up at us, he spoke, "Yes, Katie Williams is the blonde tech towards the end of the mission video and is also part of TS-5. She and Jesse are adopted sisters." A common occurrence because of the divergence. Chief Cole added, "And as a side note, Katie Williams is the designer of your cloaking systems."

We all must have looked like a bunch of stunned idiots.

"Wow," Issbeck gasped.

"That's impressive," said Simal.

All I could do was nod; I agreed with both.

Danlon just stared at the screen for what had to be a good five minutes. We all stayed quiet and waited.

"We are heading your way for a visit," he finally said.

The magistrate nodded. "Yes, I agree. That's a great idea. You and Zersus should go."

I looked at Danlon and then at Chief Cole. The chief agreed. He said he just had to clear it with his Director, but didn't think it would be an issue. Looks like Danlon and I were making a trip to Terra One, TechStar's Snowden Valley SPAR base, tomorrow morning so long as we received clearance.

I guess I'd been right when I felt things would change. And I had this strange, anxious feeling because I knew I would meet Jesse. It was like she had a secret I wanted to explore, and I hadn't even met the woman. This was going to be an interesting visit.

CHAPTER
FOUR
JESSE

DAMN ALARM! I turned over to grab the old-fashioned alarm clock and considered throwing it in the garbage for the millionth time. I smashed the top of the stupid thing. Yes I guess I'm crazy because I loved that clock. It was a piece of vintage history. Most would hate having to set it every night, that it would ring so loud it'd nearly take the roof off, that you couldn't adjust the volume, and that it would always lose time. I fixed it every night to ensure it woke me up on time, but I got a certain amount of comfort from it. I remember my dad had one like it. I guess I felt a bit of him when I looked at it. My adopted dad was the one who found it at an antique shop which just seemed so appropriate.

I flipped off the warm, toasty comforter and swung my legs over the edge of the bed. In the corner, a set of big brown eyes were looking at me with expectation: King, my shepherd, my K-9 partner, and one of my best friends. As much as he couldn't wait for me to get up so we could run, he wouldn't move a muscle until my feet hit the ground.

I saw him quivering on his bed with expectation and couldn't help but laugh, as I did every morning. And the minute I stood up, he pranced around me.

"Okay, big guy, give me a minute in the bathroom, and I'll get us out of here." I looked at him as he sat his butt down, wagged his tail, and gave me a dog smile with that pink tongue hanging to one side. You'd never know by looking at him that he was a skilled and trained military dog. Right now, he looked like a puppy. Yes, he was a deadly and enormous Shepherd, but still so cute.

I headed to the bathroom. With a quick shower and teeth brushing, I was out and dressed. I looked outside and saw nothing but white. It seemed we had our first snow of the season last night. I loved the snow, but guess who loved the snow more than I did? King was going to enjoy this run.

As soon as I opened the door, King was a blur moving past me. I turned around after locking up to find him rolling around in the snow. Every year, without fail, it'd be the first snow of the season and he felt the need to roll around in it.

"Come on, you big clown, let's get this show on the road."

As we did every morning, we headed along the path on the left side of my house that would take us into the mountains and towards a secondary path used for SPAR trail training. It led to the TechStar base, which was our final destination.

Some SPAR members lived on base to be close to the action. When I trained for SPAR, I decided early on that I wanted to keep my personal life separate so I was one of the few who lived off base. My adoptive mom and dad helped me find my place. It was beautiful, and it was me. Plus, it gave me the ability to decompress away from SPAR.

The distance was about 6 km through the mountains, and it was not an easy trail. I kept a fast and steady pace. I felt the crunch of the fresh snow below my shoes. The snow was loose, not icy, and I wasn't sliding, so I picked up the pace once I was sure of my steps.

King kept up beside me. I could see my breath leaving my body in puffy clouds from the cold. While cold, it wasn't freezing. It was perfect and refreshing. We had an unobstructed view of the TechStar Snowden Valley base as we approached the cliff edge at the top. This was where King and I always stopped for a little bit so I could catch my breath and enjoy the scenery.

From this position, you could see the front of the TechStar building. The view was stunning; the building, which looked like it was out of a winter dreamscape, sat in the valley between two large mountain ranges that met at the back.

Several roads and interlocking footpaths led towards the round silver building on stilts. The roads and paths moved underneath the centre disc where the main entrance was hidden. The middle section was several floors with windows, but if you were using your imagination, you'd think it looked like a flying saucer sitting on legs. There was another smaller saucer shape on the top where the transports land.

Towards the back of the building were three large towers. The middle tower, the smallest, held all the training facilities. Each team had their designated training space, but we also had a vast mountain training area at the back of the base. It's where we tested all the teams together and trained new recruits. It was a rough training course that flushed out people who couldn't handle it. Think "ringing out" like the old Navy Seal training. There were two other enormous towers on either side which were used as the living quarters for most of the SPAR team members, their families, and any other TechStar employees that chose to live on base.

King and I stopped at a cliff edge. We watched the transports arriving and dropping people off. Employees who lived off base, including clerical staff and visitors, would arrive via the Terra One Transport System or TOTS for short.

Chief Cole had informed us that the Coalition wanted us to work with the Kreans after the mission on Terra Four. As soon as we determined the Nomad were involved, I knew it was only a matter of time before the Kreans would want to be included. As far as I knew that was happening this morning. I'd love to say we could handle this alone, but not this time. The Krean's history with the Nomad made them the best to work with on this. It didn't mean that I had to be happy about it.

I sighed, looked down at King and said, "Looks like the show is about to begin." My stubborn streak was rearing its ugly head. I rolled my eyes at myself. "Let's go, King. Might as well face the music."

I snickered and got us back on pace with our run. King and I weaved through the bottom half of the path in a zigzag pattern and ended at the back entrance to the training tower. Once there, I swiped my comm across the security screen and held up my palm. Then, King added his paw, too. We put King and Brutus' paws in the security feature for fun. The dogs seemed to love it.

The doors slid open, and I took us through the corridors toward the centre of the building. Our next stop was the team gym. We met every morning and blew off steam before we headed down to heavier physical training.

I stepped into the elevator to take us up and heard a familiar voice calling after me.

"Hold the elevator!"

I held the doors and in popped Sid King, my second in command.

He looked like he just rolled out of bed, normal for him. Even so, Sid was a good-looking guy. Long, thick, dark brown hair pulled into a ponytail, with a thin beard across a strong jaw. He had rich brown eyes with laugh lines at the corners.

Out in the field, he was 6'2" of scary muscle. Around us, he was a big teddy bear unless we were training. His competitive streak came into play the minute we would hit the gym.

"You look like you just rolled out of bed." I raised my brows and laughed.

"Very funny. I spent the evening ensuring we had our ducks in a row with the mission report. You know, we will have to present this to the Kreans at some point," he responded.

"Yep, that's gonna happen today."

"What do you mean today?" he snapped.

"The chief asked me before I left last night to make sure we had everything ready. That's why I asked you to have the final look through. He mentioned that the plan is for the Kreans to show up at some point this morning."

I felt bad because it meant a long night for Sid, but with his photographic memory he was always the last one to go over our reports. He had a great eye and made sure we didn't forget even the smallest detail. Sid sighed, but gave me a tired smile just as the elevator reached our floor.

King came up beside me and started rubbing his head on my leg. I looked down at him, and he gave me a quick whine. I bent down to his level and rubbed his face. He was susceptible to my moods. He had great instincts about people in general, but when it came to me, he didn't like it if I was upset.

I looked up at Sid; he just shook his head, smiled and headed into the gym. I whispered into King's ear, "It's okay, my handsome boy. I'm fine. Let's go kick some butt." That worked its magic. The tail started swishing, and the tongue hung out the side of his mouth between his pants. I headed in the same direction as Sid, with King at my side.

Not surprisingly, Sid and I were the first two to arrive. We decided to hit the monitor bags. We both loved to compete and the monitor bags are perfect for a little friendly competition.

The system we installed could be set to count the number of impacts. It also gave a readout for the pounds of pressure per hit. We used it to train all SPAR teams in strength and combat skills.

"Any requests?" I asked. We were not hitting the bags without a punchy playlist.

Sid gave me a stoic stare, and I cracked up. If there was one thing he knew, I was going to pick the playlist. I loved the music from the timeframe before the divergence. I had a list of songs with a heavy beat that we would blast. It was a good hour of tunes.

Sid wrapped our hands, powered up the monitoring, and we

chose our favourite spots. The music started, and we both began. As we punched, each attack became more intense.

We used a combination of punches, elbows, knees, and roundhouse kicks. I felt the power flow through my body as it naturally followed a pattern of beats from the music. Most of my combos were unpredictable. It was my trademark and what made me good at hand-to-hand combat. Predictability was a death knell. I liked to keep my opponents guessing.

Off to the side, I noticed King swing his head around. I assumed the rest of the team had arrived and I was right. They slowly joined us on the other side of the room.

Katie Williams, my sister, selected the bag directly across from me and began pounding away. Katie's movements were slower but still fluid. People underestimated her because she was *pretty*. They looked at this sweet, blonde, petite woman and were stupid enough to think she was weak. If there was one thing that Katie was not, it was weak. I chuckled just thinking about it.

I took a bit of a break as the rest of the team arrived and joined Katie. I quickly walked around the room, watching the team's speed, skill, and punches. I gave them pointers on small things I noticed. Being the Commander was a position I took seriously. I wanted to keep them in tip-top shape, and this was one of our regular exercises.

At two of the bags to the left of Katie were Neil Fireside and Harley DeSouza, while to her right was Joe Leblanc, the team's oldest member.

Neil and Harley were the youngest. Both were gorgeous male specimens. Neil was of Jamaican descent with sleek dark skin, warm brown eyes and a smile that would knock your socks off. While Harley was a combo of Spanish and native Indian. Harley looked like he walked off a movie set. Women loved him. He had a mysterious look, dark hair and dark eye combo with full lips. He was on the slimmer side compared to Neil who was built like a tank. Both of them were like our brothers and would do anything for their team.

And then there was Joe. He was the oldest out of all of us. He came from a family of military leaders and, while he liked being SPAR, he never wanted to be in command. He said he didn't want the responsibility. I've never known exactly why, but I knew there was a reason. It's his secret to keep until he's ready to share. Joe was a large, muscular man with a touch of grey in his hair and beard with piercing blue eyes.

I watched all of them continue to kick the crap out of the bags and nodded in approval.

"Nicely done, guys. But Sid still has the highest ratings. Come on, you guys aren't going to let him show you up, are you?" I laughed as they stopped and gave me a dirty look. They quickly turned back to their bags and went at it harder.

On the playlist, I knew what was coming, and gave a shrill whistle. Everyone stopped. "Magic Carpet Ride is up next. Everyone get ready. Reset your monitors. It's competition time." The song was a remix I loved, and the beat gave us a brutal pace.

I moved over to my bag and prepped my monitor. As the music changed, I hit the bag hard and heard everyone following my lead. We moved and danced around the bags to the beat of the music, heavy and fast.

Our competitive streaks were on display. It's a perfect music mix to get the blood pumping. As soon as this song finished, another couple of tracks were coming up. I shouted to keep going without realising we had an audience. My heavy focus and attack on the bag in front of me prevented me from noticing the three new arrivals.

CHAPTER
FIVE
ZERSUS

I HAULED myself into the co-pilot seat of the Eros Hover transport, a new addition to our interplanetary fleet, and I was admittedly looking forward to the ride. Danlon was going to pilot us to our destination on Terra One.

I was not keen on this visit. I tried to spend as little time as possible on any Terra planet, even though my parents lived comfortably on Terra Two. Issbeck and I spent our teenage years there before we entered the Krean space program.

It was a beautiful and bountiful planet now. But when we first lived there, all of the Terras were simply in survival mode trying to figure out how to make the divergence of Earth into the four planets work.

Danlon slid into the seat beside me. "You ready?" he asked.

I nodded.

"You are going to enjoy the ride. These new Eros Hovers are amazing. Their response is incredible, and they travel faster than our old transports."

Based on the smile, Danlon was going to enjoy this more than I was. I would if this was a random space flight but knowing our destination dampened my enthusiasm. He rarely got a chance to use his piloting skills so this was the perfect opportunity.

I had to admire the construction of the machine. The transport had room for six people, but it was just the two of us heading to Terra One. The design of the Eros was inspired by advanced helicopters that humans used on the planets. Kreans were fascinated with them and their ability to hover, so they adapted that to a space transport. They had a similar body build to the helicopter reinforced for space travel between the Terras, from the round body at the front to a tail wing that curved up and held the engines. The landing gear popped down from under the carriage. The body was black with maroon flames down the side. I'd never seen the design before and had to admit it was what humans would call "badass."

From what I'd gathered from Danlon, the primary use would eventually be for TechStar. Slightly larger versions were created to transport the SPAR teams because most of their missions were interplanetary. I'd bet they were going to love these.

Looking over at Danlon, he looked like a kid with a new toy. It made me smile. It was rare you'd see him enthralled with technology.

Magistrate Eton had planned to join us but had to meet with the Terra Coalition and heads of Techstar to update them on everything that had occurred with my ship and the SPAR Terra Four mission.

While I would have preferred Issbeck and Simal to be with us, some issues arose with the Aries, so we decided they would stay behind.

Danlon began the pre-flight process. He asked me to check a few readings. All checked out. I could barely feel or hear the engine which was a surprise on such a small transport. Our enhanced hearing made it difficult to ignore even the slightest rumble. The Eros barely sounded like it was running. Just a tiny whisper to indicate it was on.

"Eros Hover Transport One ready to depart," Danlon communicated to control.

"Confirmed to go. Your flight should be uneventful. The

weather on Terra One is stable, and Snowden Valley's first snow-storm has passed. It's sunny but cold as hell. Enjoy."

Danlon confirmed, laughed, and looked at me as we began the lift-off sequence. The Eros moved upwards and hovered before we shot forward and zipped away from Moonbase. The first vision I saw was Terra Four. It was distinctive with a beautiful orange-swirled glow. Being 70% desert, 20% rock, and 10% small water formations, it was more unique looking than the other three planets. We were headed to the left side of Terra Four. Danlon banked and adjusted our flight path towards Terra One.

I've never been to Terra One. I've heard from others who sometimes vacation in Snowden Valley, in particular, it was all mountains and lakes. Apparently, it was magical in the winter. I couldn't understand the fascination some of my warriors had with snow. That didn't seem normal to me.

I preferred the year-round, warmer climate of Terra Two. That suited me much more. Even our warships had a standardised temperature. Kreans didn't normally take to a cold temperature.

"How long will the trip take?" I asked Danlon.

"About 45 minutes. The Eros moves much quicker than our older transports. Shaves off a good 30 minutes."

As we sat there, I couldn't help but ask what had been on my mind since yesterday's meeting. "Can you tell me about the women?"

Danlon knew I was referring to the two women we observed on the mission footage. My curiosity concerning the beautiful burgundy-haired team leader gave me an ulterior motive for asking, but I wasn't ready to reveal that to him yet.

"Do you recall when the Nomad made their move to destroy Earth? I think you would have been about 9 or 10?"

I nodded, and he continued, "I was 16, far from ready to walk onto a warship. We knew several Nomad ships had taken off into space and had abducted many humans. The leaders decided every able-bodied warrior and warrior-in-training were needed on our ships along with many of the trained human military."

I watched him close his eyes and take a deep breath. I knew this was hard for him. Many didn't know that Danlon is technically our King, even if he didn't want the title. The Nomad murdered his family—both his parents and his older sister, who would have been the next in the royal line.

The Nomad hadn't bothered with him because they didn't realise he was part of the royal family. He'd been away with a group of young boys on their first hunt. Magistrate Eton, a warrior for the royal family, grabbed all the children and managed to get them off the planet before the Nomad destroyed Allora.

I could see he struggled retelling the story, so I didn't push. I waited for him to continue.

"When Eton, our Supreme Commander at the time, and one of the humans were boarding a warship, I demanded to go with them. I could not just sit back and watch the Nomad disappear with all those people." He smiled and admitted, "I might have used my position to my advantage to make it hard for them to say no.

"Eton and a human named Lieutenant Williams agreed that I could join them, but I had to stay by their sides. At 16, I was too young to imprint on a pulse weapon, but my hand-to-hand combat skills were excellent so I had no reservations about going.

"Each warship was assigned a specific Nomad ship to follow. The one we went after was not able to outrun us. We were in a new Phantom class warship—an older version of yours. We overtook them and began boarding. It turns out the ship we chased was Curalim's."

I froze and looked over at him. He had a grim expression on his face. Curalim was the Nomad believed to be responsible for the death of his family.

Danlon continued with a scowl, "Once on their ship, we

headed down a narrow corridor, everyone firing at Nomad as we moved along it. We were coming up to what looked like doors to a cargo bay when they opened and out popped Curalim with a bunch of other Nomad. They were armed and came out shooting. They ran away from us. Eton and the Lieutenant gave chase and ordered me to try and get the bay doors open.

"There was pulse firing all around me, but I tried to tune it out while I used my tech knowledge to rework the system for the doors. While I was working on the panel, I knocked on the doors. I can remember thinking that if people were in there, maybe they would hear that. Anything to give them some hope. I heard a very faint verbal response — and then lots of yelling — I moved faster. When I managed to get the doors open, Lieutenant Williams came back. I could tell by the look on his face that he wasn't happy."

"Curalim got away?" I asked.

He gave a jerked nod.

"What happened after that?"

"With the doors finally open, Lieutenant Williams and I went in. We found about a dozen cages full of people. The first cage we came upon had two small girls inside." He closed his eyes again, probably replaying the scene, before he went on, "I can't even explain how mad I was. We could have lost those two little girls. They were so small. So young. And there were so many more people. Even a small baby boy."

He paused again. I couldn't help but feel for him.

There was much more happening besides the ships they were chasing. The Nomad had planned to completely destroy Earth. We did our best to prevent it from being obliterated like our planet, Allora, but we never could have predicted the results of our counter effects to the Nomad explosive weapon.

There were a lot of people that were lost that day. We thought they had disappeared in the divergence. But what if they didn't? Now I had to consider the possibility that they were taken by the Nomad.

Danlon looked over at me. "The girls couldn't understand me. I have never felt so helpless. Translators were distributed slowly over the population but, at that point, only the military had them. Even so, the oldest of the two, who I now know is Jesse, looked at me, and I swear she knew I would not hurt her. I do not know if it's because she knew I was young, but she also noticed Lieutenant Williams with me. The other little one was crying and hanging on to Jesse. It turned out that a lady in the next cage—I think her name was Alice—had been given a translator by the Nomad. She explained to the girls that I was there to help."

I couldn't help but commiserate with the frustration he must have felt. We take our ability to communicate with each other and other species for granted. Not being able to is a challenge but a situation with small children had to be a horrible experience.

"I'm assuming that everything came out okay, being that both girls are now grown women?" I asked him.

Danlon agreed, "It would seem."

"We managed to get them on our warship, destroyed the Nomad ship and brought them back here. Of course, the divergence happened. People, their homes — families were ripped apart, so there was no order. I wasn't sure what would happen to them, but Lieutenant Williams told me not to worry and would take care of them." He looked over at me with a smile on his face for the first time. "My trust was not misplaced as their last name is Williams."

Well, damn, so it was, I thought. "No, it definitely wasn't, and both of them grew up to be SPAR."

I knew getting on a TechStar SPAR team was a challenging process similar to what our warriors go through, but being on the top SPAR team — only the best made it. That said a lot for both women.

Even so, I found human women to be unattractive. Most were too small and looked like I could break them in two. So, it was a wonder that a human woman had caught my attention. I had noticed, based on her other team members, that you could not categorise her as small. She stood only a few inches shorter than her male counterparts. And she was quite muscular. My curiosity about her was making me anxious. I tried not to over-analyze my desire, but I couldn't ignore it either.

Typically, Krean women were the nurturers of our species. Most did not take warrior positions. It wasn't uncommon for them to work in intelligence or the medical field, we had both on the Aries, but I would love to see a Krean woman make it to a top warrior position, or maybe even become a prime.

I was just about to ask Danlon what he thought of her when he indicated we were coming in for our landing. I hadn't paid attention to our surroundings.

The view was spectacular. The mountains rose on either side of the large circular building, resembling a spaceship. We were coming in from the front edge, between the two mountain ranges, with the main building sitting like it was being hugged by those same mountains.

As reported by control when we left, it had snowed. It made the building and its surroundings almost magical. Not being poetic, that was the only description I could give it and now I understood the fascination from my warriors when they returned from a visit to Snowden Valley.

I watched as we hovered over a transport landing pad. Danlon made contact with their control. Other planetary trans-ports were coming and going. We were instructed to move to a larger area. The Eros was an unusual design, and it captured the attention of people arriving. Many turned around to have a look. I was proud of what we designed and built and noted the same look on Danlon's face as he brought us down smoothly.

"Nice landing," I said, to which he smirked.

"Did you seriously think it would be anything but perfect?"

I couldn't help but laugh. As much as we were friends, I had no misconceptions about his huge ego. Come to think of it, most would say the same about me. That was probably why we got along so well.

Danlon powered down the Eros and prepared to disembark as Chief Cole headed out to meet us. Danlon jumped out of his side of the Eros and said, "There's our escort."

I followed around to the front. Chief Cole greeted us both with handshakes and asked us to call him Frank.

We kept pace with him through the glass doors and to a set of elevators.

Frank addressed us, "The team is currently in the physical training area. I thought we'd go up and greet them. Today, they are working on their hand-to-hand combat skills. They usually start training days with a bit of a competition on the punching bags. You'll enjoy the show."

I could hear the pride in his voice. The team had an exemplary record from everything Danlon and I read about them. They were the best team Techstar had in quite some time. The other team involved in the recent mission, TS-4, was also good but TS-5, the one Jesse commanded, was better.

"Are they expecting us?" Danlon asked.

Frank looked at us and said, "Jesse is, but I don't know if she's had a chance to tell all of them yet. One of the team members, Sid, has a photographic memory, so he finished everything for the reports last night."

I looked at Frank, clearly wondering what that meant. I'd never heard of a "photographic memory" before.

He explained, "It means that he can experience things once and remember all the details. He typically will prepare his report, and then we compare it to the others to fill in any gaps."

"But he doesn't lead the team?" I asked.

"No, that would be Jesse. Sid will be next in line when the time comes. He's a couple of years younger than her," he said.

Danlon couldn't help but look impressed.

"Believe me, she earned it," Frank said.

When the lift stopped at our destination, we exited. We were greeted by a group of well-trained and toned warriors beating the living crap out of monitor bags. And what was that noise — was that music? I can't remember the last time I heard music. It wasn't unpleasant. The music carried a heavy, steady beat. The team was hitting the bags to that beat. Frank looked at us, "It's old Earth music. I don't know where Jesse finds it, but she makes the playlists they train to."

"I like it," I said. And I did. I could see all of them moving to it. I found it mesmerising and wanted to join in.

While all of them are skilled, the two on the right were far superior. One was Jesse. I couldn't look away from her. While gorgeous on the security footage, I wasn't prepared for what she would looked like in person.

She was dressed in tight clothing showing off every ripple of muscle. As I thought from the video, she was far from a small woman standing probably close to six feet. Beside her team member she stood just a touch shorter then the guy to her left. Along with her long legs, toned stomach, and muscular arms, her body was full of feminine curves. The combination made me long to get close to her.

I watched her skilled attack on the bag. We had a similar training system on the Aries. Her approach was relentless, her movements fluid, and I noted the unpredictability of her moves. Smart, strong and impressive. The hits between her jabs and kicks had a purpose behind them. If that bag had been a person, I had no doubt they'd be down.

As the song ended, Danlon turned to me and said, "Why don't you join them."

Frank nodded to the empty spot beside Jesse, "Two more songs are coming up. They typically go for three, about 15 minutes before they take stock of who's winning. But watch your approach and make sure King doesn't feel like you're sneaking up on him. He doesn't know you."

That was when I spotted the dog laying near Jesse. He was the same majestic animal that joined her on Terra Four. I'm not sure what type of dog he was, as I know very little about them, but he was quite large. He had a dark face and dark eyes. His fur was longish, especially around his face and looked quite soft. You could tell he was observant and missed very little. He had been eyeing us occasionally from his spot, alert and ready to pounce if necessary.

I headed over to the empty bag to the right of Jesse. She and the teammate on her other side didn't notice my approach, but King did. He was up and watching me approach the monitor. I powered up the sensor for the bag and noted the music change over to something different. I didn't bother wrapping my hands. I wouldn't need it. I joined the team and attacked the bag as I would in one of our warrior training sessions.

I had a very specialised style of fighting. My power came from my arms and legs, and I used them to their full strength, and length. From the side of my vision, I could see King lying back down but watching me closely. All of us kept going for what had to be another five minutes when the tempo changed again. I admired that nobody stopped, not once. I felt it, and they all had been going for five minutes before I started.

The last beat ended; I had lost track and realised that just the three of us, Jesse, the team member to her left and myself, finished the final round. I watched her freeze, look me up and down, and then those eyes of hers reached mine. I felt like a pulse blast hit me. Those damn eyes of hers were incredible. What the hell was that? I felt like I couldn't talk or breathe. I heard her teammate comment on her skills and her lovely laugh. I wanted her to direct that laugh at me.

Danlon and Frank approached. Danlon shook Jesse's hand, and it was clear she remembered him. She commented on his current position, which she clearly understood by his uniform's markings. Then the other small woman, Katie, I believe, approached. I swear Danlon looked mesmerised by her. She looked like a typical human female to me. Too small but, admittedly, very pretty.

Frank introduced Danlon to the team first. I learned that the fellow on the left of Jesse during the training was her second, Sid. The other males were Joe, Neil, and Harley. As with all humans, they had very distinctive looks which I find made it easy to remember who was who.

Suddenly, it was my turn to be introduced. "Jesse, this is Prime Zersus of the warship Aries."

I took her hand and replied, "Jesse." I watched her closely and noted that she was checking me out. I was okay with that. The feeling was mutual.

I heard Frank clear his throat, which brought me out of my trance. I could see Danlon had a stupid grin on his face. Well, shit, I was going to have to explain my fascination with Jesse to him.

Before we could continue the conversation, Frank instructed the team to clean up and join all of us in what he referred to as central comms. TS-4 will also be attending the meeting.

I followed Danlon and Frank to the lift when I felt a wet, cold sensation in my hand. I looked down to find King looking up at me. I bent down to his level, fascinated by him. He sat down and allowed me to stroke his head. I looked over at Jesse with a smile. "I've never had a pet before. I remember seeing him in the mission videos."

"He's one of our trained K-9s and my partner," Jesse explained with a chuckle. "You probably will meet Brutus as well. He is the other dog from TS-4 who was with us on that mission."

"I'm looking forward to it." With one last stroke of King's head, I stood up and joined Danlon and Frank on the lift. Before the doors closed I couldn't help but watch Jesse. I couldn't take my eyes off her and King. She fascinated me, standing there with her dog. What a beautiful sight.

Danlon cleared his throat and looked a bit uncomfortable. He was rarely a man who became anxious about anything. The tiny woman, Katie, had clearly caught him off guard. I hoped his distraction due to Katie will keep him from asking me anything about Jesse.

Danlon commented to Frank, "Jesse and Katie have grown into amazing women. But I must ask: you said their last names are both Williams. Anything to do with Lieutenant Matt Williams?"

Frank nodded. "Yes, he adopted both of them. He, his wife Alice, and their younger son, Maverick, live in Snowden Valley. Well, Maverick comes and goes with his work but he still is here a fair bit."

Danlon replied, "I'd enjoy seeing the Lieutenant again to thank him. Wait, Alice? She was on that ship, as well. With a baby, right?"

Frank nodded again. "Matt saved them all and brought them together as a family. If you have time, I'd be happy to take you two to his bar while you're here so you can speak with him. I think he'd enjoy that."

The lift stopped, and he indicated for us to follow. He led us through a beautiful office area, glass on one side and organically designed for the team members. It was almost like having the outside, inside. My thoughts wandered, and I realised that if I'd been exposed to a place like this when I was young, I might have decided to stay on a Terra.

That thought had my mind racing and questioning far too many things. It was time to rein it in and get ready for this meeting.

CHAPTER
SIX
JESSE

THE TEAM WATCHED the three men step into the elevators. Both Danlon and Zersus watched Katie and me.

I found it disconcerting. I wasn't prepared for Zersus. His strength and power were like a magnet. Even though he's Krean, damn, he was my type. His confidence turned me on. Not to mention his looks. The man gave *HOT* a whole new meaning. I've met many Krean men, but none like him. Even Danlon, who was handsome, didn't hold a candle to Zersus. I had to get a handle on my attraction. If he was here, I'd have to guess that he would be a key player in our Krean cooperative. If I had to work with him, then that ends that.

"You two ladies have a fan club." Harley crossed his arms and looked at us with a little evil in his eye. Beside him were the other guys with huge smirks.

"Please, you know that Krean men don't mess with human females," I said.

"And yeah, I also heard they don't kiss," Neil added.

Katie and I spun our heads and looked at him. "They don't?" we both asked.

He started laughing, and the other guys grinned.

What a damn shame because I'm a great kisser. Wait, what?

I shook my head at these clowns, and myself, before turning to King. "Let's go. Everyone snap to it. Shower, change, and head to central comms."

Christ. All I could think about now was kissing. I rolled my eyes and headed to the showers. I stripped off and let the water flow over me. We had to make it fast, but I needed a minute. As if this whole mission wasn't rough enough, I was pretty sure we had to work with Zersus. My breath caught in my throat, and I just thought about how he looked as he left on the elevator. Standing at least 6"5', he towered over the other men. He was wearing typical Krean military wear with dark blue cargo pants, a blue long-sleeved shirt and a vest. His position was prevalent by the number of stripes along his vest. What he wore hugged every inch of him. The man was a walking set of muscles. In my mind, I could imagine holding onto those shoulders while he … nope, not going there. Time to shut that shit down.

I finished up as quickly as I could and got the hell out of the shower. I was dreading this meeting. Katie and I changed into our standard uniform, black combat pants and black t-shirts with the SPAR identification, and exited the locker rooms. We found the rest of the team waiting for us. We had the best team SPAR had to offer.

Katie was our computer genius, designing new systems which included the cloaking tech we've been using on our biosuits, and on the Krean's warships. While all the tech specialists were good, magic happened when she got involved.

Sid King, my second in command and an all-around great guy, was the first one I noticed from the group. He was an expert mechanic and, in a pinch, could pilot anything. He also had a photographic memory. That came in handy — a lot. And Sid was one of my best friends. I talked through a lot of things with him. Maybe I should mention Zersus to him? Nah, forget that idea.

Standing next to him was Joe Leblanc, the oldest of the group. He was the most skilled in every aspect the team is trained in, except tech. He hated it. I got a kick out of it when

Katie started talking "computer," and Joe's eyes glazed over. He was a weapons expert and had built portable weapons unique to our team. Joe also spent time training recruits in everything for SPAR.

Neil Fireside was our sniper and explosives expert. He said that when he was a kid, he loved destroying everything. It wasn't any wonder that he blew crap up in his SPAR position. He also worked with Joe on perfecting the weapons we use.

Lastly was Harley DeSouza. Women flocked to him like bees to honey. The man doesn't have a vain bone in his body though. I always assumed that was the reason women liked him so much. He was another tech specialist, but his specialty was digging for information, whereas Katie's was building custom programs. Harley said Katie builds them; he uses them.

And then there was me; Lieutenant Commander of the team. I had enough tech knowledge to be comfortable working with Katie and Harley. Thanks to my dad, Matt, I was a skilled hand-to-hand combat specialist with several black belts. I was a good shot: dead centre mass or middle of the head. I tried not to mention that last detail to people I meet, especially men. It's a date killer. It's happened in the past, and it scared the crap out of them.

We made a great team. The *best* team. Our skills blended well before you added all of our physical abilities. We took pride in being the best. I couldn't imagine not being part of this team, even though I knew things constantly evolved and changed. I was hoping that didn't happen too soon.

I had a feeling that could be wishful thinking, though. As I walked up to the group, I had the sinking feeling that this meeting would change everything.

"Alright, everyone, let's go. You didn't have to wait for me, you know." I looked at them, and they started laughing. They grabbed me while King moved around the group with little yips. And down we went in the elevator to central comm; to god knows what destiny.

◆

Exiting the elevator, we ran into John Carruthers, lead for TS-4 and his dog Brutus. "Have you guys gotten started yet?" I asked.

He shook his head. "No, just basic introductions. We knew you wouldn't be long. Didn't get much training in, huh?"

"No, we just started, and the chief came in with those two."

Katie said, "Yeah, but one of them joined us."

I watched John's eyebrows raise but stopped him, "Don't ask."

The guys all started chuckling. Joe decided to add his two cents worth, "He kept up quite nicely, don't you think?"

I scowled at him and they laughed as we entered the room. The members of TS-4 were randomly sitting around the table, and they all noticed our expressions. I could see questions on their faces. They would have to wait for an explanation.

Our two Krean guests were seated at the front with the chief.

I moved to the far end of the table with King. It was the most comfortable spot for the two dogs as they could spread out, so John and I sat there regularly.

As I looked up, I found Zersus watching me. He looked a touch annoyed. He likely thought I would sit closer to the front, especially since John and I led the teams. There were seats near them, but John and I always sat back here. I didn't need to be in charge or at the front; John feels the same.

The chief stood up and just when he was about to start the meeting, an unexpected guest arrived. I could tell the chief was as surprised as the rest of us. A visit from Head Director Sheldon Cummings was rare. Thank god. Something about the man just rubbed me the wrong way, much like it did when I was six and first met him. Even so, I could accept that the current situation would be of interest to the top tier of TechStar.

"Chief Cole, good to see you." At least the man had manners as he shook the chief's hand. He asked him to introduce the

Krean guests. "I just wanted to check that everything is proceeding with our slave trade situation."

Danlon answered for the chief, "We are just getting started. I'm sure I speak for everyone when I say that we are determined to see this end."

"Good. Good. I expect nothing less, especially from our SPAR teams." He was nodding and, honestly, not really adding anything to the meeting. Thank god he decided to leave us to it. I watched both teams release their breath. None of us wanted that man to join us. He gave *useless* a whole new meaning. Every time he came around, I couldn't figure out how he made it to the position he did. Lots of friends in the right places, I'd bet.

Once he was gone, the chief got us back on track. "As I was getting ready to say, we all know why we are here." He indicated the two men beside him, "Supreme Commander Danlon and Prime Zersus are aware of our mission to Terra Four. You all will be brought up to date on what occurred on Prime Zersus' warship a few days ago." The chief turned to Zersus and indicated he should continue.

Zersus began, "Approximately 72 hours ago, as we were headed back to Terra Moonbase, we came upon a Nomad ship attempting to hide in the upper atmosphere of Jupiter."

We all looked at each other; I asked, "Did they attempt to run?"

"No. The Aries, a Phantom II warship, has a cloaking system. While previously we only had it on our transports, the warship can fully cloak. We've had a few glitches, but it held, and they didn't see us."

I laughed, and both he and Danlon looked questioningly at me. I nodded towards Katie, "You can thank her for that tech."

Katie sighed and rolled her eyes at me, "You just had to mention that?"

"Of course. Katie was integral in the customization of the cloaking systems, both enlarging them to encompass your warships and making them small enough for our biosuits."

Danlon was the first to recover and flashed Katie a blazing smile, "Thank you. Seriously, I mean it. Based on the specs we received, the new Phantom IIIs will have a more advanced shield and cloak. We couldn't have done that without your improvements, but I was unaware that you had taken them down to the biosuit level. Can I assume that you might also be able to find a way to use them on our smaller Wraith fighters? That would be amazing if we could."

Katie nodded. "Sis, can you explain what we've been doing? And it probably wouldn't take much to adapt the transport cloaks to the Wraith fighters."

She looked at me, and I explained, "We've been running the biosuit cloak in test mode for the last few months. The last mission to Terra Four was the first one where all of us were cloaked. It's a location that is particularly hard to stay invisible. We hoped the cloaks would give us an advantage. For the most part, it worked, but Katie will be making some additional adjustments. And one of the biggest issues is weapons. For the cloak to cover weapons, they must be against the body. The cloak does not cover them when we move them to ready position. Katie is working on improving that."

I could see that the two men were suitably impressed. Hell, even I was impressed. I thought it was a long shot when I suggested seeing if we could cloak ourselves.

"Yes, our traditional Terra weapons are an issue — for now — but the cloak does work with pulse weapons," Katie said.

I could see the raised brows on Zersus' face. He was probably wondering how the hell we would know that. Humans couldn't typically use pulse weapons.

"I use a pulse weapon," I mentioned.

"What? Really? You do?" he asked with clear doubt in his tone.

The chief said, "She's the only SPAR member that has been able to imprint on one of them. We've tried with others, but it never works."

I could see Danlon and Zersus looking at each other. They were shocked. I thought there had to be other humans who could use the Krean's pulse weapons but I must be wrong if they were that surprised.

Danlon was the first to break the silence, "It's rare, Jesse. Very rare. We have over 100,000 humans in our space military and out of them, besides yourself, I know of one other who is a pilot on Zersus' warship."

That was so odd. "Do you know why that's the case?" I asked.

He shook his head. "Maybe at some point, we could do a genetic comparison with you and the other person and see if that can give us an answer. If we could produce a pulse weapon that we could adjust to be accepted by humans, that would be helpful."

He turned to Katie. "Would that be something that you might be able to do?"

Katie shook her head and pointed to Joe. "That's his area of expertise. He even tweaks and fixes Jesse's weapons, so he's familiar with the pulse weapons."

Danlon asked Joe, "Perhaps this is something we could ask you to look at?

Joe grinned. He was in his element with weapons. If anyone could figure it out, he could. But in the meantime …

"Can we get back to what happened? We were discussing finding the Nomad ship. Was it a fighter?" I asked.

Zersus gave me a pointed look.

You started the conversation, buddy. So, deal with it. I gave him the same look back.

Danlon covered his mouth and coughed beside him, and I couldn't help but smile. Someone didn't miss our exchange.

Zersus scowled but continued, "We approached the ship and scanned it. It was not a Nomad fighter. Just a freighter, which we thought was odd."

I agree, finding a Nomad freighter anywhere in the vicinity of the Terras would be considered odd as hell, but based on what we knew was going on with the slave trade and the Nomad's involvement, I'd bet it was no coincidence.

"Our scans indicated a small number of crew members, all on the ship's bridge, but there were indications of body signatures in the cargo bay. There were way too many in a small space for it to be additional crew. There'd be no reason for them to be crammed together like they were."

Jesse couldn't help but compare what they had experienced on Terra Four with his description. People crammed together in cages. It also brought back some bad memories.

"We didn't know at the time why we had been called back to Moonbase, but we weren't about to leave anyone to the mercy of the Nomad. We couldn't be sure who we'd find, but it didn't feel right. I sent out eight Wraith transport ships to retrieve the people in the cargo bays. The larger Wraiths can carry many people, but their primary use is being able to attach to a ship, drill in and maintain a transfer port while being cloaked. In all, we rescued ten women and thirty children."

I watched him attempt to gather himself. It was the kids that bothered him, which didn't surprise me as it's a fact that Kreans feel children are a blessing. I'm not sure why but they have small families, so the few kids per family were important. He continued, "We used our magnetic tractor pull to capture the ship and Nomad. We brought them back with us."

I asked, "The people you rescued from the cargo bay, were they all human?"

Zersus and Danlon shook their heads and explained that some children were Krean.

The chief spoke up, "That is about the right number of children taken from the location on Terra Four, and there were a few Krean children amongst them. The older prisoners we rescued said the Nomad were anxious to ensure the Krean kids went with them."

I could see everyone trying to compose themselves. Just the

thought of losing kids, no matter who they were, was unthink-able. I asked them, "I'm assuming you've read our initial mission report?"

They both nodded. Danlon replied, "The chief sent the report to Magistrate Eton and the Coalition. We thought calling back Zersus' ship, the Aries, was the best plan going forward. Zersus has a success record when it comes to finding the Nomad. We need every advantage we can use right now."

I didn't think anyone disagreed. While I'd never seen a Phantom II in person, I heard they were impressive, but having a skilled Prime was key.

I asked, "Chief? Where does that leave us? Do we just sit back and wait to see if they can find the Nomad? And you know Creepy Blue Guy in the video is the one that was responsible for Katie and me being taken years ago. We need to find him."

I had a hard time separating the job from my feelings. I wanted this man gone. I felt such malice and evil from him. I knew there was evil out there. I always saw it in my work, but he was a whole different brand of it.

Danlon stood up and took the floor. "We have decided to team you up with Zersus and have you go into space as part of his crew to help deal with the Nomad. The number one priority is to find Curalim," he indicated to Katie and me, "the creepy blue guy." I realised Danlon knew him, and from the tone of his voice, not in a good way.

Then it hit me, "Wait, you want us to go on a warship? Like a ship out in space, warship?"

No way, nope, nada, not gonna happen. Hell would freeze over before I stepped on another damn ship out in space. The monologue played in my head. I could see Zersus looking at me oddly. I was probably wearing my thoughts on my face because I was not keen on the idea. Christ, not keen was an under-statement.

"You do not like this idea," he asked.

"*NO*," was my only response.

Danlon looked at me. "I understand, Jesse, but we need you and your team. Adding your team and skills to the Aries crew is a perfect match."

I got it. I knew he was right. I hated that he was right. I looked at Katie, saw the same look on her face, and noticed Danlon also watching her closely.

The chief said, "Jesse, we can discuss it in my office. The rest of you are dismissed. All of you get back to physical training."

I watched everyone get up and head out. I sat and looked down at King, who had gotten up and placed his head on my lap. I stroked him, not paying much attention to the others, until two large feet appeared by my chair. When I looked up, I found Zersus looking down on me.

His eyes studied me closely, and I felt it down to my bones. "Discuss it with Chief Cole. I don't have to imagine why you don't want to go, but I can guarantee that you'll be safe, and the warship is an experience I think you'd enjoy."

He turned on his heel and left with Danlon.

Once they were gone, the chief nodded at me to follow him to his office. How was I going to do this? I had no idea.

I needed to talk to Dad. Matt Williams was my hero. He rescued Katie and me, along with Alice and Maverick. I trusted him implicitly. He was one of the few people who could help me talk my way through this.

I sighed and headed with King to the chief's office.

CHAPTER
SEVEN
JESSE

THE CHIEF LED the way to his office, and we sat on the sofa. I loved this sofa and so did King, but today was not a day for pushing the chief's boundaries, so I commanded King to stay at my feet.

His office was one of the building's most relaxing and comforting places. One side was all windows that looked out over the mountains going down to the valley. There was currently a beautiful sheet of white outside due to the fresh snowfall from the evening before.

Just a bit down from the base was Snowden Valley with the original architecture that made the town so charming. Snowden Valley had grown substantially, but the town was adamant that new builds had to fit into the feel of the original ski town. My house was one of those places.

TechStar was the only thing that stood out but it was separated from the town enough that it didn't take away from Snowden Valley's character. The TechStar base blended into the mountain range. It was designed to do so for protection.

Inside the chief's office, everything was decorated in reclaimed wood. His desk, the bookcases, the coffee table, even the frame for my favourite couch—he personally commissioned the pieces in his office from a local furniture maker. I loved it so much that I went to the same person for a few critical pieces for my bedroom and was waiting on a new dining table. I wanted something big enough to have the whole team over for dinner, along with my family. My home, with all its space, was a common hangout for the team.

As we settled in, I knew the chief would be on me about going into space. I was also going back and forth in my head.

I wasn't even sure why I had such a phobia about being on a warship. We travelled regularly from planet to planet on the TechStar transports, but to me, that was like getting in a car and driving somewhere. We never left the surrounding magnetosphere that protected the five planets. So, it never truly felt like we were in space.

The thought of getting into a monster-sized warship to fly out into the wilds of space — okay, maybe an exaggeration, but I couldn't help but think it reminded me of the old westerns that were my dad's favourite movies. It was called the *Wild West* and was completely lawless. That was how I think of space. It was a lawless place. Everyone was constantly fighting to survive.

I sighed as the chief watched me mull through. He said nothing; he just let me sit and brew. When it came down to it, this wasn't just about me. This was about people who can't fight for themselves. It was the reason I did what I did.

The chief grabbed us both a coffee and handed me mine, perfect as always: one cream and sugar.

He looked down at his cup before speaking, "I know you don't want to do this Jesse, but you understand why I feel strongly that you need to go, right?"

I closed my eyes briefly. "I know, I know. Doesn't mean that it makes me feel any better about it," I lamented to him. I knew I sounded like a whiny baby. I rolled my eyes at myself, and the chief laughed.

He suggested, "I think you should go home and talk to Matt. He'll be able to walk you through your concerns, and being family, his perspective will be different than mine. Plus, he has a great handle on your mini phobia."

I started laughing, "Mini phobia? So that's what we're calling it?"

"Yep," he said with a straight face.

"It is just a small phobia." I sighed and said with a smirk, "I don't know if that's the right word. I can't help but resist the idea of getting on a warship and being stuck out there without any freedom. And what about King? I'm assuming he'll have to stay here." I looked down at him, and his head popped up, hearing his name. He stuck his nose in my hand for a rub.

It would be much better if he could go with me, but the chief shook his head. "Sorry, but he'll have to stay here. John can look after him. Brutus will enjoy having him for company." The chief put his cup down, grabbed my hand, and looked me straight in the eye. "I completely understand your feelings. Katie's, as well. You both are the strongest people I know. Having spent a good bit of time on a warship at the beginning of my career, I can tell you once you're on that ship, and considering the size of the Phantom IIs, you'll feel like you're in a small city. You'll never feel like you're in space. I just want you to know and give you my perspective."

I did appreciate his point of view. Outside of my dad, I respected his opinion as a friend and my boss.

He continued, "Plus, you're a badass, and they won't know what hit them." He gave me a charming grin, and I couldn't help but smile back.

"I'm not Wonder Woman, you know," I reply.

He shakes his head and grins. "Wonder Woman?" he asks.

I stood up, put a hand on his shoulder, and rolled my eyes. "Look it up. She's a great pre-divergence superhero!!" I commanded King to follow, and we headed to the door.

"Physical training, no skipping it," he reminded me on our way out. "Then head to chat with your dad."

King and I took off toward the elevators. Physical training was an excellent idea. I felt like punching something — again.

We spent four hours running through our obstacle course. Extreme physical training was the norm, but we all needed to blow off extra steam today. I needed it, and so did Katie. She was upset about going into space. I knew her well enough to see it was bothering her, but she rarely talked about what happened to us as kids, even with Matt.

My way of dealing with things was talking, which I did regularly and mostly with Matt. He helped me work, personally and professionally, around the walls I hit. I wished Katie would, too. But even if she didn't talk to Matt, she knew I'd be there for her. It's been that way since we left that slave ship.

We agreed to meet at Stonehedges, the bar that Matt and Alice own. I was looking forward to seeing them. Plus, Maverick had been home for a few days, and I'd yet to see him because of the chaos from the last mission.

I was always thankful that Matt Williams found us on that Nomad ship and even more that he kept us together. He immediately filed adoption papers to take responsibility for Katie, me, and baby Maverick. And it ended up that he fell for Alice, and Alice for him, so they were married five years after our rescue. Katie and I were her bridesmaids, and little Mav was the ring bearer. I kept the photo from that day with me. It was my lucky photo.

I would never forget what Matt did for all of us. While I may have lost my real family 28 years ago, I gained a new, amazing one. Even Maverick, who, when he was younger, I could have killed numerous times. Okay, maybe it was an exaggeration, but he tested me regularly. He was an incredible young man that we were all proud of.

Stonehedges sat at this end of Snowden Valley, as close to TechStar as allowed. Techstar did not allow construction within several kilometres of the base's location to keep the area secure. Everything leading into TechStar was heavily monitored.

I walked into the bar, and the rush of being home hit me. It never ceased to be my safe place. Matt was working behind the bar. Alice could be seen serving a few tables, and I noticed Maverick in the kitchen. That guy never missed an opportunity to cook. He really should have been a chef.

Matt waved me over. "You're here early."

"Yeah," I sighed. His gaze changed, and he yelled over to Henry, the other bartender, to take over for him. He came around the bar, put his arm around my shoulder and led me to our family table.

"Spill Jesse," he stated matter-of-factly. I could have sworn he had a direct line to my head.

I laughed as he encouraged me to share, "You remember I told you about the last mission … well, at least what I could tell you?"

He nodded.

While he'd been in the military, he left several years ago, shortly after Katie and I received our SPAR positions. He stayed to ensure we were well-trained and prepped for the team tests. I could tell him a bit about the mission. He'd guess or find out the rest in other ways. He might be retired, but he was still tied into what was happening at TechStar.

"I remember. Hard one to forget."

"Yes," I agreed, while I blew out a breath before I continued, "and it turns out that a Krean warship stumbled upon a freighter that was holding the people we couldn't get to."

"A Krean warship, huh?" He indicated for me to continue.

"There's been a development on how they want to proceed," I told him.

He looked at me across the table and grabbed my hand. "I was waiting for this to happen."

I frowned at him.

He continued, "I knew you would be expected to go into space someday. You're far too good at your job. I did some checking into that Terra Four mission. I heard that all of the traffickers you captured are dead."

"Shit, are you serious?" *Dead, how the hell are they dead?* It seemed there was something our Kreans forgot to bloody mention.

Matt nodded. "It's not unusual. The Nomad are known for killing their allies. They don't leave loose ends. But you know that isn't the problem. For them to be found dead as prisoners at the TechStar Lazarus base — you know what that means?"

Oh, I knew what that meant. "Inside job."

He nodded again.

We both sat quietly for a bit. I had so much running through my head. Plus, I was thinking about the fact that the Aries brought in more traffickers. Shit, I hoped they survived long enough for questioning.

"Yeah, they want the team to join the warship Aries. I don't know the exact mission details, but you get the idea."

"I do, and imagine you're struggling with it. Katie as well, but she'd never say," he sighed. "The two of you are resilient. Brilliant, too, but your survival instincts have made you both the way you are. Maverick has that, too, but not in the same way because he was a baby when everything went down. You two were old enough to remember."

He sat back. "You know your mother worries about this, too. She'll never have a reason to get back on a spaceship, but the thought that you two may have to …"

He didn't continue. There was no need. I knew Mom would worry. She was a sweet and sensitive person who had experienced many losses. I hated the idea of her worrying, but I knew there wasn't much I could do to stop it.

"Please don't tell her," I asked.

He was contemplating my request, but I could tell by the look on his face that he would say no. "We can't do that, Jesse. If I didn't tell her, she'd never forgive me for keeping it from her, especially if something happened to you two."

Mom might have been tiny and sweet, but she was fierce. I'd hate to disappoint her, and we'd be grovelling for life. "Stupid request. I take it back," and we both laughed.

I still hadn't made a clear decision. I was closer and, as always, talking with Dad made me feel better ... a bit. I had an intense desire not to let anyone down. Going on this mission was important. I couldn't argue with that point. For the people taken, for the Kreans, for the chief, for my dad, for the team and, in the end, for myself. My decision would be crucial for Katie. She would go if I did, but if I declined, she wouldn't hesitate to back me up. I didn't want to be the reason she didn't go.

Dad put his arm over my shoulder and gave me one of his big, comforting hugs. No matter how old I am, they always made me feel better.

Just as I was about to get up and chat with Mom, I looked up to see the team walk in. Right behind them is the chief and two unexpected guests. I'm surprised that Danlon and Zersus joined him. Kreans were not known to socialise with humans, especially not in a bar.

From my vantage point, I could see Danlon chatting up Katie. He was interested in her. It was so apparent, to me, at least. I nodded to Dad, directing my chin over his shoulder at the Kreans. He was about to say something when his mouth hung open. He leapt up from his seat and headed right for Danlon.

Of course he did; I don't know why I didn't realise he would recognize Danlon. Although he had been a relatively young man during our rescue, he was a grown man now and quite the man he was. I was pretty sure that the attraction wasn't one-sided, but Katie was trying hard not to show her feelings. I got up and followed behind Matt. Katie came over, grabbed me, and led me quickly away from the group.

"Oh my god. Why did they come with us?" she asked. I could see that she was fidgety, meaning something was making her uncomfortable. News flash, I'd say that was Danlon.

I had a huge grin, and she just gave me a frustrated humph,

"Could you not grin at me like that? You look far too self-satisfied."

"I can't help it." I shrugged and pointed out, "You're fidgeting."

"And what about you?" she asked.

"What about me?

"Oh, come on, you can't tell me that you aren't attracted to that massive, gorgeous male specimen called Zersus," she smirked.

"Of course I am," I admitted. What was the point of saying no? "Doesn't matter. We're expected to board his ship and work with his crew. Do I need to explain this?"

Katie shook her head and looked at the two men. "Well, thank god that doesn't include Danlon," she said and walked over to Mom, which I hadn't had a chance to do yet.

I found myself being dragged over with her. Mom gave me a questioning look. I knew she was curious about my conversation with Dad. She had great instincts and probably knew it was important. I'd tell her soon enough. As Dad said, not telling her wouldn't be the right choice so that conversation will happen. For now, though, I just wanted to enjoy the rest of the evening.

"Jesse, Katie, are you two even going to say hi?" I heard yelling from the kitchen. Yes, that was Maverick making sure he was not forgotten. As if that would ever happen. I figured I might as well get this over with and head to the kitchen. Mav grabbed me in a big hug, lifting me right off the floor.

When did he get so damn large? I heard a loud growl coming from somewhere. What the hell was that? I saw Mav look over my shoulder, and he started laughing but wouldn't let me go.

"What the hell, Mav, put me down," I demanded.

"Nope. This is seriously pissing off the big Krean over there, and I'm finding it entertaining." He had a weird idea of entertainment. I grabbed him by the ear and pinched a point in his neck. He immediately let me go. It was his sensitive point. Weird, but it worked every time.

I laughed at him and quickly moved out of his reach when he tried to grab me again. "Try that with Katie and watch the other one," I suggested, cracking up as I walked away.

Mav looked at Katie and noticed the tension while she watched Danlon. Mav winked at me. I knew he'd test out that theory. But for now, he disappeared into the kitchen. The food for the customers came first.

In the meantime, the team moved onto the stage. One of our ways to wind down and relax was to play together. We loved music, and could sing and play instruments. We were good, so when we could get together at Stonehedges, Matt and Alice kept the stage prepped for us. They would get other bands in during tourist season, but it wasn't that time of year yet. The stage was all ours for now.

Harley and I were the leads, with Katie taking her spot on the keyboard, Neil on bass, Sid playing the drums, and Joe on guitar. Harley and I took turns singing, but we could both play guitar, too. We changed that up, depending on the song.

"What's on the playlist tonight?" I asked Harley. I'm the one who led the tunes at physical training, but I went with whatever they chose here. We've perfected a lot of numbers from pre-divergence. We liked a little bit of everything, even a bit of country occasionally, and whenever we felt cheeky, we called up our 1980s tunes. Nobody had heard most of what we played, but that was okay. I felt it was important never to forget our origins.

Harley said, "Let's start with *Drive* and then hit a blues number with *Trouble with My Lover*."

Everyone nodded.

"You're the lead for those two, Jesse."

I loved both songs. *Drive* was a great start with a heavy beat, while the other was a smooth, jazzy number.

I saw Chief Cole, Danlon, and Zersus take a table near the stage, dead centre. It was a bit disconcerting with each song being about lovers. I glanced over at Harley; he smiled and winked. The bastard knew precisely what he was doing picking these songs.

With a strong beat, *Drive's* lyrics were angst-filled, about leaving and being in pain, while the second bluesy song, *Trouble with My Lover*, was about the intimacy of having his arms around me and the comfort of a lover in the middle of the night. All while Zersus sat there, watching me. It was unnerving because I felt like I was singing both to him. As I moved through each song, Harley joined in the chorus; I could feel Zersus' eyes on me. His gaze never wavered. I tried not to return his stare but found it difficult to avoid.

His deep, dark eyes in a handsome, chiselled face, were impossible to look away from. While I sang, I could only think about stroking his soft skin. No beard or stubble; with Zersus, his face was perfect in its manliness. I couldn't look away as I sang on about love. And, in my mind, it was almost impossible not to imagine what he would be like to have as mine.

As the songs ended, I was able to drag my gaze away. I needed to get my mind off of him. I practically ran off the stage in search of Mom. I suddenly had an intense need to talk to her. Mom immediately noticed the look on my face as I headed her way. I saw her glance behind me. Katie was following. Looks like the guys were going to have to perform without the two of us. Katie and I grabbed Mom and headed to the same table in the corner. I noticed Dad watching us. He winked at me. His way of saying, "Go for it."

Mom wasted no time. "Are you going to tell me what's bothering you two?" She looked from Katie to me and back again. "And don't think I don't know that it has something to do with those big gorgeous Kreans over there."

I watched her look closer at them, her eyes widening. I think she just realised who Danlon was.

"Is that…?" she asked.

We both nodded back at her.

"Oh my," she gasped.

I watched the emotions work their way over Mom's face. She grabbed both our hands. Katie gave me a brief nod, so I took the lead. "They're here because of things that have been happening that involve the Nomad."

I watched that sink in. She didn't ask us anything; she waited for me to continue.

"The team is needed on a warship."

Her grip on our hands tightened, and she glanced over my shoulder. I turned to see Maverick standing behind us. He heard. "Do you want to join us?" I indicated the seat beside me.

Once Maverick sat down, I got into the details — what I was able to tell them. I could see the concern on Mom's face, but Maverick was nodding his head. With what Mav did for a living as a security specialist, I knew he'd understand.

Once I was done, we all sat quietly. Mom was the first to move; she hugged us tightly. She whispered, "Promise me. You'll come home. Promise."

I moved out of her embrace and saw her tears and pride. "I promise."

She nodded, got up and walked away right into Dad's arms.

Maverick grabbed both our hands and said, "Damn, I'm jealous." Leave it to Mav to end with a joke.

I shook my head at him and looked over at Zersus' table to catch the chief's attention.

I nodded to him, indicating for him to follow me. Katie joined us. We took him into the back office for some privacy. Katie waited for me to lead the conversation. I knew she would go with what I decided, and while I couldn't decide for the rest of the team, I knew they would follow my lead too. The guys wanted to pursue this mission.

I turned to the chief and told him my decision, "We're in."

There's no turning back now.

CHAPTER
EIGHT
ZERSUS

DANLON and I returned to Terra Moonbase an hour ago. We'd spent the evening on Terra One and decided to stay and return this morning. I was surprised at how much I enjoyed being on the planet.

We met quickly with Magistrate Eton to confirm the mission details and agreed that the SPAR team would join us on the Aries.

I strode quietly through the busy corridors of the moonbase and contemplated the potential issues we would be dealing with. My warrior crew worked fine with humans, as we have many on the Aries, but the SPAR team differed from regular military-trained humans. Based on their training and the files I read about them, their skills were top-notch, well beyond regular military.

And then there was Jesse. First, she had reservations about being on my warship. Yes, she agreed, but I wasn't sure she did that for herself. My instincts told me that her decision resulted from her thinking about the mission and the people affected, not herself. While that was commendable, it didn't negate the fact that she hated the idea of being in space. I hoped she could adapt.

Second, I was having a hard time coping with my attraction to her. She was human. My fascination with her was confusing — maybe frustrating was a better description. If I was being honest, I wasn't attracted to many females. I found most lacking. Damn, that sounds bad and so egotistical, but very few females have attracted my attention. My brother had often wondered if my Kindred was male, which was not impossible. I'd never had the urge to find my Kindred, but it was getting difficult being without one. But I did assume mine would be Krean. Now, I wasn't so sure.

Jesse was a rare gem; my instincts screamed that I shouldn't ignore my feelings. The problem was we had to work together on the Aries. And I was in charge; it's my ship. I hoped we wouldn't clash, but she was used to being in charge. However, what I witnessed of her and her team, she treated them as equals. I hoped that would translate to us being able to work together.

I sighed to myself. I had no idea how I would deal with being around her constantly.

I reached the bay where our transports are being stocked with supplies for the Aries. I looked around and found my brother, Issbeck, giving instructions to get things moving. Issbeck was the nicest guy you'd ever want to meet until he's in "boss" mode, and then I wondered if he was more "Prime" than I was. I chuckled to myself because there was no way in hell he's worse. All joking aside, Issbeck would make a great prime one day.

When Issbeck realised I was back, he gave some final instructions and crossed over to me. "How did it go? I've passed along the instructions you gave me to have the additional accommodations prepared. Who's joining us?" he asked.

"We'll have the senior-level SPAR team joining us," I replied.

"Really? Damn, I've heard they go through crazy training to get chosen for one of those teams, but to be the top team … " I could see Issbeck was impressed. He should be.

"What you've heard is not an exaggeration, but you might be surprised to learn that two top team members are female."

"No way!"

I laughed at the look on his face. He has spent far too much time with humans. He's picked up a lot of their expressions.

"The team lead is the female from the video surveillance." I watched the expression that formed slowly over his face as that sunk in.

"WOW." For the first time in a while, Issbeck was speechless — for a moment. "I guess I shouldn't be surprised. We have a few human females on the Aries that are pretty tough and well-trained."

He was correct, we did. I didn't come into contact with them regularly, so I tended not to think about it. We also had a couple of Krean females.

I couldn't help but smile and took off towards the transport ship. I wanted to return to the Aries and ensure the SPAR team's accommodations were well managed. I figured I'd just take the stock transport over. No, of course, I didn't care about Jesse's room, no, not at all. *Right, just keep telling yourself that idiot.*

I huffed as I walked away and heard Issbeck laughing at me.

"You seem a bit overly bothered about the fact that the leader is female," he pointed out.

I didn't bother responding, which was a mistake because he was dogging my steps and peppering me with questions about her."What's her name?"

"Jesse."

"Is she pretty?"

"Yes."

"Super pretty?"

"Yes. You saw the video." It's not like anyone could miss that she's gorgeous.

"But she's human?"

I stopped at that question, turned and looked at him, "Yes, she is."

"And you …"

"Enough," I cut him off. "Get back to it. They'll be here in a few hours, and I want the Aries ready to leave the dock as soon as they are settled in."

"Don't worry, you can count on me." He smiled, took off and got back to giving orders. I figured he would want to be the one to greet the SPAR team when they arrived to get a good look at Jesse.

I continued to the transport that was prepped to leave. I could see my warship from the Moonbase supply bay and was itching to get back on board. I admit I was surprised at how much I enjoyed the time on Terra One. Snowden Valley was beautiful; if I had to choose a Terra to live on, it would be there.

Although it could never substitute for the thrill I feel when I step on the Aries.

I headed towards the front of the transport, where the two pilot seats are. Captain Cain Beaudreau was the pilot on this run. I liked the man. He was also one of our best pilots. He could fly anything, but his ability to manipulate a Wraith was second to none.

"Captain Beaudreau, did you get to spend time on your home planet?" I asked. I knew that he was from Terra One. He grew up on the other side of the mountain range surrounding the planet. I didn't know where he came from, but I'm sure it was a beautiful city. Terra One was known for its well-established cities from what was once an original part of Earth called North America. Many large cities just became resituated but were, for the most part, left intact. Snowden Valley was also one of those places. From my research, it was originally called Whistler.

"Yes, Prime, I spent a day with family and friends. It was a nice change of scenery, but I always enjoy returning to the Aries," he said.

I had similar feelings.

"How about you?" he asked.

I looked at him and kept my answer as short as possible. None of the crew knows why we were back at Moonbase.

"I went for a short trip to Snowden Valley." I noted the surprise on his face, but then an understanding crossed his features. I should have known. He wasn't stupid and probably realised that TechStar had one of its main bases on Terra One in the Valley. He didn't ask, but I could tell he wanted to. I patted his shoulder and nodded. "Let's get us back to the Aries, shall we?" I sat beside Cain in the navigator's seat and began the pre-flight check.

Everything scheduled for this transport was ready to go, with confirmation from my brother. The bay crew had to exit for the ignition. Once they were safely out of the way, we were off. The flight was only fifteen minutes to the Aries.

Looking at it from our vantage point, it was a fantastic ship. I knew they were working on a new version of the Phantoms, but I couldn't help but wonder how they could improve on the Aries.

We headed towards the central docking bay, located at the back of the left engine section, and, without so much as a bump, Captain Beaudreau had us in and settled.

I was the first up from my seat, after thanking the Captain, and out of transport when the door opened.

Simal greeted me through the bay doors, "Prime Zersus, welcome back aboard."

"Seriously? You're always so formal, Simal."

He smiled and followed along beside me as we exited the bays. Everyone else worked to unload the transport.

"Per your instructions, I've ordered the prep of the six chambers. Who are we expecting?"

I knew he was curious as I hadn't given him any details on the SPAR team, but I had been specific about where I wanted them. Their chambers would be in the same corridor where all bridge members stayed.

"The senior SPAR team from TechStar will join us for this mission," I informed him.

"I see," I'm sure he did. That should explain why I wanted them in those chambers.

"I want the team lead to have the chambers next to mine. Her name is Jesse Williams. Her sister, Katie Williams, will be placed on her other side," I ordered.

"These two women must be very special," he stated.

"There are several women on all the SPAR teams. Chief Cole explained that females typically qualify for SPAR as often as males. These two are the best."

I tried not to put too much importance on Jesse and Katie. I had an ulterior motive for that. I didn't want him to ask questions; he was as bad as my brother.

Simal didn't say anything further. He continued along beside me, and we headed to the bridge. I knew the SPAR team would arrive shortly, and I wanted to ensure we had everything ready to head out as soon as they were on board and settled.

◆

Simal and I worked on the systems prep, pulling up the needed star maps and downloading Chief Cole's intel.

I didn't notice how long we had been at it until Issbeck walked onto the bridge. That's when I realised Jesse and her team must be on board.

I turned to Issbeck and saw the big smile on his face.

Yes, they were definitely on board. Sure enough, he commented, "The SPAR team is on board and getting comfortable in their chambers. Kiv is with them and will escort them here after they have deposited their bags so they can watch us head out into space."

I could see a question in his expression, and I knew it was because of the room I had chosen for Jesse.

"Now that I've met her, I completely understand," he said.

Simal looked at Issbeck, and I gave my brother an unmistakable look. I didn't want him going into the situation about Jesse in front of anyone. Never mind, I didn't even know what I was feeling and didn't need the crew making me the topic of the ship's gossip.

Simal got the message and returned to what he was doing, but Issbeck wanted to ask me something. I held my hand up and shook my head. "Let's just get the ship ready to get on our way," I ordered.

And that ended that subject. Shortly after, the balance of the bridge crew joined us. We got confirmation from the bay that the ship's stocks and remaining crew had returned. Everyone from the ship had opted back in for this voyage, even knowing we had the mission to find Curalim. So we were leaving with our standard crew of 450, plus the SPAR team.

About 20 minutes later, the bridge doors slid open to the SPAR team. I walked over and greeted them, "Welcome aboard the Aries. If you'd like to watch us leave the dock, feel free to find a seat. We have made extra space for all of you to join us regularly on the bridge."

I watched them all smile. "Thank you, Prime," Jesse says. "We'd be happy to join and watch."

I could see the stress on her face. I also noted that Katie looked slightly tense, but neither of these ladies wanted their discomfort to be noticeable. Meanwhile, the other team members appeared to be looking forward to being on the Aries.

They spread out and grabbed a seat. I directed Jesse to the seat beside me. I noted the bridge crew observing.

I turned to the crew and introduced the SPAR team, "I'd like to introduce you all to the SPAR team. Jesse Williams beside me is their lead." I watched the raised brows on my crew, but they recovered quickly, and I continued, "Her second is Sid King, and the tech systems specialist is Katie Williams. She will upgrade and install new cloaking programs, including biosuit cloaks."

I heard the approval from everyone. I knew how they felt. I was very impressed with the improvements and additions.

I indicated the others, "Neil Fireside is their sniper and explosives expert, Harley DeSouza is also tech and systems, and Joe LeBlanc is hand-to-hand combat, intelligence and a weapons expert. They will all be key in assisting us in our mission to find the Nomad."

I watched that one-word sink in. They all understood the importance of our mission. It was time to get us out of the dock.

I requested Simal put up our exit on the primary screen so we could watch Aries' progress. I assured Jesse and her team that my warriors were experienced and the process would be seamless.

I couldn't resist watching Jesse's face as we slowly moved away from the base. The ship had to be manoeuvred backwards out of the docking clamps. Then, when we were far enough out of the dock's range, we would swing around and leave the Moonbase behind. Two of the Terras were in front of us, but we could easily navigate through them and out of the magnetosphere.

Jesse seemed to be relaxing. You couldn't feel any of the ship's movement. Stabilisers kept adjustments undetectable. I gave Simal directions as we moved past the Terras and headed towards Jupiter and Saturn. We wanted to ensure we didn't miss anything and planned to fly around both planets, running scans.

Jesse looked over at me and smiled. She was such a beautiful woman at any given time, but when she smiled, she was stunning, and took my breath away.

"That was enjoyable to watch. However, we'd like to regroup and study the mission notes, if that's okay?" she asked.

I knew they'd want to do that; however, she impressed me when she asked. I should have known she wouldn't have wanted to undermine my position in front of my crew. If I admitted it to myself, I felt she was my equal, but my domain was the Aries.

I asked Kiv to escort them to the War Room so they could have access to the details. Jesse asked if we would be joining them.

"Once we are settled into our route, we will join you."

She nodded and the six of them left. I watched her every step. She was wearing a standard military outfit you wouldn't consider feminine; plain black cargo pants that hugged her long legs and perfect backside paired with a long-sleeved shirt that fit like a glove. You couldn't miss the fact that she was all woman with that damn thing on. The SPAR logo was above her left breast. She ended it off with black combat boots and a leather belt. My mind went to places it shouldn't as I thought about unwrapping her.

As the doors to the bridge closed, I heard a throat clear. I turned to see the entire crew staring at me. Some were smiling, some tried not to, and my brother and Simal outright laughed.

"Seriously? Get us moving," I said as I settled into my seat. I hoped I could survive this trip.

CHAPTER
NINE
JESSE

THE GROUP of us climbed aboard one of the new Eros II
Transports. I had to admit it was a beautiful piece of engineering.
The Eros II had more room than the Eros I, which Danlon and
Zersus apparently arrived on.

Both resembled helicopters. Harley said the Kreans loved our
land choppers and how they hovered so they designed the Eros
to look and feel similar. Also the feature of being able to hover
worked well with Moonbase's setup.

The Eros II resembled our old combat choppers with their
vast body and entries on either side. The similarities ended there.
The Eros was visually beautiful, whereas our combat choppers
were merely functional with little thought put into how they
looked. They were meant to blend into the environment,
whereas the Eros definitely stood out. The Eros II had gold
colour across the front, continuing down the sides and over the
doors. The top, moving towards the back engine, was a dark
burgundy. The back engine looked like a fish's fin. The controls
were also similar to that of a chopper's, but the manoeuvrability
of the Eros was far more advanced. And, of course, the biggest
difference was that the Eros was space-worthy. They'd be great
for our teams.

To say we were all geeking out over the machine would be an understatement. Katie forgot the mission and why we were getting on the thing because she loved it so much. I didn't forget, but that didn't mean I couldn't appreciate Krean engineering.

We stored our gear and hopped on board. The pilot told us to strap in for takeoff. I had no problem with this ride. This was not unusual for us; we regularly moved from planet to planet for our missions, but we have never had a reason to go to Moonbase.

I was interested in getting a closer look at the location that the Kreans built. At times, when you moved between planets, you could get a brief glimpse of Moonbase if you happened to be flying within range of the moon but we had never gotten close enough for me to get a good look at it.

Moving away from Terra One, I noted we flew in a semi-circle past Terra Two. I loved that planet and didn't get many opportunities to visit. Next to Terra One, it was one of the prettiest planets, even from space.

We moved further from Terra Two, and I could see the moonbase coming into view over a mountain crater. The Moonbase settled into a section they cleared, creating direct access to space. Nothing was blocking the comings and goings of ships. I could see the many docking stages where there were several ships. They looked like they were hanging in space. Other ships off to the far side of the base looked like they were being built. It was the norm that all new warships were built in space. When ships arrived, they docked in the hanging stations for maintenance.

I couldn't help but laugh and think about the old Earth space entertainment series and how the docking stations reminded me of that. The Kreans gave us direct access to space. We had only ventured as far as Mars and had a little advancement, but nothing like we do now. It unfortunately made us prime for the picking when the Nomad showed up. While I may not have wanted to go out to space, I could appreciate how far we had come because of the Kreans.

A dark, sleek, incredible warship appeared before us, and our pilot told us, "That's the Aries."

"Wow." I could see the look on Katie's face. Yes, it was impressive.

The Eros was going in for a landing in one of the Aries' docking bays, but we first travelled along the ship's side and swung around the nose which came to a point almost like a bird's beak. The whole ship was black. You could see the bridge area at the top, with large observation windows. Below were what looked like rooms and multiple floors. Two large sections came out of the sides and looked a bit like folded wings.

The pilot moved the Eros toward the back of one of the wing sections, and I could see the landing bay come into view.

"It reminds me of a large black crow sitting and waiting for its prey," said Sid, leaning over me to get a better view.

I agreed; it did. It was ominous but beautiful at the same time.

"We are heading in shortly," said our pilot. "We have to wait for the Moonbase transport to finish unloading supplies. It shouldn't be more than 15 minutes."

While we sat there, we watched the comings and goings. Small machines were moving up and down the side of the Aries. I assumed they were looking for anything that needed work on the outside of the ship. From my research, it launched five years ago and only visited Moonbase on rare occasions. The last time must have been when their systems were updated with the cloaks, which had to be a good eight months ago or more. I couldn't imagine being in space that long.

I loved Terra One and my home, but understood the call to be on a warship. I'm sure it was no different than how we felt about being on a SPAR team.

We watched the supply ship leave. As soon as it had cleared us, we headed in. As we slowly moved into the bay, it was temporarily clear of people. The pilot landed softly, and I was seriously impressed with the Eros II.

"Thanks for the soft landing," I addressed our pilot.

He saluted and smiled back. As he powered down the Eros, I noted many Kreans heading in our direction.

The doors on either side slid open, and we exited. I was first, followed by Katie and Sid. Harley, Neil, and Joe got out on the other side. A young Krean headed toward me, and I couldn't help but feel that he looked familiar.

He smiled at me and asked, "Jesse Williams?"

I nodded.

"It's a pleasure to meet you." He had a massive grin and looked like a small boy who found a treasure. The feeling was he's up to something but still quite charming.

I shook his hand, eyebrows raised.

"I'm Second Issbeck. My brother is Prime Zersus," he introduced himself.

"That explains why you look familiar."

"I get that a lot," he chuckled.

I instantly liked him.

"Our warrior, Kiv, is going to take you to your chambers," he indicated to the fellow who came in with him. "You can drop your things off, and he will escort you to the bridge. We are stocked, and the full crew is back on board, so we're about 30 minutes from launch. Prime thought you might like to be on the bridge during that process."

Most of the team would enjoy being on the bridge to watch. Even Katie looked excited. I was the only one still not comfortable with the whole idea. I couldn't get past the feeling that something terrible was coming. I guess my reluctance about going out into space was getting to me.

"Thanks for the welcome. And yes, a quick drop of our things would be great." I noticed everyone had gathered their bags. Sid picked up mine, and I grabbed it from him. I wasn't one to let someone else carry my gear.

The warrior, Kiv, asked us to follow him. I noticed he kept looking over at me and Katie. He wanted to ask me something, so I encouraged him, "You look like you'd like to ask me a question. Please go ahead."

He hesitated. "I don't want to offend you."

"Okay, how about I tell you what you want to ask? You want to know how a woman could be leading the team?"

I laughed as his eyes widened. "You're the team leader? I had no idea. We don't see it often and spend so much time in space that we aren't exposed to much of what happens on the Terras."

I understood and knew Krean women didn't typically take lead warrior positions. We had several female Kreans that work for SPAR in intelligence. So yes, being out in space so much limited their exposure to how their species had changed.

"Well, you're missing a lot being out in space. We have several Krean females that work at SPAR headquarters. None are on the SPAR teams, but many work in intelligence operations; others are analysts and systems engineers. Perhaps it's a natural evolution. They want to make a difference like everyone." I smiled at him, and he had a massive grin.

"You're right; we are missing a lot. I'd love to see that. Maybe someday."

"Perhaps."

We headed for what Kiv referred to as a maglift. Looked like an elevator to me, but it was so smooth you couldn't feel it moving. It felt like floating up several floors. When the doors opened, Kiv explained that this level had direct access to the bridge, the War Room, and the main living quarters for the bridge crew.

"Prime Zersus has asked that we arrange chambers for you here so you can access everything."

He began sorting us into our rooms. There was a process for us to have our handprints scanned for entrance to our quarters and other areas of the ship.

One by one, we were each given rooms. I noted that Katie and I had ours side by side. I instructed everyone to drop off their gear and to meet back in the corridor with Kiv in 15 minutes.

When the door slid open to my quarters, I was taken aback. I thought it would just be a simple bedroom with a bathroom. This was far from simple. The doors opened into a comfortable living area. A set of stairs to the right led down to a bedroom. A glass barrier provided a view down to it with floor-to-ceiling windows, where the stairs are situated that gave a view into space. I laughed to myself. You certainly wouldn't have to worry about a peeping tom.

The bedroom was quite large. A desk and sitting area were on the far side, opposite the windows. The bathroom was behind the bed, under the living room. It was also a good size, including a shower with rainfall fixtures. The closet was beside the desk. I loved the space. It was not what I thought I'd find on a warship. I expected a room that was much more utilitarian. The only thing missing was a kitchen, so I assumed everyone ate in one general area.

I dropped my gear bag on the bed. I would unpack it after we are enroute. I headed back up the stairs and realised another door was across from the sofa. Another closet? I walked over and opened it to find a small bathroom. I smiled at the logic of having one off the main living area, as well. Again, surprising. The designers thought to provide as much comfort as possible to the crew.

I stepped out of my room to find Kiv waiting patiently. I was the first one back.

"Are you happy with your chambers?" he asked.

"I'm a little shocked. Are all the rooms like that?"

"Not all are two floors. That is unique to the chambers on this level, but the smaller single-level ones are full suites. When the designers put the ship together, they decided that because we spend so much time in space, the chambers should be designed to feel like home; we need more than just a bed. I would be happy with that, but it is nice to have a bit more space."

Slowly, the rest of the team joined us. Katie looked at me and said, "Wow, did you see our rooms?" She turned to the guys and asked, "Are your rooms two floors?"

They all nodded. Harley piped up, "It's the perfect bachelor pad."

Katie smacked him, and he laughed. Of course, Harley would say that. I loved him to death, but he was a bit of a player. He's never had a girlfriend in all the time I've known him. When he fell for someone, it was going to be fun. That went for the whole team, me included.

Kiv also chuckled, "We don't have much need for that on this ship."

Harley looked a touch horrified. "What do you guys do when you need … you know?"

"Oh, we know a few places where we can stop for — female attention — on some outer planets. While they aren't Krean or human, it works." Everyone snickered a bit and I swear Kiv blushed.

He indicated for us to follow him.

Joe moved in beside me, "You doin' okay kid?"

We let everyone else walk ahead, and I hung back with him. "I'm fine." I can see he doesn't believe me so I grin at him, "I can't help but feel off about this whole thing. It's not being on the ship. At least, I don't think that's it. I think it's the mission."

"Shit, you have a bad feeling?" he asked, stopping and turning to look at me.

I nodded.

Joe got a worried look on his face. "You're gonna give me more grey hairs than I already have?"

"Not on purpose," I joked as we both started to follow the rest again.

"Yeah, but we both know your feelings are not something we should ignore."

I sighed. "I don't know what it is. I can't help but think it's just my hesitation about being on the ship and nothing more. We'll see how it goes."

"You know, if you want to talk it out, I'm here," he offered.

I patted his arm and smiled. He was like an older brother. He had the calmest personality — big on meditation. He tried to get me to join him when he was in meditation mode, but I could never shut my brain down long enough for it. I found being in his company was relaxing enough. And, as with everyone else on the team, I trusted him completely.

It didn't take us long to get to the bridge. I realised now just how close our rooms were to the key areas of the ship. Before we entered, Kiv indicated another set of doors and mentioned the War Room.

"War Room?" I questioned.

"It's where we meet to plan our missions," he explained — it makes sense you'd want another room other than the bridge for that purpose. The room's name must come from when the Kreans needed it for exactly that purpose before we joined forces with them.

We continued on to doors that opened to a space that combined beautiful design with function. I had never been on a warship bridge but did not expect sleek, high-tech perfection. The first people I looked at were Katie and Harley. The look on their faces was priceless. They were impressed.

"Damn, this place is amazing," said Katie. She must have loved it because Katie hardly ever swears. Right away, she started moving around to look at everything, Harley with her. I felt like I was being watched, and when I turned my head to the left, I found Zersus staring at me.

As he approached, I couldn't help but admire the man. His uniform fit his muscular frame, and his steps were smooth, solid and purposeful. There wasn't a single thing about him that said weak. And god, he was sexy. I was surprised that seeing him lit me up like a Christmas tree. I needed to get a handle on my libido.

"Welcome to the Aries Bridge," he said. He introduced us to the crew, and I was impressed that he remembered everyone on the team and their positions. I did notice his crew watching me; I could see the quick surprise that passed over their faces when he mentioned my position, but they recovered quickly.

Zersus indicated that I should follow him. Where he sat on the bridge was obvious, and he wanted me beside him. Everyone else was distributed at different seats around the semi-circle of screens, which Issbeck sorted out for them.

Issbeck and the other warrior next to him, introduced as Simal, were laughing about something. I glanced at Zersus, and he was scowling at them. He ordered, "Move us out."

They kept laughing but turned and proceeded to begin the launch.

"On screen, so our guests can watch the process," Zersus commanded.

I noticed him glance occasionally at me. It was sweet that he was trying to ensure my comfort. "I'm fine," I told him. He looked at me for a few seconds, nodded and turned to the visual.

I watched as the dock slowly moved away from us.

Issbeck explained, "They will move the docking system away on either side. We are going to back out. Then, the Aries will swing around and head out between Terra Two and Three. We will not hit our full speed until we are well out of the magnetosphere of the planets."

We all watched. Our current view was of the Krean moon-base, and we could see that we were slowly backing away from it. As we cleared the docking station, I could see us swinging around. I don't know if Issbeck did it on purpose so we could get a final view of Terra One, but that was the first thing we saw, and then Terra Two came into view. We smoothly travelled between Terra Two and Three.

If I was being honest, it felt like we were floating. There was no motion, movement, bumping, thumbing, or humming of the engines. If you couldn't see that you were moving through space, you would have thought the ship stood still.

As we travelled past the Terras, I felt the slight power shift to the engines. It was the only indication that anything changed, and suddenly, we were moving faster. However, you could still swear the ship was standing still. Amazing, really.

Issbeck turned to us, "We are heading to Jupiter and Saturn first to make sure we didn't miss anything."

"That was enjoyable to watch. However, we'd like to regroup and study the mission notes, if that's okay?" I asked Zersus.

He nodded and turned to Kiv, "Can you take them to the War Room? We've set up the systems with everything for the mission."

We all stood up and headed for the doors. I looked over my shoulder. "Will any of you be joining us?" I asked.

He nodded. "Once we are settled into our route, we will join you."

The team and I left the bridge and followed Kiv to the War Room. Inside was a conference table with screens in the middle. Kiv hit a button to bring them all up into position, indicating we should make ourselves comfortable.

"Feel free to take a seat wherever you wish. All the systems will require your hand scans to operate." He turned and sat down at a monitor. Each of us sat in front of a screen, initiated it with our hand scans, and hunkered down to familiarise ourselves with the intel for the mission.

And so it all began. . . Where we went from here would be a crap shoot. I hoped this mission wasn't a waste of time. I quickly became engrossed with my reading and, somehow, forgot I was on a warship in space.

CHAPTER
TEN
JESSE

I was engrossed in the details of the Aries' encounter with the Nomad freighter and the rescue. As expected, the children who had gone missing from the mission on Terra Four were in that group. I couldn't have been happier that they were all rescued and returned to their families.

I watched Sid get up and head over to Kiv, who had remained with us and was helping Katie and Harley. They were working on ensuring that the systems update to their Wraiths and biosuits had no hiccups.

"Kiv, I'm assuming there's a training room here?" I asked.

He nodded. "Yes, we have a training arena with various difficulty levels."

The one thing I knew about Krean warriors was that their training methods were similar to ours. As with our rookies, they started at an easier level and worked their way up. The more complex and skilled they became, the more their training advanced. Physical skill was only one aspect of SPAR. Kreans placed heavier importance on that.

"Would anyone be willing to join me for some PT?"

As I assumed, everyone, besides Katie and Harley, jumped at the chance. I hated training by myself, so this was perfect.

"Can you take us to the training room, please — advanced level?" I asked Kiv.

He slightly bowed with a nod, grinned, and gestured for us to follow him. The training arena, as he called it, was on the next level down. He explained, "The advanced arena takes up this whole side of the ship. It needs the largest space to accommodate all physical tests."

Perfect. He escorted us in, and I was impressed. We encountered a vast selection of weapons and targets in the first section to our left. Target practice with a pulse weapon appealed to me today. It had been a bit since I had a chance for weapons training.

"Sid, I'm going to hit the target practice." Kiv looked at me strangely, and I realised he didn't know I could use a pulse weapon. I smiled as I walked up to grab a short-range pulse rifle, a slightly different design than we had at SPAR. I flipped it on. It imprinted on my hand and responded to my commands. I indicated to Kiv to turn on the targets. I raised the weapon, lined it up and started moving and firing.

SPAR and my team knew my skills with any pulse weapon. First, I was one of the few humans who could use it, but second, my skill with any weapon was up there with the Kreans, even better by many of our species' standards. I spent 20 minutes taking down every target. A pulse weapon sent out a series of invisible pulses at different levels, controlled by simple touch. They went from immobilisation to full kill settings. For target practice, short and controlled immobilisation bursts were good enough. Not a single miss in the bunch. I smiled as I hit my last target. I liked this particular weapon. It was a design we didn't have at SPAR and worked well in my hands. I had to talk to the chief about getting one.

When I turned around, I had attracted an audience, including Zersus. I had no idea he had arrived.

"How the hell did you do that?" Kiv asked.

"Do what?"

"Use that weapon. Humans can't use them."

I replied, "Most humans. I can. I always use a pulse rifle."

I watched Kiv and many other Kreans who had stopped to watch, looking shocked. They smiled and started to clap. I was glad I could entertain them.

"You are quite adept with them," Zersus said.

He turned to Kiv, "Be sure all our pulse weapons are provided for her use. Take them and leave them in her chambers, if that's alright by you, Jesse?"

I nodded.

"Kiv will give you a selection; you can use what you feel works best for you. You are used to that one, but we have many others."

I looked at him, smiled and said, "No, this one I've never used before. I love it, though."

Zersus looked at me with shock but then shook his head and laughed. I guess he wasn't expecting that.

I powered down the rifle and returned it to its spot. I headed over to the mat area where the guys were sparring. They were doing a "one on two" sequence. It was something we worked on regularly. It was rare in our jobs that we would be in a situation where we were up against just one perp, so dealing with more than one target at a time was critical.

Zersus followed beside me with Kiv. I asked them, "Would you both be willing to let me take on the two of you?"

Kiv started to laugh while Zersus looked undecided about how he wanted to answer that question.

"Oh, come on, you're not afraid of a female, are you?"

That had the effect I thought it would. They both looked at me and, without saying a word, walked over to an empty area. I took off my long-sleeved shirt to reveal my workout tank underneath. I also took off my boots and socks. I liked to spar in my bare feet when I could. At TechStar, I had to leave the combat boots on most of the time because that was more realistic in an attack scenario, but getting rid of the shoes made my movements more fluid and natural.

I was looking forward to this. Zersus was huge and probably had a good 50 kilos or more on me. Kiv wasn't exactly small either, but he was probably closer to Sid's size. My thoughts were, "The bigger they are —." I smiled at them and indicated I was ready.

I stood in the middle, and they circled. I watched how they moved. I mentally measured their strides, leg and arm lengths, and hand sizes. If I was going to win, I needed to find ways to work around the apparent difference in our sizes. They didn't realise I was regularly faced with situations where I was smaller than my opponent. There were ways to use that to my advantage.

Just as I could see them ready to pounce, Zersus' communicator went off. He looked down at it and grimaced a little. "I'm being called back to the bridge."

"Rain check then?" I asked.

He didn't want to leave, but he smiled and responded, "I'm not sure what that means, but if you're saying we will revisit this, you can count on it." He turned and left the training arena.

Kiv was standing there, unsure what to do, so I asked him if he wanted to spar with just me. He was definitely up for it. He was skilled, but I was better. We moved around the mat, jabbing and kicking. He was having a hard time getting any shots in on me because I moved faster than him. As always, I used my smaller, quicker frame to move out of his range. His long arms were not an advantage against me.

My fighting style was a combination of multiple forms of martial arts. My real father had owned a dojo on Earth, so all of us kids were introduced to different disciplines at a young age. I had been taking Judo for a year when I was kidnapped.

When Matt found out, he gave me the choice of whether or not I wanted to continue with it. I did, but I also learned to incorporate multiple other styles into one—what was once considered mixed martial arts. I mastered hand-to-hand combat using that mixed style. In most cases, it gave me an edge over my opponents.

If Zersus had been here, I doubt it would have been a simple spar. Kiv asked me to show him some of my moves. He said he was impressed with how I could telegraph him as if I knew where he would strike me. He wanted to learn how to do that.

We became quickly embroiled with having him attack me. I'd fend him off, then show him how I managed to do so. I don't know how much time passed but a throat clearing caught my attention, and I noticed Simal standing and watching. He had his arms crossed with a smile.

"It wouldn't hurt to have you train our warriors, Lieutenant Commander."

"Please call me Jesse; you know I'd be happy too, but Joe," I said with a nod, "He's the training expert."

Joe smiled and turned to Simal, "She's being humble. But honestly, I don't know that she can even teach what she knows. Most of it's instinctual."

"Interesting," Simal said with a grin. Then he let us know, "You are all wanted on the bridge."

"Alright, let's go. Someone needs to fetch Katie and Harley."

Kiv responded, "I'll go get them."

"I guess we will pick this up another time, Kiv."

"I am looking forward to it. I'm also excited to try these moves with the other warriors." He took off ahead of us to get the other two while the rest of us gathered our things.

Once I had my boots and socks back on, Simal led the way.

Sid, Joe, Neil, and I walked onto the bridge with Simal. Katie, Harley, and Kiv were already there. Zersus was with them, and something important was going on.

"On screen," Zersus ordered as soon as we walked in.

And that was when we saw what had captured their attention. Katie approached me and said, "There's more than one ship. We can only see one enough to get the details, but we are sure there are at least three. The rings mess with the scans, but subsequent disruptions in the rings' streams indicate the other ships."

I moved over to the screen that Zersus and Issbeck were working on and asked how the ships might have been able to exist inside the rings. There was no way we could get in there with the Aries. It was too large, and the rock formations would bash the crap out of it.

Issbeck answered, "The ships are small. A smaller ship can easily navigate the rock streams."

"So what are our options?" I asked. Not being completely aware of the operational capabilities of the Aries put me at a bit of a disadvantage. It was frustrating, and I didn't like being unprepared. I knew that wasn't as much of an issue with Zersus being in charge of the ship, but I preferred having all my ducks in a row. There just hadn't been a chance to fully verse myself and the team on the Aries' details, outside of some basic reading.

Zersus encouraged us to follow him. He and Issbeck led us off the bridge and into the War Room. He asked us to take a seat. With a couple of commands, a larger screen dropped from the ceiling. "Issbeck, can you put up the scans that Katie and Harley completed."

Their scans appeared in front of us. I walked a bit closer and noted precisely what Katie had mentioned. One clear ship and two spatial anomalies which could only be ships. The rock and ice formations in the stream were all irregular shapes and sizes. These three items were not.

"Are they the same size as the freighter you found previously?"

Zersus shook his head. "Based on the one ship we can see, they look more in line with Nomad fighters. We usually see a crew headcount of about 50 on them. While they wouldn't typically be used as slave transports, they could operate with a much smaller crew, allowing them room for slaves. Plus, they move quickly and are very agile in their flight capabilities. I wouldn't be surprised if that's why three of them exist. Split the amount of slaves per ship and head off in different directions. It would make it much harder for us to track."

We all agreed his summary was likely. I looked at Katie and asked, "How prepared are we to implement the cloaking system on the Krean biosuits and update the Wraith transport's systems?"

"Harley and I haven't found any issues with the Wraiths. They can be quickly updated, but we aren't sure that the biosuits used by the Kreans will be able to maintain cloaks for long periods. Our initial calculation is maybe 30 minutes. We just don't have the time to extend it further."

"Damn."

Zersus questioned me, "What are you thinking?"

"Well, you guys carry two different-sized Wraiths on this ship, correct?"

He nodded.

"And the larger Wraith transports can easily navigate the rock formations?"

Issbeck caught on at this point and excitedly agreed, "Yes, they can. We can send ten people per ship and overtake their crews. If we moved quickly, we might get enough time out of the biosuit cloaks."

"Exactly," I said.

Zersus held up his hand and asked what I guessed was an obvious question, "What about weapons? How would they stay within the cloak?"

Katie grinned at him, "We found a way around that, thanks to Jesse."

Everyone looked at her, waiting for her to explain, "Jesse is the only one that can use a pulse weapon, and the cloak works with pulse weapons. We decided to try painting our laser weapons with the chemical breakdown of the pulse weapons, and voila, our weapons were cloaked. The only negative is if the weapons are knocked out of our hands, because obviously if it leaves the cloak anything outside it becomes visible."

"That's impressive, Katie," Zersus praised her.

She smiled, "Thanks, but the whole thing wasn't my idea. It was Jesse's. And, of course, Harley helped, too." Leave it to Katie to not take the credit that was due.

I smiled at her and told them, "Don't listen to her because if it weren't for her genius, we would have never come up with this. You can have many ideas, but they won't do you any good unless someone can make them work. That would be Katie."

I watched her blush, but she mouthed, "Thanks." She's damn brilliant and needed to own it.

"So we split into three ships. There are nine of us, with Simal included, so three of us per ship and seven additional warriors each. We will leave the warship in Kiv's care. He will know what to do if we don't make it back. Plus, the Aries will remain cloaked while we are gone."

Everyone agreed, and we sat down to assemble the teams. We also needed pilots who were capable warriors, but one name caught my attention.

Issbeck said, "We need Captain Beaudreau for sure. He's the best pilot and one of the best human warriors on the ship."

Zersus agreed.

Captain Beaudreau. No, it couldn't be. I paused at the impossibility. Or was it? "Captain Beaudreau?" I was trying to temper my curiosity and anxiety when hearing that last name. "What's his first name?" I swallowed, trying to stay calm. It couldn't be.

Zersus answered with a frown, "His first name is Cain. Why?"

I saw Katie perk up immediately as the name's significance hit her. Maybe it would be a good idea to explain, "My previous last name before the war — before Katie and I were adopted by

Matt and Alice — was Beaudreau. I had five brothers that all went missing."

"Wait, you had five brothers? All from the same woman?" Issbeck is astonished. It took me a bit, but then I realised why. Families that are significant in size are unheard of for Kreans. Typically, their females could only give birth once or twice; the odd one would have three, and they never had multiples like twins or triplets. A Krean woman once explained to my mom that it had to do with the difficulty they experienced while carrying and delivering. Their bodies couldn't physically handle more.

I looked at Issbeck and explained, "Yes — all the same woman. Cain was the oldest, then Nate; next were the identical twins, Alex and Adam; Danny and I were last. We are also twins. And I know you guys find that strange, but my real dad was one of sixteen kids."

"SIXTEEN?" Issbeck shouted. "One woman had SIXTEEN kids?"

I nodded and couldn't help but laugh at the look on their faces. "Yep, my grandmother was an incredible woman." I turned to Issbeck and told him I really needed to meet Captain Beaudreau. I had no idea if he was my brother, but I needed to know for sure.

We finished planning the teams for the mission. There was no way to know what awaited us, so we tried to think of every possible scenario. When we had as much pre-planned as possible, we headed to our rooms to prepare our gear.

When I walked into my room, my thoughts were a jumbled mess. I had to really concentrate on the last bit of planning we did because all I could think about was if this Captain Beaudreau could really be my brother. I mean, what were the odds that after all of these years of separation, that he'd be on this ship. I also couldn't help but wonder if he knew where everyone else was.

Also, how had I missed Cain on the lists? Each planet had

composed a list of anyone that had lost a family member during the divergence. While each planet's list still hadn't been merged into one, I had access to all of them. I also knew my name was on the list for Terra One. I was at a bit of a loss as to why I had missed his name. It didn't make sense. I definitely had to ask him about that.

As I wandered a bit around the room, I noted all the weapons placed on the table in the living room area. There were a whole host of pulse weapons in varying sizes. I was familiar with some, as SPAR had them available for me, but I noted a couple we didn't have. I had used the small rifle in the training arena, but there was another handgun-sized one. I'd never seen one like it. I grabbed my gear belt and found it fit perfectly into one of the open pouches on my right side. Perfect, it wouldn't hurt to have an extra weapon with me.

I heard a chime, which caught me off guard for a second. It went off again, and I realised it was the door. I opened it to find Zersus on the other side.

"Can I come in?" he asked.

I moved out of his way to let him in. He walked over to the assortment of gear. He picked up my gear belt and saw how I had placed the small pulse gun in it.

"I assumed you would like that one. Most of the warriors won't use it. It was something I designed for people with smaller hands."

I was surprised, as I knew that Krean women weren't typically warriors. He must have realised my confusion.

"We have a small selection of women on the Aries, mostly human. Two are Krean females. Their positions are not as warriors, but my mandate is that everyone on the ship must train in warrior combat and can use a pulse weapon. This particular one seems to be a favourite of theirs."

I needed to change my opinion of Zersus and all the Kreans. I guess it wasn't that they were against females working with them, it was just that it wasn't the norm. It has probably taken some adjustment and getting used to it.

I stood there looking at him; he walked up close and looked intensely into my eyes. I couldn't look away; his eyes were changing colour. He moved in closer. We were toe to toe.

"I want to touch you." he said in his deep silky voice. It sent a shiver up my spine.

I took the lead and placed my hands on his chest. I could feel vibrations move through him as his arms wrapped around my waist. His thumbs stroked up and down my lower back.

I wasn't prepared for the collection of tingles. He slid his hands under my shirt to touch the skin at the top of my combat pants. He stood there, just looking at me, stroking my skin. His eyes continued to change. I could see swirls of amber threading through them.

I gasped, "Why are your eyes changing?"

I saw him frown and blink. He let me go and walked over to the bathroom. I couldn't help but wonder what was going on with his eyes. I was also trying to get myself under control. I wanted to rip the man's clothes off. I had never experienced this intense need before. And the timing seriously sucked. He was gone for just a few seconds. He said nothing but strode over to me and hauled me closer to his body. He dipped his head down into my neck. This was not helping at all, but I didn't have the strength to push him away.

He hung on to me and continued to release his breath into my neck. It was crazy sexy. He wasn't even doing anything but breathing. I could feel goosebumps all over my body. I moved my arms around his neck and stroked it, playing with the loose curls at the base. His hair was wonderfully soft and thick.

He backed up a bit and looked like he was about to say something to me just as the chime went again for the door. He dipped his forehead against mine and sighed before letting me go and heading to answer it. I took the opportunity to gather myself a bit. He made me forget where I was. I was trying to fight my attraction to him. I wanted him but wasn't sure this was a good idea. And I'm not one for casual sex. Damn.

Issbeck walked in with a question on his face when Zersus answered the door. With him was another man. He was a handsome guy, in a rough and rugged sort of way. He reminded me a bit of Sid, but he was clean-shaven and had short dark wavy hair, shaved short on the sides and long on the top, but his eyes caught my attention. They were my eyes. The exact colour, and I knew immediately who he was.

Zersus took the lead, "Captain Cain Beaudreau, I'd like to introduce you to the SPAR team lead, Lieutenant Commander Jesse Williams. I believe Jesse would like to discuss something with you. Issbeck," he indicated to him that they were going to leave. "We will meet you two in the Wraith bay."

I watched them exit and turned to Cain. I found him staring at me. He looked confused, probably trying to figure out where he knew me. I smiled to myself. He was going to be very surprised. "Cain, you're probably wondering why you're here." I smiled to try and reassure him.

In a deep voice that sounded much like our dad's, "Yeah. Do we know each other? I can't help but feel like I know you." He frowned.

I was trying hard to get a handle on my emotions, but this was all so unexpected. I nodded. "Yes," I paused and took a deep breath before continuing, "You know me, but it was from long ago."

It took him a minute. I could almost see the wheels turning, and suddenly, it dawned on him who I was. He rushed forward and grabbed me. He hugged me so hard it felt like a big bear was crushing me.

I laughed and tapped him. "Can't breathe."

He released just enough for me to take in a gulp of air. "Oh god, sorry. Jesse? You're my sister, Jesse. You're her?" he rambled, clearly in shock.

I grabbed his face, looked him in the eyes and said, "Yes, I'm your Jesse."

I watched this grown man break down and start to cry as I joined him. While I wasn't much of a crier, there are times when you can't help it. This was one of those times.

He asked, "How the hell are you here? Where did you grow up?"

I gave him a quick rundown of how I grew up. We didn't have time to get into many details but it turned out, he was just on the other side of Terra One. So much wasted time. And again, how did we miss each other on the list?

I knew we had to get moving. People were waiting for us in the Wraith bay, and we had a mission to complete. I mentioned that we needed to get a move on.

He stopped suddenly and said, "Damn, wait. Do you lead a SPAR team? Did I hear that right? That's nuts!!"

I started laughing and began gathering up my gear to go. I turned to him as he watched me. "That's right. Lieutenant Commander is my designation. I lead the TS-5 team. We're the best. I know we need to catch up, but unfortunately, that will have to wait. I want to know how you became a space pilot captain too."

He nodded, and a huge grin formed on his handsome face. He swung his arm over my shoulder. As we headed towards the Wraith bay together, neither of us had any idea how this mission would go, but you can bet that I was looking forward to getting back and getting to know my big brother.

Wait until I tell Katie. She'll be freaked out. As sisters growing up, we talked a lot about how we'd love to find our brothers. Finding just one was a good start.

CHAPTER
ELEVEN
ZERSUS

IT TOOK everything in me to leave Jesse alone with another man, brother or not. Issbeck strode beside me and was keeping quiet, at least for now.

I looked at him and noticed him watching me as we moved along. "Your eyes have gone back to black," was his only comment.

I sighed. Imagine my surprise when I walked into that bathroom and found my eyes turning amber. That meant one thing, but it wasn't as if I hadn't suspected it. From the moment I met Jesse, I knew she was special.

Jesse was my Kindred. And she was human. I had no idea how it was going to work out. A human could not feel the connection, as far as I knew. Not that it mattered; I was going to make sure that before this mission ended, she knew. I snickered to myself because I could imagine her calling me all sorts of names if I said "mine" to her face.

First, the invasion of those three Nomad ships needed to be completed. Then, I could sort through things with Jesse.

Issbeck and I reached the bay doors as they slid open to see the others prepping the three transports for the mission.

Wraith transports were our ship of choice. They were very

manoeuvrable, which we needed to traverse the rock and ice streams that made up the rings of Saturn. From a distance, the rings looked beautiful. Up close, it was a ring of destruction. Only the best pilots could navigate their way through.

Smaller ships like the Wraith transports could survive the rings, or so we hoped. The Nomad were clever and used the larger rocks to try and hide their ships. They could move with the large rocks and seemed to look like natural formations. The problem was that they weren't made of the same composition and all three were the same size. That was our first sign that something was off when we scanned the rings.

It took us a bit to determine the logistics of how many ships we needed based on the personnel volume we thought could be on their ships. This is why we chose the larger Wraiths. Like the smaller fighters, they looked like birds in flight. The central bodies were a matte black metal, with the engines running along the wings. They were designed with multiple engines so the transport could split the energy over the leftover engines if one went down. The smaller, tighter-flying Wraith fighters were built similarly and while quicker, they could only carry two of us at a time. We would need too many and that was risky. Plus the transports had wielding capabilities. It's a unique tech that we only used on these ships and would be key to the mission.

The only downside with the transports was they were slightly slower. Each Wraith could hold 20 crew. We were splitting into three ships, 10 of us per ship. That count included a pilot and navigator. Those two jobs would be critical to our survival. It would also leave room for some prisoners. We wanted to take as many as we could for questioning. With the incidences of the dead prisoners on Moonbase, this was our opportunity to get information before anyone else could get to them.

I walked up to the Wraith that was going to carry my group. I noticed Navigator Annie Sherman. Issbeck nodded towards her,

"There's no way you'll want anyone other than Cain and Annie at the helm on this trip."

I had to agree with him. Not only were Cain and Annie a great pilot duo, but they were both exemplary warriors.

Annie turned to the two of us as we approached. She smiled and asked, "Do you know where Cain is? I wanted to review our plan for the ride into the rings."

"I'm sure he will be heading in shortly. We left him with Jesse."

I watched a frown form on Annie's face and stopped just short of questioning it when Issbeck grabbed me. He excused us and hauled me away from her. I was just about to ask him why when Jesse and Cain walked in. As always when I saw her, I felt my heart pick up speed and I was a touch breathless seeing the joy on her face. I couldn't imagine how she felt finding one of the many brothers she lost. While it might just be Issbeck, me and my parents, I don't know that I would be who I am if it hadn't been for all of them being a part of my life. I was thrilled that Jesse would get the chance to have Cain in her life, even if it was 28 years later.

Cain had an arm slung over her shoulder and was jostling her. Clearly, he was saying something that was making her laugh, but what caught my attention was the "humph" that came from behind me.

I turned to see Annie with her arms crossed and eyes shooting daggers toward Jesse. I was ready to speak with her when Issbeck grabbed me again and whispered, "She has a thing for Cain."

Well, shit, that explained the look.

"We need to let her know Jesse is his sister," Issbeck coughed.

I nodded, "Yes, like right away."

I wasn't worried about Jesse. I was concerned about the damage I knew she could do to Annie. I'd prefer to have them both in one piece.

I walked towards them swiftly and said loud enough for

Annie to hear, "Clearly, you two have eased into the whole sibling thing quickly."

Jesse gave me a glorious smile; grabbed and hugged me. I'd lie if I said it wasn't perfect and settled my soul. "Can you believe it? My brother was on your ship for years. Well — one of my brothers. It's amazing."

Out of the corner of my eye, I saw Annie approach. "Cain is your brother? You're the missing sister?"

The shock was evident in her statement, but then I could see her looking between the two. If you looked at them closely, you could see the similarities. It was all in the eyes. They were unique. I noticed with Jesse that the blue would shift shades here and there, but are mostly aqua-like, similar to a clear blue ocean with dark flecks and a black ring around the outside. Cain's were identical.

She smiled with a questioning look at Annie. I stepped up and introduced them. The ladies shook hands, and Annie's face couldn't hide her relief.

Cain was oblivious. I looked over at Issbeck, and he just shrugged. All of us men, Krean or human, are dumb when it comes to women.

"Jesse, let's get everyone together and go over the plan."

She nodded and called over the remainder of her team.

Six SPAR team members and 24 warriors, including myself, Issbeck and Simal. All waiting for their instructions from me.

The bay maintenance crew pulled over a large screen for us to use. We had a list for each ship.

"Each ship will have two members of the SPAR team, two techs, one pilot and one Navigator, with the balance being warriors. The splits are on the board and the ship you have been assigned. If you haven't already, I'd like you to introduce yourselves."

I turned to Katie and Harley, "Are the suits ready?"

Katie nodded and answered, "Yes, we've prepped them all. Shall I explain to everyone how they work?"

I indicated for her to take the floor.

She explained, "Along with upgrades we have made to the Wraith's cloaking system, we have also set up a new cloaking system for your biosuits." I noticed the shock and excitement on everyone's faces. Cloaked biosuits were not something we had ever considered a possibility.

Katie held up a suit to explain. "We have been using cloaked biosuits with our SPAR suits for a while. We have had some time to refine the use, but have only used them on one mission. We have been successful in adapting this feature to your Krean suits. We know that your pulse weapons will be hidden along with the suit if you hold them close to you. If you lose your weapon, it will no longer be part of the field's protection.

"Also, we did have issues with how long the cloak operates. Initially, we could only get about 30 minutes of use out of them, but we have refined that a bit more. You should have a cloak that will last an hour. And hopefully, we will get in and out in more than enough time."

She then instructed everyone on how to activate the cloak by a small button installed along the inside of the neck. Lastly, she explained how the tech allows us to still see each other. It's really ingenious. The suits, even without the cloak, were a layer of protection. Typically, weapons fire couldn't penetrate the suits, increasing the wearer's strength by allowing our muscles to move and flex easily. They were also deceivingly light for the wearer. It took some getting used to having them on, as it gave the impression of being naked.

Everyone was very excited about the new tech; grabbed one and headed to the changing areas to get ready. I saw Jesse grab hers and, what looked like, mine.

She walked over and handed it to me. I grabbed the suit and her hand, pulling her close. She gave me a quick chuckle, surprising me by sliding quickly past me and heading to the changing room with Katie.

I hope I survive this woman, I thought as I headed to change into my biosuit. When I came out I zeroed in on Jesse in her suit immediately. Fuck! I couldn't have imagined how she would look in it. Black with a scale pattern moved up and down to shape the body, the suit hugged every inch of her. And she had a hell of a body. I knew she had muscle but I couldn't have imagined the definition and the suit showed off every inch. Add in her perfect breasts, full hips and backside. I needed to get a handle on myself or this was going to be a painful trip. Not to mention my eyes — if I couldn't control my desire, I'd be a walking advertisement that she's my Kindred.

I turned around, closed my eyes, and used my usual breathing exercises to get myself back under control. Everyone needed me to think about the mission, including Jesse.

All of us assembled back in the bay after changing. Once I had them all in front of me, I explained how we would approach. For each Nomad ship, we would approach from the side. Our Wraiths were considerably smaller than the Nomad fighters. We had a general idea of how many people were on each Nomad ship, but we couldn't be entirely sure until we could get close enough for a clear scan. The Wraiths would grab on and the latch wielder would drill to give us quick entry onto the enemy ship; the same method we used during the freighter rescue.

"Alright, let's go. Be prepared that we may have to split up to manoeuvre when we get into the rock and ice. You will return to the Aries if your Wraith is damaged and can't continue. Run a scan when you attach and clear your latch area. Once everyone is good to go, all latch wielders will drill simultaneously. Are we clear?" I needed to be sure everyone worked together.

Everyone was good with the plan. Cain and Annie headed onto our ship to get it powered up. Jesse and Joe were the two SPAR members on our ship. CeeChi and Melo, two of the Aries' techs, joined us along with three other warriors. The ships had two techs because our mandate was to get into the enemy systems and download as quickly as possible once we had secured the ships.

We all boarded the Wraiths and stored our weapons. I couldn't help but smile at Jesse having two pulse weapons. Our collection also had traditional laser weapons for the many humans on our crew. I noticed several in the weapons storage of the ship but these looked quite different from the norm. Jesse saw me looking at them.

"We've prepped the laser weapons with a sealant so they remain cloaked."

Right, I had forgotten about that. I nodded. "Thank you, I forgot that was possible. That'll come in handy for Annie and, I imagine, Joe as well."

She nodded, but then I noted a slight frown as she asked, "What about Cain?"

All of a sudden, I realised something significant. "Cain uses a pulse weapon. He's the other person we mentioned on Terra One. He's the only other human we know of that can use it."

She smiled, "Well I guess that makes a lot of sense now."

I had to agree with her, but it was also something we had to investigate further when we got a chance.

We both found our seats. The front of the Wraiths accommodated the pilot and navigator with a row of seats along each side for 12 additional people to sit. The back half was an open area used for transporting anything we might need for a mission. Since we were heading in light, we kept as much space open as possible in case this became another potential rescue mission, or to hold prisoners.

"Prime, you have the comm," Cain indicated.

"Power up, everyone. Remember to turn your Wraith cloaks on before we leave the Aries."

I was thankful that Katie had designed the cloak so that we could see each other's ships. Could our enemy figure it out? Maybe, but I imagined it wouldn't be that easy.

Cain and Annie took the lead with Issbeck's ship next to

ours. The third, piloted by Simal, followed behind us in formation. It would take us 15 minutes to get to the edge of the rings. I knew there was no way we could keep formation once we hit them, but I hoped we could get to our destinations in one piece.

I watched our approach. Looking at the rings of rock and ice from a distance made them appear dense but once we were up close, a route could be easily determined. That was Annie's job. We had the same destination, just a different fighter per transport. I could see Cain tense up a bit as we entered the rings. The rocks and ice floated, but they weren't stationary. There was movement. Not quick movement, but a touch unpredictable, so you had to be on your toes. Again, that was what Annie was there for; she kept an eye on our navigation. It made me appreciate both of their skills. Only the best pilot and navigator would have the nerve and skill to take this on.

We continued through without having to deal with any significant obstacles. A few times, I could see and feel our Wraith manoeuvring away from the rocks we passed. It was Cain's pilot reflexes reacting to rock and ice heading in our direction. The Wraith could manage a small impact, but a large rock could destroy the ship. The thought made me grab the side of my chair. I felt a hand cover mine and looked down to see Jesse's.

Across from us CeeChi and Melo were at the controls for the cloaking system. They both smiled at us as they saw our joined hands. CeeChi wasn't known for her discretion. I assumed it would be common knowledge, shortly upon our return to the Aries, that something was happening between Jesse and me. I was thankful that she didn't know exactly what that was yet.

"We are on approach, Prime."

I turned and watched our ship moving into position. We could also see the other two transports mirroring us. I was happy that everyone had made it through the rings.

Melo let us know, "All ships report clear scans."

"Give the command to latch," I said.

I watched all the other ships move to connect to the fighters.

It's a delicate operation. Our ship had to be on an even surface, but we also had to go in for a soft landing to not jolt the fighter below us.

Cain brought us down carefully. I felt the engines powering down, vital to remaining undetected. The engines could cause vibrations, and we did not want to announce our arrival.

I stood up and ordered everyone to grab their weapons. CeeChi positioned the latch wielder. Cain connected us with the other ships so we could coordinate our entry. Jesse and I were going through first.

CeeChi continually scanned to be sure the area remained clear. The best plan would be to create our entry point without surprises, and she was trying to ensure our entry remained that way. She gave a thumbs-up, and we got in position.

The wielder initiated, and I watched it create a hole through the Nomad fighter's hull while creating a permanent seal for us to pass through. I jumped in and landed cleanly, moving out of the way. Jesse followed behind me and took the rear position. We both kept a close watch for any unexpected Nomad. Joe and Melo came through next, followed by Annie, Cain, the remainder of the warriors and CeeChi last. She sealed and hid the opening of the latch.

Once we were all through, the 10 of us got into formation. We planned to split up and take two different routes to the bridge while taking down any Nomad we encountered.

"Activate cloaks," Jesse said, and we all reached up and pressed the control on the suits.

I felt a slight tingle move down my body. Once it reached my feet it stopped. I assumed it was fully activated at that point.

We moved forward, weapons ready. Because of the size of the corridor, it was easy to spread out. Jesse, Cain, and I took the front position while CeeChi and Melo pulled up the rear, watching behind us. We also carried indicators in case any Nomad approached. They wouldn't see us, but we'd see them.

And that was precisely what happened. As we moved, we

quietly took down anyone we came across. By our count, as we got closer to the bridge, we took down six Nomad. The other group, led by Joe and Annie, took down 10. That would leave a tiny group of Nomad on the bridge. We met up with the other team there.

CeeChi and Melo listened to what was happening on the bridge. CeeChi turned to us, "Prime, someone is heading this way. It might be a good opportunity for a few to move through the doorway and onto the bridge."

"I agree. Jesse, Cain, Joe, and I will go," I commanded. "CeeChi and Melo, you two get in there as soon as we have secured the bridge. I'll give you a signal through your communicator."

We moved close, two of us on each side, when the door opened. A Nomad passed through and we quickly moved onto the bridge. Jesse and I stopped abruptly as we realised who was overseeing the operation.

CHAPTER
TWELVE
JESSE

You had to be kidding me. This guy is like a nasty rash you can't get rid of. I looked over at Zersus and saw he was equally unimpressed with the fact Creepy Blue Guy was in charge.

We split up on each side; Joe and I went right while Cain and Zersus moved left.

The remaining Nomad crew was unaware of our presence, so we shifted into a position where we could take on the remaining four. We each took one, with Zersus going for Curalim. I was disappointed to be on the wrong side of the room.

I noticed Cain indicated movement to my right. A Nomad was getting up and moving in my direction. I didn't have anywhere I could go. I slowly backed up, ensuring I'm not coming in contact with anything. He continued getting closer, and just when I thought he would collide with me, he stopped at the computer next to me.

Damn, this was awkward. I was afraid to breathe. I could see the look on Zersus's face. He was restraining himself. He wanted to pounce, but we both knew the risks. They were still unaware of our presence and that was a huge advantage. I shook my head at him. The Nomad gazed in my direction. I could see a frown form between his scaled facial ridges. He shrugged and returned to whatever he was doing.

Creepy Blue Guy turned to the Nomad beside me. "Are we getting anything from them?"

Fuck, did they know we were here?

"No, master, they are just sitting there."

That was when I realised that they must be talking about the Aries. I looked at Zersus with a questioning look, and he nodded. I assumed he had given the order to Kiv to use the Aries as a distraction. Not a bad idea. Wish I'd thought of it.

The Nomad working beside me returned to his previous station, and I felt like I could breathe again. One of the other Nomad kept looking towards the door, waiting for their crew member to return. Good luck with that. I wanted to laugh because he definitely wouldn't be returning.

Creepy Blue Guy bent over a console, hit a button and commanded, "Tic, where the hell are you?"

He wasn't getting an answer.

He turned to the one beside him and shouted, "Go find out what is taking him so long. I want to know what they are up to. Our merchandise is scheduled to arrive shortly, and we can't have those damn Kreans sitting out there.

"Contact our partners and tell them our position is compromised," he ordered another Nomad. He had just turned to do so when the doors slid open, and the remainder of our team came in uncloaked.

Damn. Again, another great idea. Chaos occurred as we quickly overpowered the four Nomads before the rest of us uncloaked. Zersus was holding Curalim down, but the creep was focused on me.

"Curalim," Zersus commanded, attempting to get his attention, but he continued to stare at me. *Creepy Blue Guy* suited him because he was creeping me out right now.

Zersus pulled him up quickly, a little rough, but I liked that. Suddenly, Curalim twisted away from him and quickly moved for the console before him. Zersus didn't reach him before he inputted a command. CeeChi and Melo moved to see what he had done while Zersus tried to secure him again.

I could see the panic on their faces.

"We need to leave," they both said simultaneously. "Now!"

"He's set off a self-destruct sequence and transmitted that to the other two ships." I could see the frustration on CeeChi's face. She and Melo set up to download.

Zersus got on the comm and immediately told the other Wraith crews to get moving and get the hell off the ships. We grabbed our Nomad prisoners and started moving to the latch area.

I turned to CeeChi and Melo. "How long?" We needed to know how much time we have.

"Thirty minutes," Melo replied, as he continued to work on the download.

I asked Cain, "How much time can we give them?"

As we moved, Cain answered, "It's going to be tight as it is." He looked at our techs, "You two need to make it fast. Every second counts."

They both frantically nodded. I could see them working fast, but I couldn't help but feel anxious. Was the information worth it?

Zersus began dragging Curalim, who was not planning to make our exit easy. We should just knock him the hell out. Unexpectedly, he jabbed Zersus's hand with something that came out of his scales, and I watched Zersus pull back like something bit him. The minute that Zersus loosened his hold, the creep grabbed me around my neck. This asshole had no idea who he was dealing with.

"Leave us now. I will cancel the self-destruct if you get off the ship, but I want her."

Was this guy nuts? What was I thinking? Of course, he's nuts! If he thought I would let him take me anywhere, he was mistaken. I looked at Zersus and gave him a down signal with my eyes. Zersus blinked back, confirming he got it. I surprised the hell out of Curalim and dropped. I let my legs fall out from under me, forcing him to topple forward.

He lost his grip and the momentum forward was just enough for me to flip him over my head. Zersus was ready for my move, and hit him with pulse fire. He had it set just to immobilise. I'd have been happy to see him gone, but I knew why we needed to keep him.

"That worked. I should've done that from the start," he said, clearly pissed off.

"Can't imagine how he figured I'd make that easy."

"Right, let's move. We are running out of time. CeeChi and Melo, are you having any luck tapping into that self-destruct sequence?" I know Zersus was hoping that they could work around it. They both indicated "no." Zersus swung Curalim's limp body over his shoulder and we hauled ass back to the latch opening.

It only took us a minute to get the latch activated and back on the Wraith. CeeChi and Melo were seconds behind us. CeeChi disconnected and sealed the latch.

"Alright, everyone buckle up. It's going to be a bumpy ride," said Cain.

Priority was to get us out of here as fast as possible.

I saw the other ships detaching. We'd taken a few Nomad prisoners, along with Curalim, and they were looking pretty terrified. Lucky for Curalim, he was out like a light.

Cain had us moving a hell of a lot faster this time than what we did to get here. The ship was weaving with quick adjustments. Sure enough, I felt an impact.

"Are we holding?" Zersus asked Cain.

He just nodded, didn't look back and kept going. We were close to getting through when Annie shouted, "Large rock heading hard right."

Thank god we strapped in as Cain flew us upside down with a swift move to the left. With much enjoyment, I watched Curalim's body take a bit of a beating on that one. Well damn, we forgot to strap him in. I looked at Zersus and he winked at me. Yep, did it on purpose. We both grinned.

We had only a few minutes before the ships exploded, and we had no idea how the impact would affect the rings.

Zersus asked CeeChi to patch him into the Aries and the other transports.

"Kiv, the Nomad ships are on a self-destruct sequence. Get the Aries moving away from the rings. The Wraiths will follow. Keep the bays open for our landing. We need to move as fast as possible to escape the explosion."

We could see the Aries shifting its position, moving away from the planet. We made it through the rings, when I felt the Wraith's speed increase as we quickly followed the Aries. With bays open, we hauled ass inside just as the explosions occurred. Three ships and the Nomad we left behind were destroyed. As we landed in the bay, we observed rocks heading in our direction. Cain and Annie hit the commands, and the bay shields went up. You could hear the pinging of debris.

"Bridge, impact report," Zersus requested.

"We've sustained some damage, mostly towards the back around the bays. We need to stop and perform a check," Kiv reported.

"Take us out a bit further so we can clear the debris before we stop. Contact the engineers to send the robots to take care of it," Zersus said.

He received an affirmative from Kiv.

He also asked Kiv to send guards to move the prisoners to the ship's cells. I know that Zersus didn't want to take any chances that Curalim would wake up before we could ensure he was secure.

Katie ran over and hugged me as soon as I was off the transport. "I was so scared when we got the command that the ships were going to blow, and we weren't together."

I admitted I was anxious for her, too, but tried to keep my

emotions in check. Not easy. I watched Cain walk over to us —
no better time than now to introduce her. "Katie, I'd like you to
meet Cain Beaudreau, my oldest brother. Cain, this is Katie
Williams, my amazing sister. We grew up with our brother,
Maverick, and our adoptive parents, Matt and Alice, on Terra
One."

Cain and Katie smiled at each other and hugged. I could see
Annie behind him smiling. Katie was the first to respond,
looking over at me, "I guess if you'd decided not to accept this
mission, you wouldn't have ever met him." Leave it to Katie to
always look at the bright side.

"Yes, I suppose you're right," I agreed.

I could see Cain looking confused. "You didn't want to come
on the Aries?" he asked.

"No — umm, I have a bit of an aversion to being out in
space," I paused briefly, looking down. "I'll explain it to you one
day." Now was not the time to discuss what happened to Katie
and me, but it was a subject that couldn't be avoided forever.
Later, I would be sure to have that conversation with Cain, but
right now, I just wanted to get to my room, shower, eat, and
sleep.

I watched as the guys hauled out the Nomad to be taken to
the cells. Katie froze when she saw who we had on our ship. She
looked at me with a strained expression and I nodded. She
frowned, but then smiled, "He looks a bit worse for wear."

We all cracked up laughing.

Zersus replied, "Yeah he forgot to buckle up." Couldn't have
been better.

The rest of the team came over and officially met Cain. He
seemed to hit it off with Sid. Meanwhile, I had Harley, Joe, and
Neil take me aside. Harley was the first to interrogate me. These
guys just never missed anything.

"What's going on with you and the superhero?" Harley asks.

I couldn't stop laughing. Harley, like me, loved 21st-century
movies, and superheroes were a favourite. I was betting he

thought Zersus looked a bit like one in particular. "I think Issbeck looks way more like him with his blue eyes."

"You didn't answer the question," Neil injected.

I just raised my eyebrows, spun around, and left them standing there. All three shouted, "Hey, wait!" as I waved and headed to my room. They yelled again that they were going to get food. I was starving, too, so that was on the agenda after a cleanup.

Meanwhile, I'd let them wonder about Zersus and me. And if I was being honest, I had no idea what was happening between us. Initially, I'd convinced myself that it wasn't a good idea, but I was no longer sure. The more time I spent with him, the more attracted I was.

I sighed as I reached my room. I dropped my gear on the table. I stood there and let the tension release. So much had happened. I was on a warship in space. I found one of my lost brothers, and we had the creepy blue guy in a cell. Considering I hadn't wanted to do this, I couldn't argue that it had been an enormous success.

A shower was what I wanted; what I needed. I picked up my carry-on bag with my fresh clothes and headed for the bathroom. I quickly got out of the biosuit and headed straight for the shower. I couldn't wait to get under that waterfall and let the water wrap around me.

I made it relatively quick because I was starving. As soon as I was dressed in my workout gear, the most comfortable clothes I brought with me, I headed for the Common Room. It was on the same level as the ship's wraith bays but towards the Aries' bow section.

The Common Room was designed with comfort in mind, similar to our quarters. It surprised me, yet again, how much thought had been put into the comfort of the Aries crew. Windows were along one side of the room, all the tables were set up much like booths, the seats were quite plush, and the tones in the room were varying shades of green and blue.

I found the environment soothing. But what captured my attention was the array of food. There was a wonderful selection of dishes. I noticed not just plain veggies and meat. There also appeared to be pasta dishes, meat pies and salads, combined with a great selection of breads. The smell was terrific and I was amazed at the freshness. My stomach told me it needed sustenance. I noticed the team sitting at a larger, extended table, Issbeck and Simal with them.

I grabbed my plate, filled it to a point where it was almost spilling over, and headed for the empty seat beside Sid. Just as I sat, Cain and Annie arrived. We waved them to join us, which they did with heaping plates like mine. I couldn't contain my smile as Cain sat across from me. All those years without ever knowing for sure if any of my brothers were dead or alive, and here he was, sitting across from me now.

I asked Cain, "Tell me more about where you grew up."

"The family that adopted me lived in the Upper Lawrence area."

I was confused. How could I have missed him when I went looking for family? He kept the Beaudreau name. I should have found him.

I nodded and let him continue.

"My adopted family's name is Lavigne. I had that name until I moved to the Moonbase. They understood how important it was for me to have the Beaudreau name. It would be key if I were ever going to find family. I put myself on the list for Terra One and Moonbase. The benefits of working for Space Corp."

I couldn't understand why I didn't find his name on Terra One's list. I didn't check Moonbase, but that shouldn't have mattered. I asked, "Did you check any of the lists for any of us?"

Cain frowned, and nodded. "Well, yeah, I checked all of them. Again another advantage of working for Space Corp. Getting access to the lists is a bitch."

I agreed with him. The more I thought about it, the more I realised something didn't seem right. My confusion came out in my next comment. "Your name is not on the list on Terra One," I told him.

Cain didn't look shocked. His next statement told me why. "You aren't either."

What the fuck? That couldn't be right. Clearly I needed to talk to someone about this. I wondered if the Aries would have access to the lists. Probably a long shot because it wouldn't be information they would need out in space, but worth asking.

I asked him, "Did you look for any of our other siblings? Or Dad?" I had so many questions.

I knew he could tell I was anxious. Even putting aside the fact that there were clearly issues with the lists, there were other ways to find people.

"To answer your question, no. I haven't found anyone else," he said. He looked like there was something he wasn't saying.

"What is it?" I asked.

"Whenever I hear of someone with one of our first names, I look into it. Recently, I noticed a guy named Nate Badawi working as one of the head engineers on the new Phantom III project. He's the right age."

Zersus had come in, slid into the seat on my other side, and placed a hand over mine. I couldn't explain it, but it instantly sent a calming effect over me. It was the oddest thing. At some point, I'd ask him why that was happening.

Cain continued, "He's working on the team in charge of completing the new warships. I had planned to approach him when we were docked, but then we had to prepare for this mission." He couldn't help but sound hopeful.

I also hoped he was right. "We can talk to him when we get back."

Cain reached over and grabbed my free hand. "You can count on it."

"Anything about Danny or the twins?" Cain shook his head. Damn and again, the lists were definitely not going to be of any help.

Issbeck interrupted, "Can I ask a question?"

We both nodded.

"I'm just wondering why the Terras haven't set up a DNA matching system or a list of some sort. Almost everyone is in a similar situation, so I'd think that would make sense."

I was about to answer him when Zersus said, "Actually, I can answer that. Danlon told me that they tried DNA. The divergence didn't just change the planets, but it also affected everyone's DNA. Matching is impossible. But they do have lists on each Terra. Don't they?" Zersus asked Cain and I.

"It would appear there is an issue with the lists because both Cain and I were on them, but I couldn't find him and he never found me. Also a lot of the children younger than three or four years couldn't be identified with their last names." It was really sad because they were far too young to know what their names had been. Considering the lists were useless, I guess it appeared to not matter.

While Cain and I felt that we were related in our bones, our DNA would not match. I was unaffected by the divergence because I was away from the planet when it occurred, but any of our siblings wouldn't match us.

Cain continued, "No, I haven't found Danny, Alex, Adam, or Dad."

I frowned down at my plate.

"Wait, how many siblings do you guys have?" asked CeeChi.

We both smiled and at the same time said, "FIVE."

Issbeck and Simal stopped with their food halfway to their mouths. Even though they knew it, it still shocked them.

CeeChi and Melo had the typical Krean expressions when hearing that.

"You think that's a lot? Our dad came from a family of 16 kids," Cain told them.

"You weren't kidding? You mentioned that before. Is that even possible?" Zersus questioned.

"It's not as common as it was when our dad was born, but yes, it's possible," I replied.

"From the same female?" asked CeeChi.

We both nodded at her.

I pointed at Katie beside me and mentioned that she had come from a family of four, with three older brothers and that we hadn't located them either. Everyone at the table was quiet for a bit. We all had suffered losses. There were too many to even count, but in other ways, we were fortunate.

Cain asked Katie, "What was your original last name?"

"Prince. It's a common name, and I've had no luck finding them either. Now I know why that might be."

I could see how much that upset her, and noted the frown on her face. I made a quick head shake to Cain to leave it. Katie had been the baby, like me, but she depended on her brothers, whereas I was far less attached at the hip to mine. I was too busy trying to be one of the guys.

We finished our meal when Katie switched seats with Sid, leaned over, and whispered, "What's happening with you and the big guy?"

I ignored that for now. "Are you finding the whole list thing weird?"

She nodded.

"Yep. You and I are both on that list with our original names. I know because we watched dad put us on it. Something is definitely off about that."

"Can we access the lists from here?"

She shook her head, "No, the Aries wouldn't have that information. I mean think about it, sis. It's next to impossible to get the lists from the planets together in one, so there's no way a warship would have that information."

What she said made sense, but it was, again, another thing that made me even more suspicious. I hadn't spent a lot of time thinking about why they couldn't combine the lists, but now it seemed odd.

She nodded her agreement without me having to say anything further. All of a sudden she had a stupid grin on her face. "So back to my original question." I knew she meant what was going on between me and Zersus.

I rolled my eyes at her. "Nothing." *Yet,* I thought to myself.

"Don't give me that. You can practically smell the desire from the two of you."

"Geezus!" I couldn't believe she said that, but I had to admit I had given up on ignoring my attraction to him.

I grinned at her. "Nothing has happened," I said again.

"Yet," she chuckled. "I guess it's good we had a thorough medical before we left." She winked at me. I couldn't argue with her on that. Our checkups, for females, include checking our birth control implants. Mine isn't up to be replaced for a while yet. And we don't worry about sexually transmitted diseases any longer with the medical advancements provided by the Kreans. The birth control implants are also based on their technology. It doesn't mess with our hormones or cause any significant risks to our health. Do I want kids? Yes, eventually, but certainly not right now.

While Katie and I were having our conversation, the fact we played as a band together came up, thanks to Zersus. With much urging from everyone, we did an impromptu version of "Drink You Away." It was a good choice for an acapella performance, and we attracted a crowd. It was the perfect way to wind down from a stressful 24 hours.

Frankly, it was not how I pictured our journey on the Aries. Nor how I pictured the Krean warriors. I had thought they were all stiff and boring, which was how Zersus was at the beginning, but as we all got to know each other, it was clear that their values and views were similar to ours.

It's no wonder the two species had been able to live together comfortably.

The one thing I was dying to ask was why Issbeck had blue eyes. They were crystal clear blue. They shimmered almost to the point of him looking like they were always watery. I'm sure there's a reason because every other Krean I'd met had black or amber eyes.

As we finished our meal, people slowly got up to head to their rooms. We were all exhausted. Zersus mentioned to the crew that everyone should get a good rest. We would head back to Terra Moonbase once the ship was repaired. We weren't going anywhere for now, so it was the perfect time to rest. We would also do a final scan of Jupiter and Saturn once we could move again.

"It's 2400 hours now, so why don't we say 0800 for all of us to meet in the War Room? Some of our warrior guards are interrogating the Nomad we captured as we speak. They'll report what they can get out of them. Curalim, I am leaving for myself. I'm assuming a few of you would like to join in on that interrogation. The priority with him is to get him back to Terra Moonbase. I do not doubt that Magistrate Eton and Supreme Commander Danlon will expect him to stand trial for his crimes against both our species," Zersus instructed.

Everyone nodded.

Katie hugged me, whispering in my ear, "Have a good rest, not that I think you'll get much."

God, that girl. She proceeded to hug Cain, too. I knew she considered him part of the family already. That was just how Katie was. Sid walked out with Zersus and me.

"So we know this Curalim guy is in charge of the slave trade, correct?" He looked right at me.

"Yes, he's in charge. He's been in charge for a very long time."

Sid sighed and nodded. He knew why. The entire team knew what happened to Katie and me when we were young and that Curalim was the guy on the security tapes from our Terra Four mission. Sid's expression showed his disdain for Curalim. He stopped at his door, patted me on the shoulder, and headed into his room. That left me and Zersus alone in the corridor.

Zersus followed me to my room. We stood outside the door as I turned to him.

I gave up trying to resist this thing between us. "Do you want to come in?" I asked.

"Yes," he replied in his deep voice.

Lordy, I was in deep trouble.

CHAPTER
THIRTEEN
ZERSUS

I COULDN'T TURN down Jesse's invitation. I had an intense desire to spend time with her. And I needed to talk to her. There were things I needed to say before exploring our desires. I felt her attraction to me. While I couldn't be happier, with her being human, she may not understand the significance of Kindred. Humans did not approach their relationships the way we did.

I sighed to myself, part frustration and part fear. She had to make the choice herself. I wouldn't push her. It was far too important to me. If she needed time to think about it, I'd give it to her. If she didn't want it, I'd have to learn to deal with that choice — in time.

She took me by the hand as we entered her chambers and led me to the sofa. She sat and pulled me down beside her. I didn't let go of her hand. I pulled it across my lap and held it with both of mine. I took comfort from the gesture. This was so crazy. I had heard from many that meeting and feeling your Kindred was intense, but nothing prepared me for the raging desire that ran through me. Even this simple touch from her sent zaps of energy through my body. I didn't know where to start explaining things to her.

"Would you like me to start?" she asked.

Damn, she was amazing and somehow tuned into my reluctance. If I was being honest with myself, I was scared to hell that she was going to reject me. It was difficult for a Krean to live without their Kindred, but there had been a few rare instances where two Kreans that were Kindred weren't compatible. I didn't think that was going to be our problem..

"I need to talk to you about something important, but before I do, I need you to know that I want to be intimate with you." I figured the direct approach was best.

She whispered, "Me, too."

I couldn't hold back a slight grin at her answer. Well, that was at least one good thing and a promising start.

I took a deep breath and asked, "I'm sure you've heard of Kindred?"

She nodded.

"When a Krean meets their Kindred, an intense bond is formed. For both, it's an immediate attraction, and as time spent together grows, they begin to feel a more intense desire, and the sexual tension is quite strong." That was an understatement of how I felt about Jesse, and I'd hardly spent any time with her. She's watching and listening intently, so I continue, "You recall how you saw my eyes change colour?"

"Yes, I've never seen anything like that. They look like they are changing now. You have slivers of amber lines inside your black irises."

"I'm not surprised. That is a sign of Kindred, and we have limited control over it. It's an automatic reaction that develops the more time you spend with your Kindred."

I watched her face as I inferred she was my Kindred and was happy to see she didn't seem freaked out by it. "And I'm assuming you understand this is happening because I'm with you?" I might as well stop putting this off and just spit it out.

"But it doesn't always happen when we are together. Why?"

"Because we haven't been intimate yet," I admitted to her. "When others are around and there are distractions, I have some control over my emotions. When we are alone — well, you can see my response.

"When a Krean becomes intimate with the person that is their Kindred, that is the final attachment their body needs to complete the connection to their partner. A permanent bond is formed. My eyes would change to amber and stay that way. I'm sure you've noticed that before on some Kreans?"

"I have. There are several Kreans that work at TechStar that have amber eyes. So that means they have met their Kindred?"

I nodded.

She told me, "We humans refer to something like that as soulmates. It's the idea that we find our other half. It's a bit of a fairy tale that I never thought was real. I guess for Kreans, it is."

She wanted to ask me something else, so I didn't say anything while she gathered her thoughts. She was looking a bit confused. Her next question cleared up why.

"Why are Issbeck's eyes blue?"

It probably shouldn't have surprised me she'd ask, but that was a tricky subject. She could see I was struggling,

"It's okay; you don't have to tell me."

I shook my head. "No, that's not it. I don't think he'll mind me telling you, but it was hard for him. We all could experience it at any moment. Issbeck lost his Kindred very young.

"He met her at 18. That's much younger than most Kreans. We are barely ready to be adults, let alone be attached to someone. They met when they joined the space program. She was training to be a pilot and he, a warrior."

I explained how excited he was when he met her. I couldn't help but feel guilty that I hadn't had a chance to get to know her better. My initial impression of Shasa was not positive, but that's a story for another day.

"During her training, she was temporarily assigned to a small exploration ship. Short range, and there shouldn't have been any danger, but it went missing. It was like it disappeared into thin air. It was never found. At first, Issbeck held out hope, and his eyes stayed amber until one day, about two years after the ship's disappearance, his eyes changed to blue. That was when he knew she was gone."

Jesse was having some trouble with the whole story. "God, so you're saying that when your Kindred dies, your eyes go blue?"

I nodded.

"That must have been awful for him. Just to wake up one day and know she's gone by the colour of his eyes. I can't imagine how that would feel."

Oh, I was sure she could. While her brothers may still be alive, she had lost them at a young age. It might not seem the same, but she understood the feeling of loss.

We both sat for a bit in quiet thought. I couldn't help but be anxious. What if she didn't want to be with me? Could she handle being a Kindred? There were so many questions I had no answers for, her being human and me Krean.

She sighed, turned, looked at me, and asked, "So if we're intimate, that will form a bond for you, but how will it affect me?"

I took a long look at her. She was so lovely. She wasn't conventionally beautiful like her sister but had a unique look. The dark burgundy hair, a colour I'd never seen before, was like shining silk. I wanted to sink my hands into it. And while short, it was thick and swept over her forehead with long bangs.

And then her eyes. I could lose myself in them. They were a turquoise blue, with flecks of dark blue and a ring of black around the outer edge. The shade of blue changed — with her mood, I'd bet. I'd never seen anything like it. I loved the changes I'd see in them. And her body — I needed to stop, or I wasn't going to survive this.

I finally gathered my thoughts and answered, "I have no idea. I don't know any Kreans that have human Kindred. I'm sure there are some, as we are a compatible species, but none that I know of.

"I have a question for you. What do you feel when you are with me? Do you feel anything when I touch you like this?" I continued to stroke her hand. I clasped it harder and pulled her body closer to me. She needed very little encouragement and surprised me by climbing on my lap. She faced me, placing her legs on either side. She pressed herself down on me, and it was pretty clear from my arousal what I wanted. Not that I wanted to hide it from her. I wanted her to know how she affected me. She took a trembling breath, moved her arms around my shoulders and began playing with the hair on my neck. She slowly ran her fingers through my hair and stroked her other hand down my face.

While she did, I studied her closely. She was incredible with her heart-shaped face, perfectly formed full lips, small nose, and those damn eyes. I also touched her face. "Your eyes shift colour, too." I'd never seen that before on a human.

"My eyes change with my mood. What colour are they?" she asked

"Deep blue. They remind me of a large body of water reflecting the blue sky. I've never seen eyes that colour."

She laughed and said, "Well, Cain has the same eyes, but I doubt you've looked at them that closely."

I chuckled. "Uh, no, I don't believe I have."

I gripped her hips with my hands on her perfect ass. God, it was all muscle, round, and with my big hands, her globes fit perfectly. Jesse was curvier than our Krean females. Every inch of her was tightly toned to perfection. And that includes her backside. I found myself stroking it while Jesse brought her fingers to my lips.

"Is it true?"

"What true?"

"That Kreans don't kiss?"

I couldn't help but smile, and I was intrigued. I had a feeling she was going to show me why we should. "No, we don't. Would you like to show me what I'm missing?"

"Hell yes," she said, and I watched as her lovely face moved closer to mine.

She stroked her thumb over my lips, making me realise their sensitivity. I could feel her breathing on my lips as she moved closer. She slowly nipped lightly with hers at the edge of mine, and I felt it down to my toes, and one other place I was trying not to think of for now.

Damn, who knew that lips could be erotic. She moved to the centre before I lost my mind, sealing her lips against mine. I had no idea what to expect, but my lips relaxed and opened slightly as she laid hers against them. She shifted her lips along mine and then licked with her tongue, and that set me off. I grabbed her tight against me, moving my right hand up her back and into her hair. I latched harder onto her lips.

She continued to coax and caress mine with hers, and then I felt her tongue. She clearly wanted me to open further, so I did, and then our tongues touched. It was like a slow dance. Our lips were moving, our tongues duelling, and I could feel her rocking against me.

She slowly pulled away. "How was that?" she asked.

I smiled at her and asked, "Can we do it again?"

"Definitely, but I just want to be clear that I also want much more."

That was all I needed to hear. I stood up, carrying her. She held on with her legs around my hips, and I headed down the stairs to her bed. I planned on giving her more — much more.

She dropped her legs when I reached the bed, but I didn't let her go.

Her hands immediately moved under my shirt, up my chest, and the feel of them on my skin was almost unbearable. I needed the rest of her naked against me. My skin felt like a combination of fire and electrical currents whipping through me.

I slipped her t-shirt over her head and tossed it aside. I was greeted with a pair of round breasts, not overly large, and no bra. I smiled at the lack of a bra. I'm glad I didn't know she was without one until now because I wouldn't have made it through dinner. I pulled my shirt up and over my head, tossed it with her's and immediately pulled her against me.

I closed my eyes and savoured the feel of her. "Your skin feels good. I love your breasts." I slid my hands up and around the front to stroke them and squeeze her nipples. Their size was made for my hands. Her head dropped against my chest, and she moaned. I kept it up until I couldn't stand her moans anymore. Her shifting against me was driving me out of my mind.

I walked her slowly until the back of her knees hit the bed, then bent her back onto it. When I felt her drop onto her back, my hands moved to her pants. She had on simple black stretchy pants that formed to every curve. I grabbed them along with her underwear and yanked them quickly down her legs and off. I'd never seen a human female's body before, so I had no idea what to expect. I had heard others talk about how they were similar to Krean females. However, they had hair in the area between their legs.

In Jesse's case, there was no hair. What was revealed was a beautiful pink area that was unfamiliar to me. I reached out and touched her there, "What is this?" I asked with a grin.

She arched into my touch and gasped, "God, it's one of our most sensitive areas; just keep doing that. Don't stop. It feels amazing."

I kept stroking her slowly and moved to slide a finger further between her legs. I found her opening. It was wet and so warm.

"How's this?"

While I got a moan back, she grabbed my hand and increased the pressure I was applying. I smirked, following her lead. I increased it more, moving my finger back to the tiny nub at the top, I rubbed harder and placed two other fingers inside her while my thumb continued to stroke her nub. I slid my fingers in and out while her moans got louder. She grabbed my hand again and directed me to slide in and out faster. I felt her clench down tight around my fingers, and I heard her scream long and hard. It felt like she was having a Kindred reaction.

When she was done, she looked at me and pushed me up from the bed. She grabbed the front of my pants, undid them and shoved them down. We don't wear undergarments, finding them restrictive, so my stiff staff released in front of her face.

She grabbed me with her hand and licked it. I'd never felt anything like that. She continued to do that, and I instinctively grabbed her head. I wanted her to continue but knew it wouldn't be long before I'd be finished. I didn't want my first release to be that way. I wanted it to be inside her.

I picked her up and tossed her on the bed. Without giving her a chance to move positions, I climbed on top. She pulled me down against her and spread her legs around me. It was the most natural thing in the world; I slid slowly into her.

She was tight, hot, and a perfect fit. I'd had previous sexual encounters, but nothing prepared me for how Jesse felt. Her skin shimmered in the slight light that came through the windows. As I stroked in and out of her, slowly at first, I could feel her hands grabbing my ass.

"Faster, Zersus, god, you fill me perfectly." She could barely form words, and that pleased me — a lot. So, of course, I sped up. I could feel the heat and desire rising between us. We were both grabbing and pumping together.

I could feel her insides gripping my staff tighter as it grew.

I grabbed her hair and pulled her head back to access her neck. To complete the Kindred, I needed to deliver a bite simultaneously as I released inside her. I hope she forgives me because this is going to hurt. The pressure built up. She was screaming my name and clenched one last time as I let go. I bit down on her neck, near her shoulder. We hung on for several minutes.

I kept myself inside her; I never wanted to leave. My staff hardened again for round two. I braced myself on my hands above her, and we both looked at each other.

"Your eyes are amber," she breathily commented with a contented smile.

"Your eyes are deep turquoise blue, and your neck looks beautiful with my bite *AmKee*." I couldn't help but admire my handy work.

"That hurt like hell, just so you know," she replied, "but I don't think I've ever climaxed that hard."

"Is that what you call it? A climax?" I began moving in and out of her again, only this time I grabbed her right leg and put her knee over my arm to open her up more fully to me.

"Shit, here we go again."

Yes, my beautiful Jesse, round two was coming up.

CHAPTER
FOURTEEN
JESSE

I FELT myself waking from one of the best rests I've had in a long time, even though it'd only been a few hours. I became aware of Zersus's big body behind me and his hands stroking me.

They moved up and down slowly, over my breasts and down to my clit. I remembered him asking me what that was between my legs. I guess Krean women didn't have the same pleasure areas. We had to be similar, based on Zersus's body, which was similar to our males. I was curious about the differences.

I glanced over my shoulder and saw he was awake. He leaned forward, grabbed my breast with the hand and arm under my body, pulled me close with his other arm and moved my leg back over his hips. He was ready for round five.

I was sore from our multiple sessions through the night but had no desire to stop him. I needed it as much as he did. To say he was a voracious lover would be an understatement, and I was determined to keep pace with him. No, correct that; I wanted to keep pace with him. I craved it.

Last night, he was surprised as I took the lead at times. He had never been ridden, and it's a position I enjoy very much. And the kissing. God, the kissing. He was a quick learner, and kissing him was a beautiful experience. I can't lie; I also liked that he's never kissed anyone else. And the idea that he hasn't tried some of these positions with other women gave me a weird sense of satisfaction.

I felt his cock pressing to enter me, and while I was wet enough, I felt his large size slide into me with a touch of pain — an enjoyable pain. I was overly sensitive from a few rougher rounds last night. He was also learning that my clit was my "magic" spot, his words, and he loved to play with it.

He raised his head and moved in to whisper in my ear, "My beautiful *AmKee*." He had called me that multiple times, and I knew it was a word to express his affection, but I couldn't help but wonder why it didn't translate.

I moved my hand over my shoulder and grabbed his neck as he continued to move in and out. His pace was picking up, and I could feel the energy building through my body.

I had never climaxed like I did with Zersus. I imagined some of it involved us being Kindred, and I knew I'd never experience this again with anyone else. He said he wasn't sure humans felt the ties, but I could assure you I felt everything intensely. My initial feelings for the man grew tenfold in just a few hours.

He grabbed my hand from his neck and placed it with his at my clit. He wanted me to participate. Again, it was another thing he immensely enjoyed.

Also, as I learned last night, his cock grew as he closed in on his climax. Uh yeah, one *HUGE* difference between human males and Kreans. It surprised me the first time it happened. He was already larger than the few men I'd previously been with but then getting bigger inside me was insanely pleasurable.

I wasn't the type to sleep around much, but I'd had my share of lovers over the years. Most of my relationships didn't last long, but I wasn't one for single nights of sex.

The energy built between us and we both exploded. He continued to stroke me through my climax as I felt him release inside me. The contentment I felt was glorious. I turned over to face him. He pulled me close and continued to stroke my back. I felt every caress down to my toes. It was soothing and electrifying, both at the same time.

He gave me a soft kiss. "You look like you want to talk." he inquired.

I nodded. There were just so many things I wanted to know. "I want to know about you. We know nothing about each other, even though I feel like I've known you forever."

He smiled, "That would be the Kindred affecting you. I'm surprised you're feeling it, but I'm glad to hear that. What do you want to know?"

I thought for a minute. I started at the beginning. "How did you grow up?"

"You know we arrived here a little over 28 years ago?"

I nodded.

"I was 10; Issbeck was six when we first arrived. We were both born on a warship. My dad was a warrior and my mom, a teacher. I think we had been here about a year after the divergence when my dad decided to move us to Terra Two. Issbeck and I spent the rest of our years in Florence-Pisa Meld. I'm not sure what I expected, but it was so…" he paused for a second in thought, "peaceful. I know things were chaotic after the divergence, but the worst was the first year, so by the time we got there, it was settled a bit. Things never seemed that bad to me."

I thought briefly before responding, "Maybe it's because your entire existence on the warship was constant chaos? It was just something you were used to?"

He absentmindedly nodded, "Maybe. I never thought of Terra Two as home. It always felt like I was biding my time to get my feet back onto a warship. As soon as I turned 18, I entered the Space Corp program. I've worked my way up to my current position. I became one of the youngest primes when the Phantom IIs were launched."

You could feel the pride from him. He should be proud. He earned it. I couldn't help but feel a bit reticent. What did that mean for us? His life was on this ship. Then I thought of something. "What's with the no kissing thing? 'Cause that's just bizarre," I said in my usual cheeky manner.

He threw his head back and laughed. I loved his laugh. Kills me every time. He leaned in and kissed me before answering, "Honestly? I'm asking myself the same question. I have no idea why we don't because it's something I want to do non-stop now. I think it's just not a way that we express ourselves. We tend to hug and rub to express our affection."

"And bite, dammit," I said and frowned at him, attempting to be serious.

Of course, he laughed again and pulled me closer. "Sorry about that. I probably should have warned you. It's just a need to mark. It's a way to prance our Kindred around in front of people, and then they know you're mine. I realise that may sound barbaric to you, but I hope you didn't mind too much." And he grinned … again.

I shook my head and laughed at him.

"What about you, Jesse? The only thing I know about you is your current life and what happened the day of the divergence, but tell me about your life with your brothers," he pressed.

I sighed. It was painful to remember but at the same time, wonderful.

"My brothers … I loved them so much, but what a pain in the ass they were." I giggled a bit. "Danny and I were the youngest; we are fraternal twins."

He frowned, "What does fraternal twins mean?"

I always forget that Kreans don't experience multiple births. "We humans regularly have multiple births. In my family's case, we had two. Danny and I are fraternal; Alex and Adam are identical."

"I'm still confused about what the difference is?" he asked as he continued to stroke his hands down my back. He was seriously distracting me.

I tried to concentrate on what he asked. "Well, not to get too medically technical, identical means that both foetuses come from one fertilised egg. Fraternal comes from two separate eggs, which would be me and Danny. Identical is always two boys or two girls who look exactly the same. Most people can't tell them apart. Fraternal twins can be either sex and usually don't look alike. Does that make sense?"

"Sort of. I have to admit that it's a bit crazy."

I grinned at him. I guess it was to him."Well, from my mom's point of view she only had to get pregnant four times to have six kids."

He chuckled, "I can see that being a plus."

"Of course, you know that Cain is the oldest, then there's Nate," I stopped and thought about the fellow that Cain had mentioned for a second, "then the twins, Alex and Adam, and then Danny and me. Our dad was Charles Beaudreau. Mom was Elise, but she died before I knew her. I was two, and Dad said she died in a car accident. The war with the Nomad had just started but we weren't feeling it yet. My Dad always said that while he missed her, he was glad she never had to experience it." I moved in closer to Zersus. Being closer to him made the pain of losing all of them a little less difficult. And he knew. He stroked me, held me tight and kissed my forehead.

Although I'm not sure I could move. I knew we had to get up, shower, and head to the bridge.

"Come on, *AmKee*, up you get. Let's shower together."

I watched him grin at me. "Hell no, I'm not showering with you. We will never get out of here. You go first, and then I'll take mine."

He gave me an exaggerated sigh, making me laugh. He kissed me quickly and headed off to the bathroom. While he was showering, I grabbed the clothes we had left strewn all over the bedroom and put them on the bed. I grabbed mine and planned to take them into the bathroom with me. I was a quick showerer and didn't waste my time with a lot of froufrou crap. I never bothered with makeup. My hair was short for a reason. I'd finger it into place, and it dried in minutes. Then I was good to go.

I heard the shower turn off, and he walked out naked. I laughed at him as I approached and dodged him as he went to grab me.

"You need to be faster than that. And I put your clothes out for you," I shouted as I dashed into the bathroom, locking the door because I didn't trust him. I chuckled as I showered and quickly dressed. To my surprise, as I left the bathroom, he was also ready, although I could tell it took everything in him to leave. If anything, duty comes first.

"You ready?" he asked me.

I nodded, moving closer to him. He pulled me towards him and planted a quick kiss on my lips. He grabbed my hand, and we headed up the stairs, out the door, and toward the bridge. He put an arm over my shoulders as we approached and stopped me before we entered.

"Issbeck is going to know immediately. He is my brother, and he will sense our connection. I'm sorry I didn't mention that before, but I didn't want you caught off guard."

I considered what he said, "Not like the eyes aren't a dead giveaway. Will he be okay with it?" I was concerned about what he told me about Issbeck losing his Kindred. And I couldn't help but feel for him and his loss. I even felt some understanding of how difficult it must have been. And he was so young when it happened. It made me sad.

"Of course he will. His instincts told him that I was forming an attachment to you when he met you. He won't be surprised." Zersus smiled at me.

I was still a bit nervous about this, but I liked Issbeck. I hoped the feeling was mutual. Knowing that he lost his Kindred, I couldn't help but worry that he could feel uncomfortable about Zersus and me being together.

The doors to the bridge opened as Katie, Harley, and CeeChi headed out. They stopped when they saw us and looked at Zersus's arm around my shoulder. Katie squealed and jumped on me.

"Geez, could you let me breathe, sis," I told her.

She laughed, "I'm just so happy. You did what I thought you would last night, right?"

I could hear Zersus rumble beside me, and I just shook my head at her antics.

Zersus was the one to answer, "Yes, we *are* together."

I noticed CeeChi look at my neck. Her eyes widened; she looked between us. I could see her get a bit emotional. She grabbed one of my hands and one of Zersus'. "I am so pleased for you both. Prime is a good man; you are the perfect Kindred for him."

To lighten the mood, I tapped her on the arm and she snapped out of it, but she had an enormous smile.

Harley was the last one to come forward, but instead of hugging me, he put out a hand to Zersus to shake his and asked, "You know how important she is to all of us?"

Zersus' mood switched to serious at Harley's question. "Yes, I completely understand. I swear you have my word that I'll never hurt her, and I will do everything in my power to protect her ..." He paused, winked at me and continued, "As much as she'll let me."

"You're lucky you added that in," I commented, giving him an exaggerated scowl and just like that, the mood lightened, and we all laughed.

Zersus addressed the reason we were there, "Anything to report on the information you gathered from their ships?"

They nodded.

Katie spoke up first. "We hit the jackpot. We were just heading to grab a quick breakfast. We've been at it all night, but Melo is in there, and he can give you a quick rundown on what we found."

"Alright. Jesse and I will see you back here when you're done. Don't rush and enjoy your breakfast." Zersus and I watched them leave as we entered the bridge.

As expected, Melo was sitting at the system off to the right, going through the data from the Nomad ships. Issbeck and Simal were chatting about the ship's repairs at the main consoles, and a couple of other warriors were looking at star charts to the far left.

The entire bridge was built like a semi-circle. Where you entered was dead centre, a large central screen was split into two large sections at the front and it usually showed us the space we were travelling through. There were steps that led down into a lower area, filled with transparent screens of varying information. In total, nine people could sit at those stations. Zersus, rather than being the type to have a "captain" style seat, simply took the centre console position, and things were relayed to him based on their level of importance.

I liked that he put himself at the same level as his crew. It said a lot about the man and also his ability to lead. His crew had a tremendous amount of respect for him, and I could see why.

Before he could lead me over to Melo, Issbeck stepped before us. I held my breath for a second. My eyes met Issbeck's, and I saw many emotions cross his face; all were good. He stepped towards us and zeroed in on the bite mark on my neck. I heard him gasp a bit, and then he smiled. He grabbed and pulled me into, yet again, another bear hug. I started to laugh, trying to pry myself out of his death grip when Zersus gave him a bit of a growl.

Issbeck let me go as Zersus pulled me back against him. "I was just giving her a *welcome to the family* hug," he complained. Zersus scowled at him, and Issbeck ignored him, looked at me and let me know, "I'm so happy for you two, but don't let him get away with being grumpy. You give him hell."

"Oh, you can be guaranteed I will," I agreed.

Zersus just crossed his arms and looked at us both with frustration. "Do I not get a say in this?"

We both replied *"NO"* at the same time. We could hear everyone on the bridge snickering. A small smile crept onto Zersus' handsome face.

The three of us moved over to where Melo was, and Zersus

requested that he give us a rundown on the data they'd found. Melo grinned, congratulated us, and indicated the screen before him. "We've combined the data we took off all their ships. We've managed to filter it down to the main points on this screen. Issbeck had us transmit some of the information immediately to the Supreme Commander; you will see why when you read it. Fast action by Terra Moonbase was necessary."

As Melo finished his explanation, we were already reading. The team had found several plans. I realised why Issbeck had felt it necessary to send the info to Danlon.

The first significant point in the information was a plan to remove a couple hundred people from Terra Three. There were details and specifics on who was being taken. They were brazen, taking people who would be missed in larger numbers.

Terra Three was the planet that housed much of our entertainment industry, including actors, actresses, and musicians. A number of the group were actresses. Damn, there had to be a hundred young people under the age of 18, and many were marked as Krean. I could feel Zersus tense beside me.

"Get SC Danlon on the comm so I can talk to him," he commanded Simal.

On top of that, we found out the Nomad had been doing this for years. There was a list of people taken that seemed endless. It was similar to a shopping list. I pointed to the planets named and asked Zersus, "Do you recognize some of these planets?"

"Yes, some are familiar. I've heard of a few others but don't know their exact star locations. There are only a couple here I am unfamiliar with, but I would think that a visit to some of our allies could get us the information we need."

I nodded to him, and we went back to reading.

I noted that another species was mentioned as the Nomad's partner in moving the people around. I'd never heard of the Obsidi. I asked, "Who are they?"

I watched a frown form on Zersus' face. "That's unusual. They are a peaceful species. Very religious. Their ships are not warships. It's strange to me that they would participate in this. We haven't encountered an Obsidi ship in some time though, so who knows."

Zersus sat down, leaned back, and crossed his arms. I could see he was thinking. "But what if they had no choice?"

"Explain. Are you doubting their participation?" I asked.

"We all know the extent the Nomad will go to destroy a species and their planets. The Obsidi would be an easy target. They would also be the last ones we would ever suspect. I'm not one to give the benefit of the doubt so easily, but something just doesn't feel right."

I watched Issbeck, Simal, and Melo nod so I had to consider their opinions and try not to let my distaste for the slave trade cloud my judgment. After all, they knew the Obsidi species, and I didn't.

"Prime, I have the Supreme Commander," said Simal.

"Patch it in over here." Zersus moved to the next screen.

Supreme Commander Danlon appeared. He was frowning. He looked at me and squinted. He zeroed in on my neck, but that was for another conversation, although he did grin a bit.

"Danlon, my warriors have told me they sent you information we retrieved about the plans to move the large groups of people off Terra Three?"

Danlon nodded. "Yes. Several SPAR teams were dispatched to the coordinates immediately. We managed to stop most of the operation. There were many from both our species, mostly children. Unfortunately, one small group was able to get away, and we could not track them. We estimate about 20 people were taken. We were also able to apprehend some of their accomplices. The SPAR team set up fake bio signs, and they took the bait."

"Were they Obsidi?" Zersus asked.

"No. I know you found that information in the database, much to my surprise." He paused. *Huh*, so Danlon was just as surprised as Zersus about the Obsidi's participation.

"So if not Obsidi, then who?" Issbeck asked.

"The group we detained is Chatoch. They are an insectoid species and not pleasant. If they had gotten their hands on our people ..." I could see Danlon rub his temple and sigh. I could tell from his posture and general stance that he was pissed. "Sorry, I am just pissed off that we could not stop them completely. I swear this is not going to continue!"

I could see the frustration and determination on his face. I wanted to make sure that didn't happen, too. I'm sure all of us wanted to find all of the lost and bring them home. I looked at Zersus, Issbeck, Simal, and Melo; they felt the same. When I looked around at the rest of the crew on the bridge, they had similar expressions. We had some work ahead of us.

Zersus asked Issbeck, "When will we be ready to return to Terra?"

"Simal and I received a report from the engineers that the repair-bots should be done in approximately eight hours. We took a lot of damage at the back, near the rear thrusters, so the repairs are taking a bit longer because it's delicate work."

Zersus nodded, turning back to Danlon, "We will be on our way as soon as possible. In the meantime, we will continue interrogating the Nomad we have in our cell chambers, along with Curalim."

Danlon tensed up when he heard that name. "I want that man on Moonbase as soon as you can get him here. He has a lot to answer for." He quickly signed off.

I knew Danlon had a history with Curalim but didn't know the full story. I had a bad feeling about the creepy blue guy. Something about him didn't sit right with me. And how could he get so much control over so many species? I guess not all of them fought the Nomad like ours did.

I looked at Zersus, and he grabbed my hand. "You hungry?" he asked.

"Starving." I pulled him up from the chair and put my arms

around him. He rested his chin on my head. I looked at Issbeck, "Have you eaten yet?" I asked.

He nodded. "Simal and I ate a few hours ago; you two go ahead. We will keep on the engineers to try to get us moving as soon as possible."

"We plan to chat with Curalim once we've eaten." Zersus mentioned. "Melo, if you and the rest of the tech team come up with anything else you feel is important, let us know immediately, and we will head back."

Zersus guided me out of the bridge and headed for the Common Room. Food first — then Creepy Blue Guy.

CHAPTER
FIFTEEN
JESSE

WHEN ZERSUS and I arrived at the Common Room, it was bustling and full, unlike the last time. Many of the warriors were taking the opportunity to get a bite to eat and relax. Everyone else's jobs were on hold, except for the engineers, with the ship down for repair.

I noticed that Cain and Annie were in a back corner together just as she stood up and strode away. She looked pissed. Cain looked frustrated. The best thing right now would be to leave him alone. However, when Cain noticed Zersus and me together, he nodded for me to join him.

When I reached his table, I sat across from him. Zersus went to grab our plates. As soon as I sat, Cain asked, "You and him?"

I looked at Zersus over my shoulder, looked back at Cain and smiled. "Yes."

"You know that Kreans take permanent mates, right? I've heard about their Kindred partners and how attached they become to them. Honestly, sis, you shouldn't get involved with him because if he finds his Kindred, he'll leave you. I'm not saying that to be negative about Zersus because I think he's a great guy, but it's the reality of their species."

I looked at Cain, smiled at the fact that he hadn't noticed my neck, and dropped my collar. As soon as he saw the bite, he sat there with his mouth hanging open. "Holy shit. Seriously? You're his Kindred?"

"So it would seem," I smiled.

Cain grabbed my hands and squeezed. "I'm so happy for you!" I could see a frown form on his handsome face as he added, "But how will the two of you make that work? Never mind the fact you're human. How does that work? That is just so weird. Do you feel it? I've heard it's pretty intense for Kreans."

I held my hands up. "Whoa, one question at a time. You're making my head spin." We both laughed. "First, I have no idea how it'll work or why me, but you know what? I'm not worried. We'll figure it out. I'm confident we can find a way to make it work. And do you know why? Because when it's important, you always find a way."

I noted his expression change when I said that. I wasn't just talking about Zersus and me. I could tell something was brewing between him and Annie.

As Zersus came over with our plates, Cain got up, congratulated him, gave him the standard, "*take care of my sister,*" and left. He looked happy but a bit melancholy at the same time. It took me a minute to realise Zersus was talking to me. "Everything okay?"

"It's fine; I think he's just dealing with some things." I smiled at him. He bent down to kiss my forehead and dropped the plates full of food. The smell was mouthwatering. It looked like a beef stew and he included biscuits that were still warm. I couldn't wait to try them. Dunking those biscuits into the stew was going to be so good. We both dug in, and it was delicious. All of the food was fantastic. They had an excellent chef. I was just about to ask Zersus how the food was stored on the ship when Sid, Neil, and Joe arrived. They were obviously looking for us.

I could tell by the look on their faces they knew. Katie and

Harley must have told them. They were all smiles, hugs, and back slaps for Zersus. Quickly, though, they got serious.

Sid asked, "Are we going to talk to that piece of shit in your holding cell?"

Zersus grinned and nodded. "We were just finishing up and planning to head there now. I'm assuming you three would like to join us."

"Damn right, we would," said Neil. He wasn't a man of many words but wanted to watch Curalim squirm.

"Let's go." We followed Zersus. Time to face the devil.

◆

As we approached the sliding door to the cells, the warriors on guard stood at attention. "Prime," they addressed Zersus and gave slight bows. I noticed many warriors did this, even though I could tell it made Zersus uncomfortable.

Zersus introduced them as Hishto and Ren, putting his arm around my waist and pulling me forward. He was making sure they understood I was important. It was unnecessary, but I loved that he had no reservations about us being together.

I noticed both warriors quickly realised who I was to Zersus without him having to explain. I smiled at them both, and they tried to fight a grin. Zersus shook his head and led us into the cells. He gave the order to prepare Curalim for our interrogation. Zersus' warriors had already questioned several other Nomad with little results. They knew nothing. Curalim would have the information, so the creepy blue guy was last on the list.

The holding cells were in the ship's bowels and were not built for comfort. Anyone relegated to a cell got a bed and a small washroom; the space was minimal. I'd guess about three metres by two metres, just enough for one person. The front had metal bars and a charged force field. It was prudent to have a double system to contain the prisoners, as you never knew their skills or if they would attempt to escape. My mind returned to the incident on the Nomad ship where Curalim had jabbed Zersus. It was hard to tell if that was a needle or something inherent to his species.

As we approached, Curalim got up with his attention focused on me. He sniffed the air and closed his eyes as if savouring a scent. Suddenly, his eyes snapped open. He roared and approached the barrier. He began banging on it. If I was being honest, it was a tad comical. All of us stood there and watched him lose his shit. I assumed at some point he'd stop and maybe tell us what had his pants in a twist, but for now, we dragged some chairs over and sat down in front of his cell to watch the show.

Eventually, he realised he wasn't going to get a reaction out of any of us. He stopped making a spectacle of himself, but he continued to stand there, holding the bars and staring unblinkingly at me. His stare was creepy. I rolled my eyes and looked over at Zersus.

Zersus was the first to ask, "Are you finished having a tantrum?"

Curalim turned with a look of pure hatred to Zersus. "You took what was mine?"

That was when it dawned on all of us what was going on. It had to do with me. He was upset because of me. What I couldn't understand was why.

"I can smell it. He marked his scent on you. His stench is combined with your smell," he scornfully admitted.

What the hell? This guy is a fucking weirdo. I couldn't hold it in. "Oh, I don't know, I kind of like his smell," I said with a smirk. There was no way I was letting this guy get anything out of me other than disdain. "I like everything about him. Guess your shit out of luck, huh?"

I could see the anger and rage in his eyes. He was pissed. I stood up and walked closer, Zersus warned me to keep a distance from the electrical barrier. I looked Curalim in the eye and let him know how I felt. "You don't think I remember you? I remember everything. You're the one that took me from my family. You planned to take me when I was a small girl, right? Well, I guess you lose."

He kept his mouth shut, but I could feel the anger rolling off him. It wouldn't do him any good, so he might as well forget it. He would tell us what we wanted to know, and then we'd take him to Terra Moonbase. I'd never have to think of him again.

Zersus stood up and walked towards me, at which point Curalim stepped back. Interestingly, he had an aversion to Zersus. Or is that fear?

Zersus addressed him, "Let me tell you how this will go. We're going to ask you questions, and you'll answer." Zersus turned to one of the warriors on guard and nodded. I wasn't sure what that meant until we all noticed a mist forming in Curalim's cell.

Curalim realised quickly what was going on and tried holding his breath.

Sid stepped forward, watching him closely. "Is that an interrogation thiobarb?" he asked Zersus.

"Yes," Zersus replied. "He'll only be able to hold his breath for so long. We can start with our questions once he's taken a good long breath. No matter how much he struggles, he won't be able to resist telling us what we want to know."

I could see Sid, Joe, and Neil looking confused.

Joe asked, "Why didn't they use that on the prisoners we caught on Terra Four."

The guys knew they ended up dead, but they didn't know when it happened. I spoke up quietly, "They didn't get a chance. They were killed before they could be transported to Moonbase so they couldn't be interrogated. That is why the group recently captured on Terra Three is probably being kept on a warship. I gave the chief the idea, so I'm sure he mentioned it to Danlon."

We went back to our seats.

The five of us sat there and waited. It didn't take long for Zersus' prediction to happen, and Curalim had no choice but to breathe in the mist. I could see him stagger and sit. Zersus asked Sid, Neil, and Joe to go first with their questions. We all had enough questions to keep this guy up all night. Their questions centred around what had been happening with the disappearances. We wanted answers. Surprisingly, he didn't know who the traitors were. In his arrogance, he said he did not need to know, just that there were many and they were helpful when needed. I could tell the guys were pissed off. We had hoped to get more answers.

When they began the questions, I noticed that the warrior guards had started a recording system. It was similar to what we used along with a camera recording, so I assumed that was also happening.

I'm not entirely sure we were prepared for some of his answers. Confirming what we suspected, that the slave trade had been going on for years. Of course, we knew the intensity had increased significantly over the last year. The ultimate end to it was for the Nomad to weaken our hold on the Terra planets and for them to invade and take over. In Curalim's bizarre mind, his people believed that spreading us all over the universe while making a little profit by selling us off would make the Terra's easier to conquer. And now that we had a robust five-planet system, they wanted it even more. Bastards wouldn't get it. I'd die before I'd let that happen. And if you looked at the guys' faces, they would also.

It was taking considerably longer than they had expected. They underestimated us and didn't realise how completely the two species, humans and Kreans, could combine our strengths. They were faced with a situation where they had two determined species that would fight them. I made a note to talk to Zersus about that. I felt it was vital that we made our strength the number one goal going forward. My instincts told me Curalim displayed a touch of fear when discussing this subject.

It took several hours for the guys to finish their questions while the guards continually flooded the cell with mist. I guessed we didn't want him coming out of it before the interrogation was over.

Once the guys were done, Zersus stood and walked towards the cell. He had asked me to stay seated, which annoyed me a bit, but I knew there had to be a reason for his request.

He began his questions with, "Who was in charge of the destruction of Allora?"

I lifted my brows. Not what I was expecting him to ask, but I had to admit I was curious.

I could see Curalim trying very hard to hold back on answering. You could see sweat on his brow, his hands fisted, his back straightened. It was no use, and he couldn't resist forever.

Zersus suddenly shifted to give him a view of me. "Why do you want her?" he asked softly.

Curalim lost concentration and replied, "I saw her when she was little. I wanted her, so I took her. Then your damn people took her away from me. I will take her back." It was all stated matter-of-factly, and he genuinely believed he would get me again. Not sure how he figured that would happen but before I could go down that road, Zersus asked again.

"Who was in charge of the destruction of Allora?"

Curalim was so busy concentrating on me that he slipped up and answered, "I was."

He turned raging eyes to Zersus. Aha, got you asshole.

"It was a shame your parents managed to get away. If I had gotten rid of them, you wouldn't be here to stand in my way. No matter, she will be mine, and you will lose." He smirked at Zersus. I guessed he was looking for a reaction but props to Zersus that he hadn't even flinched.

Neil leaned over to me. "Damn, he's tough ... I mean Zersus, not Creepy Blue Guy." He winked at me, and I couldn't help but smile.

The other guys nodded, and Sid said, "I agree. He's no pushover. Perfect for Jesse."

I punched him in the arm, and he faked like it hurt. Bunch of

clowns. I was fortunate to be able to call them my friends —
sometimes.

Zersus continued his questioning. Most of his questions
centred around the attack on Allora. It was information that the
Kreans had wanted for a long time. I knew Zersus was doing
this for Danlon. I had always felt Danlon was important to the
Krean people, especially Zersus, but I hadn't had an opportunity
to ask why.

Zersus looked over at me as he finished up and asked me if I
had any questions for the *"Creepy Blue Guy."* I shook my head.
He was the one who tried to take me and Katie as children, and
he lost. That was good enough for me. I honestly couldn't care
less about his opinions on what he thought about me. My main
concern was ending his slave operation. I was hopeful that his
capture would put a huge dent in it, if not end it.

We got up and turned to leave. As we reached the doors,
Curalim yelled, "Oh, how are your dear brothers, Jesse? Your
father? Found any of them yet?"

We all stopped, and I turned to him. He was attempting to
use something he knew to get to me. I knew he wasn't lying
because he was still under the influence of the mist. I looked
over at Zersus. He nodded and acknowledged, "We can discuss
it later alone."

"Okay, but we can come back and have another go at him?" I
asked.

"Definitely."

I looked at Curalim, smirked and promised, "I'll be back,
asshole." I turned around and left with the guys.

Zersus told Hishto and Ren to send off the recordings to
Issbeck. They both looked upset. While they were both too
young to have experienced the destruction of Allora, I was sure
their parents were present during that time. I had no idea what
to say to them. How could you comfort someone whose entire
planet was gone? The Nomad had destroyed so many lives.

I assumed that Issbeck would get the interrogation details off to Danlon.

I took one final glance back to see Curalim watching me.

I'd definitely be back, but I wanted to talk to Cain and maybe take him with me. I would find out if he was bullshitting or if he really had any useful information about my brothers and father.

CHAPTER
SIXTEEN
JESSE

AFTER THAT "LOVELY" visit with Creepy Blue Guy, we decided to head to the War Room and work on the data. There was a lot more we could learn.

We found that Katie, Harley, and CeeChi had already situated themselves there instead of the bridge. There was more room to work. Everyone hunkered down and started scanning through the information. It would take a lot of time to review it.

I was going through a list of people's names and having trouble making heads or tails of the codes next to them. I know that Katie was running an algorithm in an attempt to determine the combinations' meaning.

"Holy shit." Katie's exclamation in the quiet had us all looking at her. She was staring at the screen in front of her.

We got up and moved to stand behind her to view her screen. In front of her were several names. Damn, they were Katie's brother's names — her real brothers lost years ago, like mine. Again, there was a set of codes beside their names.

I was almost sure the code somehow included their ages when they were taken and said as much to Katie.

She nodded. "Yes, and I think the date taken is another

sequence, as this set of eight numbers appears to be a date." She pointed to a sequence. "This looks like the same date we were taken. All of the entries correspond to year, month, day."

"That makes sense. So male or female is first, age second, date next." I pointed to a set of letter sequences toward the end. "What about this?"

Zersus joined us and said, "I think that could be who took them."

"Look here; this set is an 'O,' and then on this one is a 'C' and then an 'F,' and so on. I think that could refer to who assisted them with the transfer?"

"If that's the case, we know the Obsidi is one, and the Chatoch, but who are the others?" I asked.

Zersus stopped for a second and I could see the wheels turning. I knew he was running through all the species that begin with an "F," trying to find a likely one. I could tell when he realised he may have it. He turned to us and said, "I'd guess it's the Feranth."

"Why them?" I asked.

He gave us a quick rundown on them. I winced thinking they may have their hands on some of our people. Out of all the species helping the Nomad, they are the only ones that make my skin crawl.

Katie asked, "What about the "N"?"

Issbeck piped up, "Probably the Niri." When did he show up? I guess I wasn't paying attention.

"The Niri?" I asked.

Issbeck explained, "They are a robot race. They wouldn't keep the humans themselves. They would sell them for tech parts they need to survive."

Zersus commanded, "Let's rundown these species. We need to know what sort of ships they have. Their weapons capabilities, homeworlds, who they might be in contact with and anything else that could be relevant. The more information we have, the better." Zersus split us up into four groups, each taking a different species. We'd use whatever we could find on the Aries systems about them, for now.

The first group, Zersus, Simal, and Melo, took the Obsidi. Next was Sid, Katie, and me; we focused on the Chatoch. Issbeck, Neil, and Harley had the Niri while Joe, Kiv, and CeeChi started on the Feranth. We quickly checked the ship's repairs and were assured it should only take another four to five hours. We agreed to work for a couple of hours, take stock of what we had, and then get some rest.

We hunkered down and started digging for information. At one point, I looked around the room, and everyone was engrossed in their research. After a few hours, we stopped and looked at everything we'd gathered.

Zersus' group gave a rundown on the Obsidi. They were a humanoid species considered very peaceful and religious which we knew. They had a beautiful planet in the sector where the Allora had once been, but it held very little in the way of resources, so not much to attract the Nomad. And they carried no weapons. I wondered how they defended themselves. They were an easy choice as a target for the Nomad to force them to help. Everyone agreed. The only thing we found of interest is that the Obsidi have many spaceships and could communicate effectively with all of them. Perhaps this was why the Nomad wanted to partner with them. This ability could be worth a lot to a species like the Nomad — to any species. The Obsidi kept this a well-hidden secret. We all agreed they were an odd choice as an ally to be working willingly with the Nomad. That left a question as to what their role was. We would make it a priority to find out.

The Chatoch was an insectoid type species, as Danlon had mentioned, very hard to kill and quite advanced. Their hand weapons use was non-existent. Their multi-limbed bodies made them fast-moving, but they couldn't hold weapons so they depended on their strength, speed and their pincers, which carried a toxin that caused paralysis. Their body's outer shell was difficult to penetrate with a pulse weapon, but if you hit a gap in their armour, they would quickly go down which meant accuracy when shooting was critical. They had been known associates of the Nomad for a long time. Their treatment of slaves was typically to sell them. They did not keep them as they had no use for them. They didn't have a home planet; they just roamed space to trade for necessary supplies. That fact will make finding them a challenge. I couldn't help but think we were lucky they didn't make it off Terra Three with everyone they had planned to take. From a spaceship's point of view, theirs were no more advanced than ours. It was hard to say how many ships they had.

Issbeck's group shared the Niri were a robotic race with no organics. No one knew what happened to the people who made them, but now they repaired themselves. They had no use for organic species but would trade slaves for mechanical parts they would need to survive. They were scavengers. They walked upright on two legs. Their hands were typically whatever scraps they could use, so it varied depending on how old the robot was and if they needed replacement parts. Like humans, no two were alike because of this. They had no faces, just two black holes for their eyes. They did "see and hear," but it's believed that they just interpret input, which is why they can be easily fooled. It wasn't that hard to outsmart them. Generally, they were not a combative species, so getting to them might be a good place to start. As far as ships were concerned, they seemed to be falling apart, from everything Issbeck's group could find. They had very little defence and seemed to be an odd partner for the Nomad. Zersus suggested they may be disposable allies.

Last was Joe's group which researched the Feranth. To say they were concerning was an understatement. Out of all the species, this was the one that worried me. They appeared to be humanoid, but it was hard to say for sure as no one had ever reported seeing what they looked like under their armour, and their size was of some concern. Of all the species we'd examined, they were the only ones that would take the slaves to their home planet. The rumour was they ate their slaves when they were done with them, which really was an awful thought. They had a small cluster of planets, one in particular where they mined deranthium, the primary ore they needed to power their ships and run their planet's energy. They kidnapped slaves from all over space, worked them to the bone, and then ate them; at least that was the lore. There was also the theory that they kept women as sex slaves because no one had ever seen a female Feranth. It wasn't far-fetched to assume they didn't have females of their own since women and children seemed to be one of the main targets of their slave abductions from the Terras.

The Feranth's home planet was heavily protected and hard to get to. In combat, they moved slowly because they wore heavy armour. They depended heavily on their weapons, so we would have the advantage if we could disarm them. They were just as fragile as we were in battle if injured. Their fighting skills were on par with ours. Krean pulse weapons could penetrate their armour when set to maximum. Not ideal because it would kill them and prevent us from taking them as prisoners. Getting our hands on some of them would be ideal, but they didn't like to be taken alive. Their spaceships were also a huge concern. They had many battleships and typically attacked in a swarm. We would need to be careful with them. They were also long-time allies of the Nomad and, while they typically did not get involved in the Nomad's wars, they needed slaves. We had to prioritise getting our people off of their planets.

Altogether, we would have our hands full.

I could see a few yawning. We were ready to take a break. Harley and CeeChi wanted to stay and continue analysing the data.

Zersus asked if I would join him in his room. Seriously, did he even have to ask? At least I'd get to see his personal space. Hopefully, get to know him even better.

Imagine my surprise when I realised he placed me in the

quarters beside him. The noticeable difference when we entered his space was obvious. It was clear this was his home. It had a personal, warm feel to it. It was clearly a "man's" space but still welcoming. While the furniture was similar to my chambers, he had added art, carpets, a throw over the sofa and even, what had to be, customised curtains. Unusual, considering you didn't need them in space. However, they made the room feel more personal.

He came up from behind, wrapped his arms around me and whispered, "Do you like it? You're the first woman I've brought here."

I felt the thrill running through me at the thought. I smiled, turned in his arms and nodded. "I love it. It has you written all over it."

He picked me up, my legs wrapped around his waist, and carried me down the stairs. He had a thing for carrying me. He didn't stop in front of the bed this time but continued to the bathroom. I bent back a bit, looked at him and raised my eyebrows. What was he up to?

He laughed and gently placed me on the vanity. He started to undress me. "Since I didn't get a chance to have time with you in the shower this morning, I figured I'd take my opportunity now."

I couldn't help but laugh — no argument from me. I loved the idea.

We shed our clothes quickly and it was clear he was more than happy with this plan. His cock was hard and ready. He turned on his shower, which was larger than the one in my chambers, so *"yeah"* for the boss's shower. He directed me under it and dropped his head to kiss me. The man had no reservations about kissing now. And he was a naturally great kisser.

His chest rumbled as he pulled back, looking me in the eye with those beautiful golden, amber eyes, and said, "How I could have thought kissing wouldn't be enjoyable is beyond me." He dipped in and slowly ran his tongue over my lips, much like I did when I was giving him his first kissing lesson. Then we both opened, deepening the kiss.

He lifted me again, bracing me against the shower wall. I knew what was coming. He placed his elbows under my knees. Damn, good thing I'm flexible because I was almost bent in half. I was entirely at his mercy, with my pussy open for him to do what he wanted. He took complete advantage thrusting in hard and to the hilt, then moving his cock quickly in and out. I swear my eyes rolled back at the feeling of his enormous cock inside me. He was pumping hard. Gone were the gentle rounds of last night, making sure every thrust counted.

I could barely hang on. The angle that he hit with each thrust rubbed along my clit, building my orgasm, and he knew that. I'm unsure how he came up with the position, but we would do it again if I had anything to say about it.

"Oh god, Zersus. Harder. Faster," I commanded.

"You like it like this?" His chest rumbled as he thrust harder. I was ready to explode. His cock was swelling, and I knew what was coming.

"My beautiful *AmKee*," he practically purred in my ear.

"Zersus, I love your cock so much, don't stop."

And he didn't until we both came together. I think I might have passed out for a moment. That was the most intense session we'd had so far. Could anything possibly get better than that?

As I was thinking how amazing I felt, he was stroking in and out of me. I touched his handsome face and stroked his smooth, sculpted jaw. His skin was so soft, like a baby's, which was surprising considering how tough he was as a warrior.

He leaned in for a kiss as he slowly released me. My legs didn't want to cooperate as I tried to stand. He had to brace me.

We both laughed and went about cleaning up. He wouldn't let me wash myself, determined to do it himself. I loved how his hands travelled over every inch. Then, he let me return the favour. I hadn't yet had a chance to explore him, so I took my time. He stood tall. His legs were muscular, strong and long, attached to what had to be the best ass on the Terras. He had small dimples at the base of his back that I traced up and over the muscles in his back. Then I moved around to his front, where his abs were clearly defined. Top that off with strong arms and a tightly sculpted chest. And damn if it wasn't all mine. Okay, now, who sounds barbaric? I laughed at myself. I swear he knew what I was thinking but only bent down and smacked a quick kiss on my lips.

He grabbed the towels as we left the shower. When he finished drying us off, he picked me up bridal style and headed for bed. I hoped he was going to let us rest. I needed a power nap. I noticed his brows scrunched together and he asked, "In the shower, you said you loved my cock. What is that?"

I looked over at him and started to laugh before realising he was serious. I reached for his cock which was semi-hard. "This is your cock. Is that not what you call it?"

He pulled back, looked at me with a frown and said, "Who came up with that word? It makes no sense at all. That part of my body is my staff."

I rolled away from him and couldn't stop laughing. "Your staff? Why staff?"

"Because it's long, sticks out straight, and when it's hard, it's like a weapon."

I howled at that. I was having a hard time breathing, I was laughing so hard.

He grabbed me and pulled me on top of him. "Woman, are you laughing at my staff?"

And that just made it worse. God, I loved this man … and his staff.

He moved his hands between my legs and asked, "What about this sweet little nub? What do you call that?" His hand moved further down. "And this?"

I smiled at him, resting my chin on his chest. I took a long look at him. "That's my clit — the little nub as you called it." I considered his second question and couldn't help but answer,

"The other is my pussy." I could feel his chest rumble as his full laugh erupted from him.

"Humans are so strange."

He wrapped his arms around me. I settled with my head on his chest as he stroked his hands down my back, and I could feel myself slowly relaxing. I was sexually sated, relaxed, and happy.

CHAPTER
SEVENTEEN
JESSE

I woke up with a jolt. I was a touch disoriented for a second, but then I realised where I was. We'd fallen asleep in Zersus' bed. It dawned on me what woke me; my communicator. I had slipped it back on when we got out of the shower.

I activated it and saw an urgent message from Harley. He said he'd found something important, and I needed to return to the War Room.

Zersus was still sleeping soundly, so I asked if he was needed. Harley said no. I decided to let him sleep. He had to be running on fumes and needed the rest. I couldn't help but wonder what else Harley could have found that was so important.

I quickly dressed and took the short walk back to the War Room. When I entered, the only person inside was Harley.

"What's up? What did you find?" I asked him.

When he turned to me, his look made me edgy. He nodded towards the monitor before him but didn't say anything. His expression was grim as he turned towards the screen.

He pointed to a spot on the list of names. There were three of interest: Charles Beaudreau, Alex Beaudreau and Adam Beaudreau.

"Just the three?" I asked.

He nodded.

"So that means my dad and twin brothers were taken and are not on the Terras." I noted the sequence beside their names. It was the same day I was taken, but the letter beside their names was an "O." If we were right, the Obsidi took them.

I sat down to think. At least I knew Cain was fine and where he was. Nate was still a question, but Cain and I would check into that as soon as we could return to Moonbase. And so far, nothing about Danny; I could still hope he was safe on a Terra but the list issues weren't helping that circumstance.

"What's up, Jesse? You look like you have something on your mind," Harley knew my "*thinking*" look.

"You weren't down there when we interrogated Curalim, but his last words to me were about my dad and brothers."

Harley sat there for a second, letting that sink in, "Damn, so you think he has information about them? Didn't you guys give him the thiobarb?"

"Yes, which is why he wasn't lying about that."

"Right." Harley nodded. "That makes sense."

I rose quickly, but Harley grabbed me.

"Whoa, Jesse, I can see that look on your face. Don't go down there alone; take one of the guys with you. I'll go with you, just give me a minute to shut this stuff down."

I reassured him it was fine, "There are two guards there all the time. I'll be fine, but when Zersus wakes up, I'm sure he will head here looking for me." I smiled. "Give him the rundown on what you found. I might even make it back before he gets up.

"Oh, and I almost forgot. When we were down there the last time, we never did ask him about the coding because we didn't know about it. I'm going to ask him about that, too. Maybe I can get some sort of confirmation about his partners, and if our guesses on who they are is correct."

Harley agreed that was a good plan, but he said again, "Be

sharp. I don't trust anything about the Nomad, especially that guy."

I gave him a thumbs up.

As I left the bridge, I contemplated waking up Zersus to take him down to cell level with me but it would be a short visit. The less time I spent in Curalim's presence, the better. I'd have the guards mist him again, ask the questions, and that would be it. Then I hoped I'd never have to talk to him again. While I knew I could fight back now and wasn't a child, I couldn't shake the creeps he gave me. I guess it was a little "six-year-old-Jesse" showing herself.

When I arrived at the cell doors I used my hand scan to open them, while realising the guards weren't outside. I figured they must be inside dealing with the prisoners. The cells seemed unusually quiet though, and I cursed myself for not having a weapon with me. I moved cautiously forward wondering where the guards were. I felt a quick prick to my neck. My movements became jerky. I felt myself losing the ability to walk. I couldn't lift my arms. Everything seemed to tilt, and I realised I was falling but someone caught me before I face-planted.

That someone was Curalim.

"Well, hello, my dear. I was so hoping you would come back and I could avoid having this lovely warrior go look for you."

I couldn't move or talk but could hear and see everything. I realised quickly that one of the warriors was working with him. I could see out of the corner of my eye the other warrior — I couldn't remember his name — at the door on the floor. Hishto, that was his name. Oh god, please tell me he isn't dead.

As if he knew what I was thinking, Curalim said, "Oh yes, he's quite dead. We can't have him running to someone and telling them about my plan, can we?" He smiled one of the most evil grins. "Now, be a good little girl and be quiet. What am I saying? Of course, you'll be quiet, won't you?"

I watched as his creepy hand stroked down my face.

"I'm going to take care of a few loose ends."

He walked over to the cells containing the other Nomad. I noticed Ren watching with a painful expression as he kept looking back at me. There was commotion in the cells and then quiet. The same thing happened in the other two. I knew, without even asking, he had eliminated the other Nomad. No loose ends seemed pretty damn clear.

While Curalim was *cleaning up* the loose ends, the warrior, Ren, leaned over me and whispered, "I'm so sorry, but he knows where my family is. They were taken several years ago off of Terra Three. I didn't want to do this because you are Prime's Kindred, but it was the only way. I promise I will do what I can so Prime can find you."

Was he stupid? Why didn't he just interrogate him in his cell? Something else must have occurred. I was pissed but the worst of it was, I understood. He was young, and it must have been a considerable loss. I understood that better than most. I did not doubt that Curalim wouldn't tell him anything and that his hours were numbered. I just couldn't tell him that. I was furious with him, yet I wanted to cry for him as well, knowing he was going to die at the hands of this madman.

Curalim, having completed *getting rid of his loose ends*, headed back to me. He picked me up and told Ren, "We must get moving before they miss her. Get me to the launch bay, and then I will tell you what you want to know."

It was like being in a dream. The feeling of knowing every-thing going on, but not being able to react to anything. Curalim was carrying me bridal style; oh, the irony. Surprisingly, he was trying not to jostle me too much. It sucked, and I wanted to jump out of his arms and punch his lights out. The three of us avoided the lift system, took a weird in-direct route, and ended at the bay level.

On the bright side, I was not experiencing any breathing issues. I had no control over my limbs and I couldn't vocalise anything, or I'd scream my head off.

The poor warrior in the cell chambers, I felt horrible for

Hishto. I didn't know if he had family, but he didn't deserve to die. The other Nomad I cared little about but it showed how cruelly Curalim looked out for himself and didn't even care about his own people which didn't bode well for me.

Damn, Ren was making sure we got to the transport bay without an issue. I was worried about what would happen once we reached it. I hoped it was empty. Everyone was on standby mode because the ship was being repaired, but I wasn't sure if the bay would be empty.

As we approached, Curalim ducked into an alcove and ordered Ren to check who was in there.

I saw him turn to Curalim and say, "I told you that the bays are probably only on short staff right now because the Aries is in stationary mode for repairs."

"I remember quite well, but I do not want any surprises. Report back here and let me know what we can expect. Remember, I get on a fighter and you get what you want."

I knew he was lying. If I had to guess, he would kill Ren and anyone else in the bay. God, I hoped it was empty. At this point, I didn't have much sympathy for Ren.

It didn't take long, and I could see Ren returning from the corner of my eye.

"There are two warriors, but I've told them I will relieve them. They will leave, and then I'll let you in. This particular bay has only the smaller Wraith fighters. They are short-range but can easily carry the two of you."

"That will do just nicely," replied Curalim. He turned to me, stroking my cheek again. "Almost there, my dear. We will be gone, and they will never find you."

Even immobilised, I could not stop the shiver that went down my spine when he touched me. Could this guy get any creepier? I had no idea where he was taking us, but I knew one thing. As soon as this drug wore off, he was going to regret that he ever messed with me, my team, the Aries warriors, and mostly Zersus.

As if he could read my mind, he spoke again, "Oh and dear, don't get any ideas. Remember, I know where your family is. I will make things difficult for them, so be a good girl and cooperate. It will keep them healthy and alive." He laughed maniacally. "Well, of course you are going to cooperate, aren't you?"

He gave that creepy-blue-guy-smirk. It was precisely the same one I saw on his face the first time, 28 years ago.

I didn't like being threatened, and what he didn't know was we were making headway on tracking down the people taken, including my family. He told me something I wasn't sure of — my family was still alive. We would get to them before he did.

That list worried me. It was a map of every person removed from the Terras. We hadn't counted but, just from observation, I'd guess there were thousands taken over the last 28 years and that didn't include those who had gone missing during the years we were at war with the Nomad, and as a result of the divergence. It was heartbreakingly in the millions, maybe more. Were the ones we thought dead still alive? We had so many questions. It seemed an impossible task, but we had one thing that I don't think Nomad, like Curalim, ever had; love and hope.

As he hid us in the alcove, I heard the bay doors open again as the two warriors left. Even though I couldn't feel my limbs, I could feel some of my tension release. The last thing I wanted was for any additional people to be hurt because of this man. I already knew Ren's life would end at his hands.

"Time to go, my dear. The smell of this ship nauseates me. I will feel much better once we are on our way. Shall we?" Dickhead, as if I had a choice. He picked me up and quickly walked over to the bay doors as they opened. Ren directed us in, quickly checking the corridor, and then closed the doors and secured them.

"I've set up a Wraith fighter for launch. It's the one closest to the exit. You can place her in the back navigator seat," Ren instructed.

Curalim placed me there and tried to make me comfortable. I

found it a touch comical that he was treating me like a piece of glass, but being that things would get worse if we could make it off the Aries, it didn't matter.

"How do I activate the new cloaking system?" He turned to Ren, who shrugged.

"I have no idea. I'm not a pilot. I'm unfamiliar with the controls. If I had to guess, I'd say a command is required to activate it." He turned to move to a monitor. I expected he was attempting to find information on how to work the cloak. Sure, I knew how, but I wouldn't tell the asshole even if I could right now.

Curalim walked over to Ren and I saw him watching over his shoulder. He then worked beside him. He was trying to get into the system, but I could see that it was not something he was familiar with, frustration evident from his expression. I had to admit that the Aries' systems were not for the faint of heart. You had to be technically competent to get around it. I wasn't even sure if Ren could do it.

I was wrong in that hope. I noticed Ren pointing to something he found. He kept working and announced, "I think I figured it out. There is a sequence you have to set, and then it automatically activates. It will drain some of the energy from the ship, so you won't be able to move as quickly."

"Good to know. Thank you, Ren, I appreciate your help," Curalim said as he moved his hand onto Ren's shoulder. He quickly extracted a needle and jabbed him in the neck. "I am sorry, young man, but I do not leave any loose ends, and you are a loose end," he said as he sat him down against the wall beside the computer system. I had no idea if he was already dead or just heading there. He might not even survive the ship's ignition and launch.

I watched Curalim climb into the Wraith. I looked worriedly at him.

"Do not worry, my dear. I am an excellent pilot and have flown a Wraith many times, albeit an older version. The cloaking system is quite genius. I understand you and your team are responsible for that. Although I doubt you thought it would be used against you," he chuckled.

I glanced toward Ren as the Wraith's top closed down on us.

He continued, "Oh yes, he is dying. I cannot imagine how he thought I would tell him something I had no idea about. I suppose I could figure out where his family may be, but I really do not care."

And with that, he grinned, turned to the controls, and powered up the Wraith. He had strapped us both in and put us in hover mode, and I assumed he commanded the force field on the bay to clear. I could see a bit of Ren from the side, and it appeared he was protected where Curalim had left him. I was sure that wasn't on purpose. We shot forward quickly, and I watched him code in the cloak activation.

The larger Wraiths could carry a group through space for a reasonably extended period but these smaller Wraiths are short-range.

I hoped that Zersus would realise I was gone. We had ties as Kindred. I had no idea if Curalim understood the extent of what that meant. Zersus had explained it to me and one thing that stuck in my mind was that he said it created an invisible bond. He could tell if I was still alive — almost acting like a homing beacon. I had no idea how that worked, but it gave me hope.

I knew one other thing that could help the team find me, but I wasn't sure if she had finished installing the new feature into the Wraith fighters. If I could move, I'd cross my fingers right now.

Suddenly, Curalim turned in his seat and reached over to inject me again. What the hell was that? I could feel myself losing consciousness, and the last thing I heard was, "We cannot have you know where we are going, my dear. Have a good sleep — for now."

CHAPTER
EIGHTEEN
ZERSUS

As my senses cleared, I realised Jesse wasn't beside me. She must have gotten up and let me sleep. While I appreciated it, I preferred waking up beside her. I never wanted to be apart from her. I knew that wasn't very realistic. There would never be a point where I'd want to rein in Jesse's independence. She was too strong for that.

We didn't even have any idea how being Kindred was going to impact us. She was human and SPAR and worked from Terra One. I was a Krean Prime on a warship in space. I had no idea how we would meet in the middle, but I couldn't help thinking things would work out because we wanted them to. Our desire to be together would help us figure it out.

After quickly showering and dressing, I headed off to the bridge. I figured I'd find Jesse there or in the War Room. Just as I reached the bridge, I realised I had forgotten to turn on my communicator. The doors of the War Room opened, my communicator went off with dozens of messages, and the room was in chaos. I detoured and headed there instead. Everyone turned and looked at me.

Katie approached me and grabbed my arm. "Where's Jesse?" I could see the panic on her face.

I answered, confused, "She's not with me. I assumed she was here." I quickly realised that was wrong, looking around the room. She wasn't there.

Katie shook her head. "I got here, and only Issbeck was here, no one else, but we found that on the screen."

I looked towards where she was pointing and stepped forward to read. There were three names highlighted. Damn, they were her relatives. That couldn't be good. I recalled what Curalim had said to her as we left the interrogation. "She must have headed down to the cells."

At that exact moment, the communication system went crazy. A couple of messages were coming through from different locations on the ship. Katie quickly put them up on screen. Harley was on one, and Simal was on the other. I had a horrible feeling about this. They both started talking simultaneously; I put up my hand and directed, "Harley, you first." I could tell he was in the cells from the comm video, so I wanted to know what was going on.

"They are all dead down here. Curalim is gone."

Wait, what? Gone? How was that even possible? Then what he said sunk in. "Who is dead?"

Harley looked down from where he stood. "A guard is dead, and all of the other Nomad as well."

Simal cut us off, "I'm in the small Wraith fighter bay, and Ren is here. He's barely breathing. You need to get down here NOW!"

I didn't need to ask why; Katie and I took off. Something was very wrong. I also sent Issbeck a message to meet us down there. We arrived at the bay at the same time.

Issbeck asked, "What's going on?"

"I'm not sure, but from what Harley told me, Curalim killed Hishto, all the Nomad, Jesse is missing, and Ren could be dying," was all I could say.

As we rushed into the bay, I saw Simal sitting on the floor holding Ren. I also noticed Divi, our Krean medic, was checking on him. "He doesn't have much time, but he wanted to talk to you," she informed me.

She and Simal stepped back as I knelt next to Ren.

He grabbed my hand. His breathing was difficult, and I felt his life slipping away. "Sorry, Prime," he was struggling to talk, and I had to lean down to hear him. "...let him take her."

He gulped and closed his eyes. I thought he was gone but then he opened his eyes wide and said, "My family. He knew. Used that. I'm sorry." He gasped a few more times, closed his eyes, and stopped breathing.

I had a mix of rage and sadness. He was one of the warriors that could have gone far. I had no idea that his family were amongst the taken.

I stood up and looked down at Ren, gathering my thoughts, but then what he said sunk in. "Fuck ... Curalim has Jesse." I looked at everyone.

Katie ran to the system and started punching buttons. She looked like she was getting worked up about something. Knowing that Jesse was missing made her look crazed.

She turned and looked at all of us just as CeeChi, Harley, and the rest of Jesse's team came rushing in.

Sid was the first to yell, "Where in hell is Jesse?" As he looked down and noticed Ren's body, he said, "Shit, is he dead?"

I nodded at him. "Yes, Ren was killed by Curalim after helping him." I held up a hand as I noticed them all getting upset. "Ren thought Curalim would help him find his family. He let Curalim take Jesse."

I could feel the rage building but Issbeck came over, put his hands on my shoulders and said, "You can feel her. You know she's fine, yes?"

I nodded. Yes, I could feel Jesse. The delicate pulse that bound us together was there and clear. It could help me locate her, but only as we got closer to her. I could feel it diminishing as if she was being dragged away from me, and I felt panic in its place.

Neil, Joe, and Sid peered down on Ren's body with a look of confusion.

I asked them, "What's bothering you?"

Joe was the first of the three to respond, "Why didn't he just use the thiobarb? It's not like Curalim wasn't locked up."

Neil and Sid frowned and turned to me also for an answer. I sighed and tried to gather my thoughts to answer them. Lucky for me, Issbeck understood that I was overrun with emotions and couldn't get the words out.

He said, "He couldn't simply use it. It is controlled by the bridge. A request has to go into the system and then get approval from one of us. It's a two tier system of approval because it's a drug that could be misused."

I shook my head. "But if he'd asked I would have approved the request. I wish he'd just asked." I closed my eyes and tried to control my anger. Even though I understood, it didn't excuse what he did.

I heard a sharp whistle and turned to see Katie, Harley, and CeeChi over at the systems with big smiles. Considering the current circumstances, I failed to understand their expressions. "Please explain why all of you look like you just won a prize because right now is not the time for smiling."

Harley stepped forward. "Because Curalim was dumb enough to take one of the few ships in this bay with the newest version of the cloaking system installed."

I looked at everyone standing with us; nobody seemed to know what that meant. Hands on my hips, I roared at them, "Explain, NOW!"

Katie took the lead, "Well, because you gave us full access to update and improve everything, we had been working on a new tracker for the cloaks. We wanted to be able to tag every ship with a unique signature. Something that only we could track. We had installed it on just a few of these small Wraiths first." Katie looked down at Ren, with a realisation on her face. "Oh my god, Ren knew." She looked at all of us and yelled, "*HE KNEW!* He was running security in here when I was making the installations. He knew which ships had the new tracker system installed. I had explained it all to him. He was interested, said he was a geek, loved systems, and hoped to work on the bridge at some point."

I could see the sadness run across Katie's face, but it didn't take me long to realise that Ren had probably prepped the ship that Curalim had taken. While I wanted to hate him for letting Curalim leave with her, he did what he could to protect her and ensure we could find her.

I looked at Katie. "Tell me we can trace it."

She gave me a crazy nod, with a smile, and indicated the screen. We had a clear picture of the movements of the fighter Curalim had taken.

I moved over to the comms and sent a quick message to our engineers. We needed to get the Aries moving, or we would take one of the larger Wraiths to go after her. Issbeck caught on to what I needed and sent commands to our larger bay to prep a series of Wraith transports. Either way, we might be needing them at some point.

"Prime, we were just going to contact the bridge and let you know the repairs are completed," said Zetz, our head engineer. "All engines are powered up and ready, running at optimum. All damages repaired."

"Perfect, thank you, Zetz," I signed off and turned to everyone.

"Let's get up to the bridge. We have a ship to track and my Kindred to find."

The minute we arrived back on the bridge, Issbeck, Simal, and I moved to the controls and got the ship moving.

I had Katie to my right; she was transmitting the coordinates from the tracker on the Wraith. I noted Harley, CeeChi, and everyone else at the consoles. We had a full bridge, and everyone was working on trying to track that ship. I had a quick thought about how important Jesse was to all of us. I should not be surprised, she was a remarkable woman and easy to love.

I noticed that the Wraith had put a fair amount of distance between itself and the Aries. I thought that was odd.

"Isn't it strange that he managed to get that far in a Wraith fighter?" I asked. I could see everyone looking at me, and they had thought the same.

"Do we have any thoughts on that?"

CeeChi was the first to take a guess. "What if they met up with a larger ship?"

Yes, that could be an explanation. "Wouldn't that shut off the tracking system?" I turned to Katie for an answer.

She shook her head, "No, not necessarily. I designed the ships to be traceable even in our bay and when they are off. It's like installing a permanent beacon that never shuts off. Once that code was entered, it was activated. It doesn't turn off without another code. Ren clearly didn't give him that."

"Woman, you are an absolute genius. How in the world did you come up with that idea?" Issbeck asked. Katie shook her head and looked over at Harley.

They both sadly said, "It was Jesse's idea."

"Why am I not surprised?"

Sid shrugged. "I swear she comes up with every possible scenario. Good thing she did in this case."

I watched Neil step forward, a man who spoke very little, and asked Katie, "Does Jesse know which ships you installed the systems in?"

She shook her head.

"I'm going to guess that she's hoping the ship she's in is one of them," Neil said. We're all thinking the same thing.

Sid and Joe came forward, and Joe commented, "She absolutely would be hoping that — I think we need to follow that trail and get her back. No one gets left behind — ever, but especially Jesse. She is our leader and our best friend."

I could feel their confidence that we'd get her back. I got out of the funk I'd felt knowing Curalim took her. He'd made a colossal mistake. We would get Jesse; she had left a trail of crumbs for us to follow."Let's set a course for that signal. Make sure the Aries cloak is running. I want to be sure that we aren't announcing our arrival."

Katie turned to her system and an image of the Aries on her monitor. From what I could see, she had also improved the cloak on this ship.

"Did you just improve the cloak on the Aries?" I asked her.

She nodded and said, as she was punching buttons, "Sure, I figured while we were down and getting the repairs completed, I might as well."

I couldn't help but grin and noticed everyone else shaking their heads before we turned to our screens.

"Hang on, Jesse, we are coming," I said and heard affirmation from everyone.

CHAPTER
NINETEEN
JESSE

THROUGH THE TINY slits of my eyes, as I tried to pry them open, the first thing I noticed was a black ceiling. My brain was trying to decipher what I was looking at. I could confidently say this wasn't my room on the Aries. The ceiling was too low. As I squinted and began to adjust my focus, my memories started coming back to me. I sat up quickly, my head spinning. I brought my hands up to my head and just held it for a second. Not that it helped much. It felt worse than a really bad hangover.

Remembering that some sort of drug had immobilised me, I could still feel the lasting effects. I tried to lift my arms higher and, while they were no longer immobile, they felt like dead weight. I tried swinging my legs over the side of the bed and attempted to stand. Nope, that wouldn't work. My legs were not ready to hold my weight. I sat my ass back down, and shook my head in an attempt to clear it a bit more.

I started to scan the details of the room. While my brain wasn't quite fully functioning, I could admit the space was nice. The bed was enormous; I'd say myself and two Zersus could easily fit in it. It was soft and comfortable with plush grey bedding. I noted the door, which was kitty-corner to where I was sitting. As my eyes moved around the room, I noticed what looked like a reasonably comfortable couch and set of chairs against the far wall to the right of the doors. A beautifully designed, wood table and chairs sat to the left of them. Further past the table was an opening that led to a bathroom. And lastly, small doors were on either side of the bed where I was sitting. I leaned over and grabbed one to open it. There was nothing inside. I guess both were closets ... his and hers, I huffed. I'd be damned if I was going to be the *hers* to Curalim's *his*.

I tried to stand again, only this time much slower. I leaned over on the bed to take some of the weight off my legs while I gained some strength and stability back. Slowly, I felt my limbs begin to cooperate.

It took a bit, but I started moving around the room. It was decorated in a very tasteful manner, nothing that indicated it was Nomad. Their ships were cold and impersonal. While I had only been on the fighter recently, I'd seen plenty of images of their ships in my position with SPAR. And not like I could forget the ship I'd been on at six years old. It was anything but pretty. Comfort was not a word that I'd use to describe the Nomad.

Part of our training was to be fully versed on them, their people, their ships, and any other intelligence we gathered. Too bad we hadn't found out about their participation in the slave trade earlier. Doesn't matter. We knew now, and we would stop them. I couldn't explain it, but I felt it down to my bones. But first, I had to get the hell out of here. I moved over to the doors, and they slid open. Outside were two guards. I'd never seen their species before, they were definitely not Nomad.

Both were extremely tall, close to seven feet, I'd estimate. There was no lack of muscle and apparent strength, but I'd describe them as sleek. They were also pale-skinned, almost like porcelain. Each had identical tattoos on both sides of their necks, peeking from the edge of their clothes. Their arms, which were also visible, had beautiful tattoos as well. The markings looked the same on both. There was no difference, so I assumed they weren't tattoos, but perhaps species markings? They had long white hair in multiple braids down their backs and silver-grey eyes shining at me.

They stood there and stared at me. I found the whole situation funny and started to laugh. They grinned back, bowed, and spoke in sync, "Miss Jesse, we are instructed not to allow you to leave."

The one on the left said, "We would like to welcome you to a Peaceship of the Obsidi."

The Obsidi — well damn, that answered who they were and the ship I was on.

"We would ask that you please move back into your room. Curalim will be along shortly. We will notify him that you are awake," the other one spoke this time.

As I was heading back into the room, the one on the left mentioned, "If you would like anything to eat or drink, we would be happy to have it brought for you once Curalim and you have had your visit." And damn if he didn't bow again. They are nothing if not polite.

"Thank you." I figured I might as well be equally polite. It might benefit me to develop a good relationship with them.

I stepped back into the room and the door closed behind me. Well, so much for that, I huffed. I went over to the couch and sat. *Wow, comfy.*

When I thought about it, it was clear the entire room was quite lovely. I felt the Obsidi wanted to ensure I was taken care of. Maybe something else that could work to my advantage.

As I was considering what I could do to get out of this mess, the doors slid open and in walked Creepy Blue Guy. Okay, Curalim, but I liked Creepy Clue Guy, and I believed that if the shoe fits — for him, it did!

"Hello, my dear. Did you have a good rest?"

Was he fucking serious?

He walked over to join me on the couch. I noticed he didn't attempt to touch me but did sit close enough for me to feel like he was invading my space. I got up and moved to one of the single chairs. He smirked at me. God, I hated that smirk. While I did not suffer from nightmares about the time Katie and I were taken, the one thing I've never forgotten was that smirk.

He sat back, crossed his legs and put his arm on the back of the couch as if relaxed and having a routine visit with a friend. *Who does that?*

I mirrored his movements. I sat back in my chair, crossed my legs and put my arms up on the sides. "Actually, yes, I had a good sleep. Very comfortable bed. I'll have to see if I can get one at home."

He laughed, sounding more like a maniacal cackle, and I found it interesting that he could. I didn't think it was customary for Nomad to have a sense of humour. When he stopped, he looked right into my eyes with his weird, yellow, reptilian-shaped ones, and I saw no humour in them.

"You are mistaken if you think you will leave. We are on this ship for now, but that is temporary." His voice was cold and laced with venom. He glanced at his communicator, abruptly rose and headed to the door, but before he exited, he turned back to say, "I will be sending someone to give you something to wear. I want that uniform gone. I want his scent gone. I will return later so we can have a lengthy chat. You need to understand that you are mine now." And then he left.

I didn't realise I was holding so much tension in my body until he was gone. I let out a huge breath and relaxed. One thing I knew, and had a feeling that Curalim didn't, was that the ties that bind me to Zersus were intense. They would never be gone. I'd rather die than ever let that creep touch me, but I was going to do everything in my power to make sure that didn't happen and get back to my man.

Then I thought about his comment. God only knows what I was going to be expected to wear.

◆

"You expect me to wear this?" I held up the scraps of fabric and addressed my question to the small porcelain doll that had come into my room with this so-called outfit. Christ, this would barely cover my important bits.

She bowed, tilted her head, and nodded.

I sighed. God, this was awful. Sure, it covered the essential parts, but the outfit was minimal. That was the best description I had for it.

The young girl came forward. She was really lovely, but quite different compared to the men guarding the room. She had long, straight silky-gold hair to her waist and barely came up to my chin. Her build was tiny in every way, almost fairy-like and delicate.

She took my hands and the strangest thing happened. I felt a calm and gentle feeling run through my body. I looked down at her, with her long, sleek gold hair, and her silver-grey eyes glowing at me. She smiled and softly said, "I know you do not wish to wear this. I would not either, but it is Curalim's order. I would ask that, for now, you please put it on. More will become apparent soon.

"I will leave you to change. I will be back with nourishment. We have a wonderful selection of foods from our culture that I think you will enjoy." And with that, she bowed and left me alone.

I looked down at the "outfit" and sighed. There's no point in putting this off; I might as well get it over with.

The outfit, if you could call it that, only covered my hips and breasts with what looked to be a leather type fabric. When I put on the breast piece, it clung to me quite well, so thank god they wouldn't fall out. My breasts, while not overly large, were barely contained. If I raised my arms, they would pop out, so note to self: no arm raising.

The upper part had armbands that surrounded my biceps. They seemed like they would be loose, but they sucked onto my arms when I put them on. It was the strangest thing because they had seemed inflexible.

The bottom piece could be described only as underwear, and while covering my front, half my ass was hanging out. Thank god for the sweeping fabrics which flowed from the top of the bottoms. I turned to look behind me and could see that my butt was a bit more covered than I had originally expected by the slits of silky fabric. Lastly, I'd been given what looked like a pair of sandals. Similar to the armbands, as soon as I put them on, they formed perfectly to my feet. They were the only part of the outfit I liked. When I walked around in them, I found them to be very comfortable.

Just as I finished getting the shoes on, the doors swept open again to the young girl and the two guards. They were bringing in many plates with food. At that point, my stomach growled. So yeah, I was hungry.

All three of them bowed — I sort of wish they would stop doing that — I asked the first thing that came to my mind. "What are your names?"

They all smiled at me, and the young girl answered, "I am Surly. My father is the Peacekeeper of this ship."

Okay, that must mean he's crucial to the ship's operation. Information to file away. The more info I can get, the faster I can get out of here.

She then turned to indicate the two guards. "They are Haso and Chim. They are brothers and my father's best guards. They will not allow anything to happen to you."

My brow furrowed. Huh, that's not normal. They are here to protect me?

Surly must have seen my confusion because she said, "You will understand soon."

Haso and Chim placed the plates on the table and left. However, I noticed they both turned back to take a long look at me. They were grinning as they left — damn outfit.

Surly asked me to sit, and she began dishing food onto a

plate for me, and then one for herself. I was happy she was going to join me. I had a ton of questions for her.

She surprised me again as we sat by saying, "While I know you don't like the outfit, it certainly suits you."

I looked down and raised my eyebrows at her.

"Haso and Chim liked it."

I laughed. "While I appreciate that, I am taken."

"Oh, I know, I see you still wear his mark. He will show up soon enough."

And now that had me sitting and just looking at her.

"Eat," she said.

"Alright, but only because I'm hungry." I watched her smile at me. The meal was surprisingly good. I had no idea what I was eating but most of it seemed like vegetables, an assortment of meats and the best-doughed buns I'd ever had. I loved them. They were round and golden, lush, soft, sweet, and melted in my mouth. I dipped them in the gravy that came with the selection of meats. Now, did I want to know what I was eating? That would be *NO*. I was just going to enjoy it and keep my ignorance.

Surly and I chatted during the meal. She was more than willing to tell me about the ship, her father, and the Peace troops on board. As we finished and moved on to what I assumed was dessert, I asked her, "Why would your people be involved with the Nomad?"

Surly stopped and considered the question before answering, "It is not really for me to explain. My father will soon; however, know that we do not help them. We subvert what they do and try to help the people they try to destroy."

I sat back in my chair and looked at her. Instinctively, I knew she was telling the truth, but what that meant wasn't clear.

We had both finished, and I assisted Surly in cleaning things up when the two guards entered the room.

"Curalim is returning."

I watched Surly tense up. She turned to me and said, "I must leave. I do not wish to be in his presence. I will be back." They all bowed again and left.

I decided to return to the single chair and sit down. I wanted to gather intel from him that would be useful. Curalim was clever; that much was obvious, but so was I. I also wasn't a six-year-old child anymore.

No more than 10 minutes after Surly left, Curalim walked in. He looked around the room and quickly found me. He walked forward. "Stand up," he ordered.

I had considered telling him to fuck off, but then I realized that I might get further by letting him think I was cooperating with him, so I stood. I watched him look me over. He motioned for me to turn around. I did, rolled my eyes, and then looked at him over my shoulder. I gave him a nasty look, partly because I knew he would expect that from me but also because I was seriously pissed off about the outfit.

"Very nice. Although, we do have to do something about your hair. What in the world did you do to it?"

I was confused. What the hell was he on about? He tried to reach up to touch it, but I backed away.

He wasn't happy about my reaction. "Firstly, we have to do something about the length, but what is this colour? It is quite awful."

My hair was burgundy. I'd had a small genetic change that meant I didn't have to constantly colour it. One of the only cosmetic changes I had ever done, simply for convenience. I smirked at him, "It's permanent. So sorry to disappoint."

I could tell he was not happy. He grabbed my arm, led me to the couch, and pulled me down to sit beside him. "Shall we sit and have a chat?"

I backed as far away from him as I could get. "Talk about what exactly? I can't imagine why you'd think I want to talk to you." I was done trying to be cooperative.

As before, he moved his arm over the back of the couch, close enough to grab my hair. He pulled it back so that my head was forced over the back of it.

Relax, Jesse. Get information, remember.

He bent forward over me. He watched me for what seemed forever but then suddenly let me go. He sat back, crossed his legs, and continued to study me. I'm unsure if he expected me to say anything, but I stayed silent. I sat there and stared back.

He gave an exaggerated sigh. "I thought you were smarter and would learn that cooperating would be better for your health. I admit I am thrilled to see you are not going to, my dear. You should know I have little patience for people who do not follow the rules, but I am sure I will have fun teaching you that lesson. You will learn."

I crossed my arms over my chest and looked him in the eye. "Well, it might be helpful to tell me the rules. I'm not a mind reader." Okay, it was a smart-ass response, but I was being honest. Tell me the damn rules, asshole.

He grabbed my arm, yanking me up to stand close to him.

It took everything in me not to retaliate.

"As you wish. Rule one. You do not leave this room at any time. The guards are permitted to restrain you if necessary. Rule two. When I enter the room, I want you down on your knees, head down. If you do not cooperate, I will break a bone in your body. You will not be given medical attention, and I do not care how it heals." He pulled me closer. "Are we clear so far?"

I tilted my head and looked up at him through my lashes, feigning fear and stuttered, "Y-yes." Asshole.

"Rule Three. When we are on my ship, you will wear nothing. Nomad typically do not wear clothes in their own living spaces. You will be without, as well. You will only be given clothing when we travel or are outside my living space."

I almost laughed in his face. If he thought being naked would make me uncomfortable, he was sadly mistaken. It levelled the playing field. No clothes on me or him meant no weapons. I could deal with that.

He opened his mouth to continue with what I was sure was *Rule Four* when he received another message on his communicator. It took him a minute, and I saw anger cross his face. I hoped it was my team coming for me.

"I will take my leave, but rest assured my dear, I will be back." He moved towards the door but turned back just as he was about to leave. "Remember the rules. Next time I return to this room, be prepared to greet me properly."

He walked out, and I gave him the finger. I called him every swear word I could come up with and I'm sure I got creative with a few extras. I needed to get the hell out of here.

CHAPTER
TWENTY
JESSE

I HAD no idea how much time passed after Curalim left, Surly returned, accompanied by the two guards. Rule One came to mind, and I scowled at Haso and Chim. They had their usual smile and bowed, ignoring my nasty look and addressing Surly. "Princess, the time to visit your father is now."

Wait, did they call Surly a princess? I'll be damned, they did.

I turned to her to ask her, but she cut me off, "It will all be clear very soon. Shall we?" She directed me to leave with her and the guards. Wait, we were leaving. What was up with that? Haso and Chim led us down a hallway.

Based on the room, I assumed the ship would be nice, but I was unprepared for how beautiful it was as we moved through it. The walls on the ship were almost transparent. Corridors and hallways could be seen everywhere, with many Obsidi moving through. And the walls had a slight shimmer. As we turned down another corridor, it felt like the whole ship gave off a gentle and calming vibe, much like Surly did when she held my hands.

It gave me a clearer understanding why Danlon and Zersus had been surprised to find the Obsidi had partnered with the Nomad — the vibe from the ship, from the guards, and from

Surly didn't fit. I couldn't explain it, and I couldn't shake the feeling that we had their participation all wrong.

As we walked through the halls, I noticed many people stopped and looked at me. Many males followed us. Were they looking at me or Surly? What the hell?

"Really, what is it with the people on this ship staring."

Haso and Chim looked over their shoulder, scanned up and down my body, and Haso commented, "It is rare we have such an unusual beauty on our ship, and the outfit suits you."

I stopped and stood with my hands on my hips and scowled at them.

They turned to me with a questioning look.

"Seriously, you like this outfit?"

They both energetically nodded and answered together, "YES." And just had to add a grin.

I exaggeratedly sighed and crossed my arms. "Christ, I feel like the Princess from the Trilogy," I said under my breath.

Surly gasped. "You have a princess that wears that?" she asked me wide-eyed, with surprise.

Well, that opened up a can of worms. I looked at them and started laughing. I couldn't stop. How would I explain to them that I was talking about a character in a movie? They probably didn't even know what the hell that was. I bent over, trying to catch my breath from laughing when Surly approached me and laid a hand on my shoulder. A sense of calm flowed through me.

"Thanks." I smiled at her. "I'm referring to a character in a story who wore an outfit a bit like this." I tried my best to explain it to her.

"Why make someone wear something like that in a story?" she asked. Clearly even she thought the outfit was atrocious.

I shrugged. The boys bowed again and indicated we should continue.

We walked through many hallways, moving upwards. We were obviously heading to an essential area of the ship heavily populated with more Obsidi, and the surroundings were even more beautiful.

As we moved through the hallways, I noted male and female Obsidi were distinctly different. Both were quite pale skinned. The males we came across looked very similar to Haso and Chim; tall, sculpted and tattooed. Whereas the females took on a very similar look to Surly, with delicate faces and a tiny, almost doll-like stature. It made the females look almost ethereal. Surly in particular as she was the only one I noticed with the gold hair. I am going to assume that is because she was royalty.

We approached a set of opaque glass doors. Surly put her hand up to be scanned, and the door slid open to the bridge. Off to our right stood a huge, older Obsidi. Even more sizable than Haso and Chim but with a gentle face. His hair was silver, not white, and it held more braids than the guards. I had to wonder if that was a sign of position.

The man approached us as Surly rushed to him. He hugged her — reminding me of Matt's hugs. He smiled and moved to face me. He was an extremely handsome and distinguished older man, but the resemblance to Surly couldn't be missed. I'd guess he was her father. Which meant he was in charge of the ship.

He came up and put his hands out for me. My instinct was to put mine in his. Surly calmed me, but I felt complete trust, honesty, and warmth when he touched them. I couldn't help but smile at him.

He smiled back and welcomed, "Hello, Jesse. It's my pleasure to host you on my Peaceship. My daughter has told me you are quite strong and partnered with a Krean?"

I nodded.

He directed me to follow him. "Come and join my daughter and me in my pashon. Thank you, Haso and Chim; you can return to your regular duties."

I guess I won't be needing guards anymore. Surly and I accompanied her father into the room that he referred to as pashon. It was styled for comfort: no desks. Simple, just sit and relax. He indicated I should take a seat. Surly sat in the one beside me, and he sat across from us.

"I will begin as time is of the essence. I am Rushim Arou. I am the head Peacekeeper of the Obsidi. Humans and Kreans would refer to my position as King, however we try not to use that title. Your capturer, Curalim, has no idea Surly and I are on this ship. We were waiting for the perfect opportunity to release the Obsidi from our forced association with the Nomad."

I looked at them both. "Forced association? Are you referring to working with the Nomad concerning our missing people?" I figured being direct would get me answers faster.

To my surprise, he nodded."Unfortunately, we have been forced to work with them. I will explain this quickly, yes?"

I nodded.

He continued, "Almost 30 years ago by your time, the Nomad took over one of our planets. It held a good portion of our population. In the takeover, they killed a number of our people, including my wife and son. Surly and I had been away on sabbat when Nomad overran our ship. They did not understand the importance of Surly and myself, and our people went along with that. We were given no choice but to assist them or they would destroy our planet. We knew what they had done to Allora, the Kreans' planet, and while I knew my wife and son were dead, I did not want any further destruction to occur to our planet or people."

He stopped to gather himself. I understood. While they hadn't successfully destroyed us, what happened to Earth, the split into the four planets and our fight to survive after that — yes, I understood.

"The Nomad wanted our ships, which are quite advanced with special forms of communication. They are quick, can hold many people, but most of all can move freely through space without people feeling threatened."

I nodded. That was what Zersus had said. The Obsidi were

no threat. That was a massive advantage that the Nomad needed.

"We also knew what had occurred with your planet and quickly figured out the Nomad had additional plans for your species. We felt the need to try and protect your people as much as possible."

"Protect us?" I asked.

Rushim nodded. "Yes, we knew we couldn't stop it — yet — but what we could do was make sure people were taken to places where they would be safe. So that was what we did. We have kept a list of where we took them so that when we could finally contact you and were ready to fight against the Nomad, we could hopefully return them. Also, the places we took them are unknown to the Nomad. They were so busy moving so many people that they never caught on. Our plan was to protect and build, until we were strong enough to fight them. We feel that time has come." He sighed. "I hate to admit it; we were never designed to fight. That is something we have had to learn."

I nodded my understanding. "Fighting comes in many variations," I replied. "Our entire population had to modify our lives to adjust to the new version of our world."

"Yes, you have. We were aware of what happened to your Earth, but we were thankful you had the Kreans. They are a robust species. I knew that you would both benefit from being allied."

He was right, but now I needed to ask, "So where do we go from here and how do we deal with Curalim?"

"I assumed you would want to know. Curalim is not currently on the ship. We arranged a little situation that would require him to leave. A problem occurred with one of his other slave transports requiring his attention. He will be gone for a good while.

"In the meantime, we have sent out a beacon for your Kindred's ship and are moving in the direction of the Aries. We are hoping that we will meet up with them shortly. That is why I wanted you on the bridge. When they arrive, you can immediately speak with them. We have also planted a beacon at our previous location so Curalim will appear to think we have been captured." With that, he stood and asked, "I assume you would like to change?" He couldn't resist a smile as Surly tried not to laugh.

I rolled my eyes and agreed, "Please!"

He indicated that I follow him. Surly grabbed an outfit out of Rushim's closet. I'm not sure how that would fit me, but at this point, anything was better than this awful thing I currently had on.

After changing, I felt so much better in the Obsidi uniform. It was similar to what Haso and Chim wore, but it hugged my form. I was amazed. I would have never guessed it would fit me. Plus, while their clothes looked hard and uncomfortable, they were the exact opposite. I also noticed that it changed colour as soon as I put it on. So odd, but I loved how it felt and was hoping I could keep it.

I walked out of his bedroom with a smile. Rushim nodded. "It suits you," he said and led us onto the bridge. Rushim indicated I should take a seat beside him. Surly was seated on the other side.

"We have managed to pick up a faint trace of the Aries. It is moving closer to us. Are you feeling your Kindred?" he asked.

"Is that what I'm feeling?"

He nodded.

"Our bond is new, and I'm not Krean, so I'm just learning what these feelings are." Clearly, I had a lot to learn. I was anxious and felt like I wanted to punch the crap out of someone. My damn emotions were all over the place. At the same time, I was feeling tingles and excitement. All of the feelings were increasing, definitely like a beacon drawing me to it. I had to mention this to Zersus. He hadn't been sure how strong my attachment would be. Well, I can answer that now.

Rushim smiled. "I am confident you will learn quite quickly.

You are resilient. I am aware of your run-in with Curalim as a child." Rushim had tapped into who I was, but he knew much more about me than I thought. "I do hope you do not feel that our people are bad, but I will understand if you have difficulty trusting us. We have much to answer for and will do everything we can to help."

I nodded but corrected him, "Truthfully, I can't help but trust you. It's just an impression I get from both you and Surly. You're not the first, and you won't be the last to be manipulated by the Nomad. What matters is what you do in the future."

He looked intensely at me. He nodded his head. "I was right about you. I felt your flow when I held your hands. You have a positive energy; it's powerful. Stronger than most I meet. I look forward to meeting your Kindred. You would not be partnered with someone who was not an equal to you."

"He is a wonderful person." I truly believed that about Zersus. There would never be any other man for me.

I liked to think I wasn't a negative person, but I didn't give my trust easily, which is why the intuitive feelings I had about Rushim and Surly were so strange to me. I had to believe my feelings were genuine and happening for a reason.

One Obsidi sitting at a console told Rushim, "Peacemaker, we have the Aries tracking on long range. They are reaching out to attempt to contact us."

"Accept their request." He turned to me and asked me to stand before him. "The comm is yours, Jesse."

I stood up and faced the extensive monitor system in front of us. Their bridge was quite large, with many Obsidi running the ship. The tension was there but we were soon to be on the same side.

Suddenly, something amazing appeared in front of me. I was looking at the bridge of the Aries with my team, the fellow Kreans who were now my friends and, most of all, the man I loved. Zersus.

I could see the relief on his face, but he was still scowling. He was pissed and hadn't spoken with the Obisdi; he didn't know what I did.

"Jesse, are you okay? Are you being held prisoner?" he demanded.

"Prime Zersus, I'd like to introduce you to Peacekeeper Rushim Arou, head of the Obsidi people." I moved to the side so Zersus could see Rushim and Surly behind me. I watched the interest cross his face, but he remained quiet and stoic.

"They have many things to discuss."

Zersus nodded. "Issbeck, do we have an estimate on when we should reach their ship?"

"Yes, Prime, another 30 minutes at most. They are moving towards us fairly quickly, so that will reduce our travel time."

Rushim checked with his crew, and they confirmed.

"We will happily come aboard your ship, Prime, when we arrive. However, I'd advise we not remain stationary. We want to avoid any potential contact with Curalim, as he likely won't be alone."

That made sense as the Obsidi ship would be vulnerable to attack.

I could feel the tension leaving everyone and noticed a much more relaxed group on the Aries. I saw Sid stand up. "Not to take over or anything, Zersus, but uh, Katie, can we cloak and move together? I have to agree with him," indicating Rushim with his head, "we shouldn't stay in one place even if we are cloaked."

I saw the wheels turning in Katie's mind. "Maybe. As long as we stay joined, it should work." She sat down at her system, and I watched her working on something when I heard Rushim's ship getting a signal. "

"Peacekeeper, she is sending us information. Accept?"

Rushim nodded his head to allow the transmission through. We received Katie's specs on how we should prepare before we reached the Aries. Rushim ordered the specs be sent to their engineers so they could get their Peaceship ready to join with the Aries properly.

Rushim asked, "Would you two like to talk more? I can arrange for you to talk in private in my pashon."

I looked at Zersus to ask him, but decided we should wait. Shortly, I could touch him, not just talk. I'm sure he picked up on my thoughts because he let Rushim know that he would rather talk and touch me in person. Rushim chuckled a bit at him but said he understood.

When the screen was off, I sat and anxiously watched us speed towards the Aries.

We had just enough time before our two ships met to figure out the logistics that Katie had sent over.

I did wonder about something and asked Rushim, "How is that you can see the Aries?" As far as I knew it should be cloaked.

Rushim grinned, "Yes your ship's cloaking system is quite genius, however, useless to our sensors. But you need not worry. That is not something Curalim is aware of and being that we do not carry weapons, we are not a threat to your warships."

Thank god for that. They certainly weren't a threat, but their lack of weapons was worrisome.

Along with the entire bridge of the Peaceship, I watched our approach to the Aries. The details that Katie sent asked us to find the smoothest and most easily accessible outer portion. The idea was to have a smooth, flat section of our two ships meet. There had to be a perfect connection, so the techs on the Peaceship decided on the best spot to match with Katie's spot chosen for the Aries.

Her idea was to use the same technology on the Wraith transports to create a portal between the two ships with a latch wielder. It would accomplish many things. One was the ability to travel between ships, but it could also create a situation where the cloak could be extended to protect the Peaceship while it was attached. It was a similar principle we used with the weapons we carry with our biosuits, just on a larger scale. A force field would be kept in place to protect the two ships.

I watched the pilots on the Peaceship slowly manoeuvre us into place along the port backside of the Aries. The Aries was still in space, allowing all of the position changes to be taken by the Peaceship. Ever so slowly, it moved in closer and closer, and then I heard it. A slight clang rang out, indicating that we were attached. The techs on the Peaceship created a magnetic field that would help ensure we stayed that way.

I headed with Rushim, Surly, Haso, and Chim down to where the latch wielder would penetrate through the two ships. You could see the forcefield in place, and I heard the wielder working.

Before we knew it, there was a hole in the side of both ships. On the other side, the first person I saw was Zersus. Rushim indicated I should go first. I didn't need to be told twice.

CHAPTER
TWENTY-ONE
ZERSUS

IF I COULD HAVE, I would have run through the damn hole the second it opened. Jesse barely stepped through and I grabbed her, hauling her against me. I tucked my face into her neck. We both were emotional, me just breathing her in and her crying. There wasn't a single person talking. They just stood and watched us try to get a grip on our feelings. I have no idea how long we were like that but when I glanced up, I noticed we were alone.

She looked up at me, as I rested my forehead against hers. I closed my eyes and took a long breath of her scent. "I would have never stopped looking for you," I told her. I bent down and kissed her. It was a *welcome back, and don't you ever leave again,* kind of kiss.

She stopped me and gave me a long glance with those gorgeous eyes. "You need to know I felt it. I felt you getting closer. Every inch of me was anxious, excited and tingling."

I was in shock, but only for a second. She was Kindred to me in every sense of the word. When I moved away, I couldn't stop the huge grin that formed on my face. She laughed and slapped my chest. I swung my arm over her shoulder and we walked out into the corridor. Everyone was standing there clapping and shouting. Even Rushim and Surly joined in. Having her back was an incredible feeling.

Cain and Katie grabbed her from my embrace, and mauled her to death. I couldn't suppress a larger grin. Cain was the first to say, "Damn, sis, I just found you. You're not allowed to do that again."

Everyone laughed at him except Katie. I knew how worried she was. I don't think she's had a chance to sleep. Most of us haven't slept, but Katie looked like she was going to drop. And there was no sleep in sight just yet.

I told everyone, "We need to head to the War Room to discuss details. We also need to get the ships moving. Issbeck and Simal, please head to the bridge. We need to coordinate with their bridge and ensure we move in tandem so that the force field and wielder hold. Cain, you're our best pilot, so I'd appreciate it if you could lend your expertise in helping Simal."

He nodded, "Absolutely, whatever I can do to help." I watched Simal pat Cain's shoulder and turned to head to the bridge.

Cain gave Jesse a final hug and followed him.

I asked, "Rushim, would you like to communicate with your ship?"

Rushim nodded, and Issbeck asked him to follow him while everyone else moved to the War Room. I watched Jesse take Surly aside and introduce her to Katie. When Surly held Katie's hand, I watched contentment wash over her face.

She looked at Jesse with shock, "Wow, did you feel that?" she asked.

"Yes. She and her father had an immediate calming effect on me," Jesse replied.

I knew what Jesse was referring to. It was well known there was a reason the Obsidi were called Peacekeepers. The Nomad was the only species unaffected by them, which isn't surprising based on their cold nature.

Surly looked at us and said, "But for Katie, it's a different feeling. It is not the same for everyone."

I admit being intrigued by that, but we arrived at the War Room as I was about to ask her to explain. Once inside, everyone started asking questions about what happened with Curalim. It was like twenty questions being thrown at Jesse all at once. Poor Surly looked completely confused; I just laughed and told her it was always like this with them.

"They are a team, but they are major pains in the ass —" I received multiple gasps, shocked looks, and a smack from my Kindred "Jesse's words!" I'll have a permanent smile forever, so Jesse was free to smack away. Shortly after, Issbeck arrived in the War Room with Rushim.

Katie asked, "Are we moving together alright?"

"Perfectly. Both ships are moving at the same speed, although slower than we would like. We are monitoring both sides of the latch to ensure it stays stable, and the cloak is covering both ships nicely. Brilliant idea, Katie," Issbeck praised her.

Rushim walked over and indicated that he wanted to shake her hand. Here we go, I thought. Sure enough, I watched the amazement fall over Katie's face as he enveloped her hand with both of his. He turned to me and nodded, saying, "Jesse's sister is quite brilliant and a lovely person."

I watched Jesse look at Katie with such pride. They weren't blood sisters, but I couldn't imagine them any closer.

I stepped forward and dropped the screen at the end of the table. Danlon's face came up. Issbeck had been tasked with getting us connected to him for a chat.

Rushim was the first to address him, "Supreme Commander Danlon, it is a pleasure to meet you. I apologise for taking so long to remove ourselves from the Nomad situation."

Danlon nodded and moved aside as Magistrate Eton joined them. I watched as a smile spread across the magistrate's face. He addressed Rushim, "My friend, I thought you had perished. I heard about your wife and son. I'm so sorry we couldn't be there to help."

So they knew each other. Rushim assured the magistrate that there was nothing the Kreans could have done. At the time, we had our hands full helping the humans. He said that he had been quietly positioning things behind the scenes to protect his people so they would be prepared when it was time to ally with us.

Rushim filled us in on what had transpired with them over the last 28 years. Details were given about the people taken and about the Obsidi's attempt to protect and move as many as they could. It turned out they had moved all their own people along with ours to many locations. He instructed his ship to send all the information to Danlon.

Then Danlon asked the obvious, "Where is Curalim right now, do you know?"

"I can only give you his last location based on where we knew he was headed. We will transmit that information to you as well. However, I would guess he is long gone. We also placed a beacon for him to give the impression that you captured us. We feel it is important for them to think we are still working with the Nomad. He also had no idea Surly and I were aboard the ship, or even alive. You will have everything sent to you that we have on the Nomad. I know it is important that you capture him, and we will do everything we can to assist."

Danlon thanked him.

I turned to Rushim and asked something I had been wondering, "I'm assuming you have other ships out there?"

His answer surprised all of us. "We have approximately 90 ships in various locations throughout multiple star systems."

"But how do you communicate with all of them?" I asked. I couldn't imagine how one kept track of that many ships all out in space.

"We have a very unique communication system. It occurs between us telepathically and allows us to never lose track of each other. It was what the Nomad was after, but they were disappointed. We led them to believe it was the ships that are organic. They would never have given us the freedom we have if they thought the key to our communication was our people. We would, however, be happy to share our communication with you. It would just require the presence of Obsidi on your ships."

Magistrate Eton felt it would be a good idea. We were almost ready to launch the new Phantom warships, and they would be a perfect testing ground to add Obsidi to the crew complement. We would also want to keep up communications with all of the Obsidi ships.

Jesse asked, "How many crew do you have per ship?"

I was wondering the same.

"There are approximately 150 Obsidi per ship, but they can carry 250. We must leave much of the ship open, or the Nomad would suspect us of not doing our part."

I couldn't help but wonder just how many Obsidi were left.

As if reading my mind, Rushim answered in a whisper, "There are only about 100,000 of us left."

Magistrate Eton sat back as if someone struck him. He stepped away from the monitor, and everyone was quiet until he returned. He was upset; it was apparent.

The magistrate invited Rushim, his daughter, and any other Obsidi from their ship to find a home on any of our planets if they wished. "I wish I'd known." The magistrate's distress was palpable. I had no idea how many Obsidi perished, but I knew it had to be a significant number.

I noticed Surly was a bit teary. Since she was sitting next to Jesse, she grabbed her hand and let her know she'd be happy to show her Terra One and her home. I smiled because I was looking forward to seeing Jesse's home as well.

Danlon mentioned that my parents, whom he was also close to, lived on Terra Two, and that might be an excellent place to settle some Obsidi while providing some protection.

"My daughter, our people, and I would be honoured to be a

part of any Terra." Rushim bowed in appreciation and then requested to speak with Danlon and Eton alone.

I wasn't that surprised by the request. Once Danlon and the magistrate agreed, we all left so they could have some privacy. Surly asked if she could go back to her ship. Harley piped up and volunteered to take her to the latch. I didn't think much of it but noticed Jesse wink at Harley. I turned to Jesse. "I think you owe me for making me worry about you like that. I awoke, and you were gone. A little scolding is in order — hmmm?" I whispered in her ear. I could see the intense desire form in her eyes; she would enjoy my need to scold her, almost as much as me.

She had no sooner spoken her agreement than I picked her up and threw her over my shoulder. I took off down the corridor towards my room.

"I'll talk to you guys later," Jesse yelled to everyone as they all howled in laughter.

I had her to my room, through the doors, and was heading down the stairs to the bed in seconds. She was struggling to get me to let her down. I chuckled, smacked her ass a couple of times, and kept going. She wasn't getting down or going anywhere other than my bed for at least the next couple of hours.

Considering what went down with her going missing, she would be lucky if I ever let her out of my sight again. That seemed a bit extreme, but my emotions were on overload. And they said Kreans were cold. Not when it came to our Kindred.

I tossed her on the bed. Before she had a chance to move or talk, I was on her and had her mouth in a kiss. I couldn't even imagine why we Kreans had an aversion to kissing because kissing Jesse was pure pleasure. Having her mouth under mine stoked my desire even more.

I pulled back after another deep, meaningful kiss that told me Jesse was more than ready. I had my hands on either side of her head with them in her silky, short burgundy hair. I loved her hair. It was thick and soft. I revelled in it for a minute. She had her eyes closed. She was enjoying my stroking of her head and hair. I moved my left hand down and followed the shape of her face.

Her eyes opened, looking right into mine. So many emotions passed over her face, but the one that made my heart squeeze was the slight sadness. I know it reflected what had happened and, while she was back with me, it had affected her more than she wanted to admit to herself. She was not an emotionally closed person but admitting to a weakness was something I knew she hated.

I smiled at her and lifted myself a bit off her. She snaked her arms around my neck so that she moved with me. I rolled over on my back and took her with me as she straddled my hips and sat up. I looked her over for the first time and noticed her outfit.

It was an Obsidi piece, similar to what Surly and Rushim wore, and it looked amazing on Jesse. I stroked my hand down the leg of her outfit. The feel of it surprised me. I had expected it to have a rough, rigid texture, almost like what you found on Terra called leather, but this material was soft. It was almost plush. I found it very strange, and when I pulled a bit on it, it moved and stretched. However, as it moved away from Jesse's body, it changed to a harder texture. It was the most bizarre fabric I'd ever seen.

Jesse chuckled. "I can tell from the look on your face you're as surprised as I was by the material. It's wonderful, isn't it?"

"It suits you," I told her while I kept stroking down her legs. "I noticed how perfectly it fits you, but I thought it was a rough material."

"I know. When they gave it to me I thought it would be too large, but the way the material works, it forms to whoever wears it so they don't have to make multiple sizes since it'll fit every-one. It also changes colour based on the person wearing it. When they gave it to me, it was black; I put it on and ended up with this. I've never worn anything like it."

That is different. The colour suited her perfectly. It was

varying shades of tan mixed with burgundy. It swirled depending on where it hugged her body. I was amazed. Clearly, the Obsidi had perfected clothing because Rushim and Surly's outfits suited them well, too. I imagined how helpful something like that would be for our warriors.

"I know what you're thinking," said Jesse. "I asked if there was a way we could get them to work with us on getting this for TechStar. It's also a protective material."

"Protective, how?"

"Haso and Chim told me it stops any weapons attacks. It is impenetrable. I'd love to see SPAR and the Krean warriors wearing it."

That would be fantastic.

Jesse put her hands on either side of my head and smirked. "Now, can we forget about the outfit and get back to my scolding?"

I couldn't help but laugh. Leave it to her to look forward to that. I swiftly sat up with her still on my lap and without any more words, I began to release her from her outfit, top down.

It didn't take me long to realise she had no bra underneath, and I took quick advantage. While she pulled my shirt over my head, I grabbed her breasts and slowly kneaded them. I loved their size; they were typically larger than Krean females. Jesse's breasts were perfect, with dark pink nipples. I pulled her up to meet my mouth and slowly sucked and licked one nipple and then over to the other. God, she tasted good.

I watched her as I kept moving between the two. She threw her head back with a moan, her hands grabbing tightly onto my hair. The little bit of pain was worth every inch of her that I was able to taste.

I swung her around so her back was on the bed again. I wanted her pants off. We both quickly got rid of the last barrier between us. Once we were completely naked, I turned her over with her ass pulled up towards me. She had shown me this position during our first time together. I loved it, looking at her perfect ass as I pumped my staff into her in one hard stroke. I wanted to add a little extra to this round.

She moaned loudly as I quickly filled her over and over. I raised my hand and smacked her. Jesse gave me a quick yelp, looked over her shoulder, and smiled, giving her approval. I was not into hitting a female, but smacking her ass during sex was as pleasurable to me as it was to her. Each time I did it, I could feel her clench and grip my staff harder.

I watched her ass cheeks redden. They looked so perfect, round and quivering. I could feel her reaching her climax. I wanted to go with her. Bending over her body, I rested my one hand down on her left side; my right reached under her to find her sweet nub. I picked up the pace, and I pumped hard; I rubbed her as I was losing control. I felt her go over the edge, and I followed right along with her.

As we came down, I swung us on our side, remaining inside her. I never wanted to leave. With my other hand, I brush her hair off her sweaty forehead. She turned her head to kiss me, but then I watched her close her eyes, and she promptly dropped off. I couldn't help but smile. I kissed her cheek, hugged her close, and allowed myself to sleep with her.

Something stirred me a bit later, and I noticed Jesse was gone. I shot up from the bed in a panic. It took a bit to register that she was in the bathroom. I took a massive breath as I heard her. That scared the shit out of me. I didn't know how soon I would get a handle on her being taken from me.

She opened the door, smiled when she realised I was up and strutted towards me. She climbed in, pushed me back down and moved on top. "I checked with the bridge. With the ships attached, we have to move a lot slower. It'll be several hours before we reach Terra." She grinned at me. "Any ideas on how we can fill the time."

I laughed and grabbed her. "I can think of a few."

◆

Several hours later, Jesse and I were up. I watched her put the Obsidi outfit on again. It was apparent she liked wearing it, and I had no complaints. It hugged every inch of her body. You could see it shift with her when she walked. The colour also seemed to shift with her movements. She was ahead of me as we walked towards the bridge, and I appreciated the view. The pants hugged her long legs, great ass, and then curved to her tiny waist. I had no idea how, but it made her look like a warrior while showing off everything feminine. Fuck, I loved the damn outfit — and the woman wearing it.

When we entered, we found everyone there. Even Cain and Annie were present. Annie hugged Jesse, whispering, "Don't do that again." I noticed Annie glance at Cain with concern.

I laughed as Jesse hugged her back and agreed, "I don't plan on it!"

Annie nodded and went back to the navigation system. She was assisting Simal with something. He gave me a nod.

Cain approached and grabbed Jesse, saying, "We have news about our family."

"Really? What sort of news?" she asked.

I hoped it was good news because Jesse could use that.

Issbeck and Rushim waved us over to where they were sitting. Issbeck nodded to his screen.

I saw a list of names again, similar to what we had retrieved from the Nomad ships, only this list had actual dates and planet names beside each person. And right there were her dad's and brother's names. I looked at Rushim, feeling Jesse's emotions rolling off her, and asked, "We know where they are?"

I looked at Jesse to see her and Cain with arms around each other. They were both emotional. I can't even imagine how they must be feeling.

Rushim said yes and explained, "We had all my ships keep a clear log of who they took and where we placed them over the years. It was all added to a database that I knew we would turn over once we could rid ourselves of the Nomad. From what Cain has told me, it appears that his and Jesse's family were amongst some of the people we moved at the beginning."

Jesse asked, "Do you know those planets?"

"Yes, but they are a very long journey," Rushim replied. He also added, "I know that Curalim made reference to your family and knowing where they are, inferring he could hurt them. I can assure you he does not know where they are. He does not know where anyone is. He never has because it is not something he feels is important. As cold as that may sound, it is probably the best possible scenario."

As good a news as this was, I couldn't help but feel frustrated. We had to get back Jesse's family. I could feel Jesse's intense need to get to them. I pulled her into my body, and she let me hug her in front of the crew and her team. "I promise *AmKee*, we will figure it out."

When she moved away from me, Rushim grabbed Jesse's hands. "I know you want them back. And that was part of the plan, to eventually get everyone back. We will, and Obsidi Peaceships will participate as much as possible. We will devise a plan when we get to your Moonbase."

I watched her close her eyes and take a deep breath. We both knew he was right.

We also learned from Rushim that he had moved many surviving Obsidi to the same planets. He had no particular plan at the time other than saving them. They were also clearly listed, so they would be easy enough to retrieve. I suspected Danlon and Eton would approach the Coalition to allow the remaining Obsidi to find a home on the Terras, especially since so few were left.

One problem I could foresee was the Obsidi ships would have minimal participation in retrieving the missing people. It would be far too obvious and attract the wrong attention. I looked over at Jesse and could see her in deep thought.

When she glanced at me, she said, "I'd guess you are

thinking the same thing I am. We must send out several ships to gather everyone, but Obsidi ships can't be involved."

I nodded and saw that Rushim was watching with a regretful look.

"No, not right away. We will have to be very watchful for the Nomad and their other allies, and I do not want to take the chance that one of our ships could be boarded by them. We do not carry any weapons on our ships," he replied.

"Right, and with Curalim thinking your ship was taken captive by the Aries, he will move on and continue working with the other Obsidi ships. It is a good plan." I had to admire how Rushim had fooled and manipulated Curalim. I doubted that happened often.

Simal told us, "Prime, we are on the final pass along Mars and will swing around towards the Terras. We should reach the Terra Moonbase in about an hour."

I asked everyone to take a seat and requested that Simal send a message to Danlon with our estimated arrival. I also told him to remove the cloak now that we were in range of Moonbase. We received a message with instructions to come in from the angle between Terra One and Two so that it would look like we were bringing the Peaceship as salvage.

I sat down with Jesse next to me. She grabbed my hand and kept it on her lap. I noticed Issbeck looking over at us; he winked at Jesse and returned to what he was working on with Rushim and Cain.

As I glanced around the bridge, I saw that everyone was together. Over to the left by systems, Surly was sitting with Katie, Harley, CeeChi, and Melo. The rest of Jesse's team, Sid, Joe, and Neil, looked like they were reviewing information about the Obsidi ships with Kiv; Issbeck was with Rushim, going over some final details along with Haso and Chim; Simal, Nate, and Annie took us in and coordinated with Rushim's ship. It was a beautiful sight to watch us all working together.

I felt a tug on my hand, looked over, and saw Jesse looking at me.

"We work well together, don't we?" She smiled at me. She just read my mind. Yes, we did work well together.

But even knowing that, I couldn't help but wonder what would happen from here. Jesse and her team worked out of Terra One. Once we got to Moonbase, would her team's mission be over? I found the thought frustrating because I wanted to continue what we started.

I couldn't help but feel unsettled, even with her holding and stroking my hand.

CHAPTER
TWENTY-TWO
JESSE

As we approached the space between the two Terras, I noticed Rushim and Surly sitting forward with awed expressions.

I asked, "You've never seen the Terras?"

Rushim answered, "No, we kept our distance. I admit it was purely intentional."

"What do you mean?" Zersus asked.

"I felt that if I came here, I would not be able to resist contacting Eton. He is a very old friend, and it would have been hard for me to be near without alerting him. I had to wait until the time was right." Rushim continued, "Jesse's arrival on our ship created a perfect way for us to make a move while leaving Curalim with the impression we are still their allies."

We watched Simal, Nate, and Annie navigate us closer to Moonbase. One of the complex sets of docking stations was on our entry path. The new ships are being completed to the left. From what I could tell, it looked like six new warships in varying stages of being built, with one finished.

I wanted to get back home. I was ready to get off the warship. I didn't want to admit that to Zersus. I'd hate for him to be disappointed. There it was again. How were Zersus and I going to deal with this? I was worried. We both loved what we did, but how would we continue to do that and be together? There had to be a way. Before I could overthink it, Danlon was suddenly on our viewscreen.

He welcomed us and asked for a private conversation with Zersus, myself and Rushim. I wondered about what Rushim had discussed with him and Magistrate Eton. Maybe we'd find out.

As the three of us headed to the War Room, Zersus gave final instructions to Simal to complete the docking process. First, they needed to arrange for the release of Rushim's Peaceship. It would be moved to an area where captured ships were held. The crew would be removed from there to make everything look legit. I assumed this was for show because we suspected there might be eyes on what we were doing.

We entered the War Room, having a seat, and bringing up Danlon on one of the smaller monitors. "I won't waste time. We have arranged a meeting with the Coalition and a few other key players. They were notified of your arrival and should be here within the next hour. Once you get the ship docked, I would like the three of you to head to Command. Zersus knows where that is. The rest of the crew will remain on the ship for now." He looked at Rushim. "Is Surly okay remaining with the rest of the bridge crew, or would you prefer for her to join your ship?"

Rushim answered, "I will leave that choice to her. I believe she has become quite attached to a few people here." And with that, he smiled over at me. I also had a sneaky suspicion that Surly liked our tech, Harley.

"Alright then. I will let you know when everyone has arrived, and you can make your way here."

"Confirmed, Supreme Commander," Zesus replied.

I turned to Zersus and Rushim. "I guess this will be a long evening."

They agreed. Zersus wrapped an arm around my shoulders and squeezed as we got up and returned to the bridge.

We let everyone know we would be the only ones leaving the ship. Sitting with Harley, I approached Surly and asked her if she wanted to leave and return to the Peaceship. I noticed her quickly glance at Harley and shake her head. He grinned as he spun back to his monitor.

I couldn't help but smile as I walked back to Zersus. Just as I went to sit, he dragged me onto his lap. I laughed at him and swung my arms around his neck, "Prime, we are on the bridge. Do you think this is appropriate?"

"Yes." He pulled me closer so that he could nip my neck and quickly kiss me. I could hear the approving rumble from Issbeck and Simal. Laughter was coming from everyone else.

"Well, okay then," I said, snuggling in with him.

It wasn't long before we heard from Danlon. Everyone required for the meeting had arrived. I'll admit I was a touch nervous. Not about the mission or anything that had happened but just how Zersus and I would deal with our situation.

As long as we were still on the ship, I could avoid the subject. As soon as we left, I would have no choice but to face it head-on. As we walked to the transport bay to take one of the supply shuttles across to the station, Zersus grabbed my hand. He brought it up to kiss my knuckles and whispered, "I know what's going through your head. I can feel your emotions. Everything will work out, you'll see."

How could he be so sure? God, I hoped he was right.

◆

The flight over to Moonbase was a quick ride. Zersus led me through a vast set of corridors. The moonbase was a beehive of activity. The way it was built reminded me of a spider. From space, you could see the central round portion and, from there, the numerous outer legs. There were more than a dozen that went in all directions. It made the loading and unloading of ships much more manageable.

The Moonbase, while beautifully designed, could only be

described as efficient. It was silvery grey steel and blended nicely with the moon's rock and ice terrain.

The placement of the Moonbase also gave it direct access to space from all angles. Someone had considered how to get the most out of its location. I admired that while it was built for what was supposed to be military use, it still had an inviting and comfortable atmosphere. I assumed that the command area would be similar.

From everything I'd heard, the base had another offshoot section where space military personnel lived. That was well hidden from view. It was built between two mountain ranges on one side of the moonbase. They had to be close enough to get to the base quickly, but they also wanted the residence protected. I'd love to know precisely how that all worked.

It was a long walk through the corridors, but we eventually reached an area opening to a circular walkaround. There was glass on one side looking out over the base, the hub of activity, and all the ships docked. I stopped momentarily and admired the sheer ingenuity that had gone into everything.

I felt Zersus come up behind me. "Impressive, isn't it?"

I nodded.

He continued, "I felt the same way when I saw the TechStar base on Terra One."

I smiled up at him, and he motioned for us to continue.

Rushim came up on my other side and said, "I hope I get to see your home, Jesse. Your team was telling me about it. It sounds quite lovely."

"It is Rushim, and you're welcome any time. You'll like my parents." I smiled at the thought of them.

"Yes, and the Techstar base that the SPAR teams work out of is quite the sight to see," Zersus added. "I am also looking forward to seeing Jesse's home. I didn't get an opportunity to do that the last time I was there."

I could feel he meant it and was excited to show it to him. I joked with him, "Just don't forget I share my home with King."

"You share your home with another man?" Rushim questioned with a frown.

Both Zersus and I laughed while I shook my head. I explained that King was my canine partner. I could see the slight frown on Rushim's face. He probably had no idea what a dog was.

We reached a sizable, panelled section as one slid open. Danlon stepped out. "Ah, you are all here. Good. Good. The Coalition is here, along with a few others. Come in and find yourselves a seat."

The Coalition Magistrates, including Eton, were around the table when we walked in. Beside them was another man I didn't recognize but assumed he was military based on his uniform. And lastly, my boss, Chief Frank Cole, and TechStar Head Director, Sheldon Cummings. Out of all of them, the only one that made me uncomfortable was Cummings. I'm not sure why. His presence didn't seem strange, considering he knew about the mission and had introduced himself to Danlon and Zersus back on Terra One, but I couldn't shake my discomfort.

I was still glad that Zersus was with me, and again, he sensed my feelings because he steered me away from Cummings and seated us closer to Danlon while Rushim took a seat next to Magistrate Eton. Eton introduced everyone around the table. There was my Terra Magistrate, Phillip Corden, and a pleasant-looking older woman, Magistrate Madeline Simpson from Terra Two. Next to her was Magistrate Lillian De Haro from Terra Three and the other Krean, Magistrate Savo from Terra Four. The person I didn't know was introduced as Commandant Ed Foster, the head of the human Space Military program, as I suspected. Finishing up with the chief and Cummings.

Danlon began by explaining that everyone had been versed in what had occurred during our mission; however, the group had questions for us.

First, they asked Rushim to give a quick rundown on the

Obsidi and their participation with the Nomad. They wanted to hear it from him.

While Rushim went through everything, answering questions along the way, I could feel Cummings watching me. It was a touch disconcerting and weird. I also noted that Zersus was frowning at his obvious stare. When Rushim got to the point where Curalim had arrived with me, Cummings piped up and asked, "So how exactly did Jesse end up with him?" He looked at me and snidely said, "I thought you were supposed to be the best of SPAR?"

I could tell the chief wasn't happy with Cummings' questions. I looked at Cummings, prepared to answer him, and noticed he wasn't even looking at me. He was watching my hand joined with Zersus'. He didn't like it, but I couldn't figure out his problem. It didn't make sense. He was wearing his animosity for Zersus on his sleeve. Was I the only one that noticed it? No, I wasn't. I could see several people noticing his odd behaviour.

Before I could answer, Rushim continued, "When Jesse arrived with Curalim, we were informed that he had immobilised her. She was unconscious. Certainly not in any condition to argue about being removed from her ship and crew. I am sure Prime Zersus will fill in the rest of the blanks about how she ended up like that."

I looked at Rushim and, for the first time, saw the tough side of him. He certainly put Cummings in his place. I wanted to laugh. Cummings cleared his throat and returned to brooding.

Rushim finished providing his details. The magistrates were upset but expressed that, while they weren't happy with the Obsidi's participation in what the Nomad were doing, they understood.

Magistrate Simpson spoke up first, "Peacekeeper Rushim, I am sorry to hear about what happened to you and your people. Considering that could have happened to any of us sitting here.

"I understand you lost your family and that it was your

mandate to keep the rest of your people safe. I can't fault you; I know the rest can't either." I noted all of the other magistrates nodding.

Rushim bowed his head. "Thank you, Magistrate."

She continued, "I understand you have committed to helping us going forward?"

He nodded. "Yes, I promised Magistrate Eton that I would do everything I could, and so would my people."

All of the magistrates expressed their agreement with this plan. They were about to continue when Cummings decided to speak up again. "How can we trust him not to turn his back on us? He did on the Nomad."

I tried not to roll my eyes at the man. What the hell? I wanted to reach across the table and throttle him.

Magistrate Eton got to him first, "Please do not, first and foremost, refer to us in the same breath as the Nomad. And secondly, I trust this man more than I do most. I will personally vouch for him and his people."

Hidden meaning: you being the "most" asshole. I'm not the only one that got the reference. I felt Zersus give an extra tug on my hand. The chief had been quiet until this point. He looked over at Danlon, who nodded at him. They both stood up and walked over to Cummings. Behind us, the doors slid open and several warriors walked in.

"Sheldon Cummings, you're being placed in the custody of the Krean Moonbase to face charges of conspiracy against both humans and Kreans."

I sat there in shock.

Cummings stood up. "What is the meaning of this? You can't arrest me. Do you even have any idea who I am?" He directed that at Danlon, who just laughed in his face.

"Of course, I know. Based on the evidence we have gathered, we know you have been one of the key players in the slave trade. We know that you had a hand in making sure our recent prisoners never made it to interrogation. And we know you were one of the key people feeding our military secrets to the Nomad. We can't imagine how you thought you'd benefit from a relationship with them, but we will find out soon enough."

The chief handcuffed him as he continued to scream and yell that he was being framed. Danlon and the chief just laughed and handed him over to the warriors. They had instructions to place him in a holding cell for the time being. He was still screaming on the way out of the room. Thank god, his voice was cut off as soon as the doors slid shut.

The chief sat down, giving me a wink. I couldn't say I was surprised that Cummings was involved in something illegal, but this was not what I expected. Another thought occurred to me. "You don't think he's the only one, do you?" I looked at the faces around the table.

I watched all Coalition members look at me, along with Eton, Danlon and Ed Foster.

Eton answered, "No, we don't. We think that there could be several high-level TechStar individuals involved. Which is why you two are here."

Zersus and I looked at each other in confusion. Magistrate Eton asked Danlon to explain.

"We have decided to create a new security section called The Guardians. It will be led and trained on Terra One by Chief Frank Cole. He'll explain more about that later. Commandant Foster and I will be involved in anything space-related."

"We want the two of you to work with all of us to choose the people in Guardians top positions. They will come from the current SPAR program and the top space military. We must fill the six new Phantom ships, find primes, and assign the ground Terra teams. Jesse, your SPAR team members will be the first asked if they want to participate and become Guardians or remain with SPAR. TS-4 will also be asked. The chief has assured us that the remaining SPAR teams are ready to move up to higher-level teams for TechStar. It will be a natural progression, but we want them to decide for themselves."

"I'd be surprised if they said no, and of course, I am not either. It's a yes for me."

Chief smiled at me and said, "I knew you'd say yes."

I looked over at Zersus. Danlon was waiting for his response, too.

"Of course, I'm in. I assume my part will be finding suitable people for the new warships?"

Danlon nodded. "Yes, and I would say the first Prime should be your brother, Issbeck. He would make a fine leader for the Phoenix, the first new Phantom III."

I could see Zersus agreed with the choice, beaming with pride for his brother.

"So we'd be located at Snowden Valley's TechStar base?" I asked. I was worried about Zersus and how he'd feel about that.

Magistrate Corden from Terra One answered, "We thought about it and felt that keeping you in Snowden Valley was the best plan because it allows you to keep an eye on SPAR. However, we will build a separate operations base for the Guardians. A stretch of land on the other side of Snowden Valley is not part of TechStar but is available to build. We will locate the new facilities there.

"As far as everyone else will know, it will be a new base for an elite SPAR program, which explains why it is separate. What you do will be more secretive, and very few people will know the truth. Chief Cole will be your only direct TechStar contact and will directly report to the Coalition."

At least he was one person I could trust. This was a lot to absorb, but we needed to face this ongoing issue with the Nomad head-on. It would take some time for us to put the teams together, but I didn't doubt we could do it.

I looked at Zersus again. I needed to know he was on board. If he wasn't, then neither was I.

"Are you okay with this? It will change everything for you, and I know you've always preferred space." I couldn't help but worry about what he was thinking.

He leaned over and kissed my cheek. "Where you go, I go."

I heard Magistrate Simpson chuckle while everyone else smiled.

I looked at Zersus. "I guess it is true."

"What's that *AmKee*?"

"Home is where the heart is."

"I have no idea what that means but it sounds reasonable." He brought my hand to his lips and kissed it lightly. He closed his eyes briefly and said, "My parents always told me that finding your Kindred makes everything clear in your life. I never believed it. I always thought my life was perfect and I needed nothing else. I was so wrong, and now I understand. Wherever you are, I will be. It doesn't matter if it's on a warship or a Terra. As long as you are there, I know I'll be happy. You are my Kindred, my partner, my life."

My heart exploded. I could feel my eyes tearing up. I blinked and was sure my smile was a mile wide. When I looked at him, I felt the same. I had never thought how much I was missing until I met him. I placed my other hand on his face and brought him close so we could rest our foreheads together. I closed my eyes and could feel him squeeze my other hand. I looked into his wonderful amber eyes and whispered, "I love you."

CHAPTER
TWENTY-THREE
JESSE

THE COALITION MAGISTRATES EXCUSED THEMSELVES. Eton asked Rushim to join him for a little "catching up" while giving him a tour of Moonbase. Zersus and I remained with the chief, Danlon, and the commandant to discuss further details. It centred around the immediate recruitment of specific SPAR members which would be my team and TS-4. The chief wasn't overly concerned that it would leave SPAR short-handed, which I was worried about. The Nomad may step up their intended program with our capture and interrogation of Curalim. The chief assured us that plenty of well-trained recruits could fill the positions on the lower end. Having the well-oiled group of TS-4 and TS-5 to start the Guardians was vital because we worked well together on missions.

The Commandant asked us to call him Ed and said he would list the top-tier Space Corp members best suited to the Guardians. When we mentioned Cain and Annie, he nodded and said, "They would be clear choices."

Zersus chuckled a bit, which caused Ed to raise an eyebrow at him. Zersus explained, "That's a good thing because Jesse and Cain are siblings."

Ed froze. "Well, I'll be damned. I've been around Cain

throughout his training and he told me plenty about his family."
He shook his head with a bit of a sigh. "I'm happy for you both. I
guess that makes him a perfect candidate to join the Guardians.
Let me go and get a list of the people I think are suitable. Chief,
can I send you the list to arrange a full security check?"

The chief nodded and replied, "That's a great idea. I have a
couple of key people I know that work for TechStar we can
recruit to do the security checks."

"Perfect." Ed got up. "I'll get on that right away. I have
another meeting to attend, so I need to leave, but I'll get that to
you in the next day or so."

Danlon said, "I'm sure I don't need to tell you but for *our eyes
only*. Don't share this with anyone else, including assistants."

Ed frowned, sighed, and said, "Fully understood." He shook
hands with all of us, gave me a big smile, and left.

Continuing with Zersus' end of things, Danlon said that
several of the Phantom IIIs would be ready to launch shortly,
with the first one ready in a few weeks, and felt that several of
the warrior crew on his ship could be promoted to positions on
the new ships.

Zersus agreed and began making a list of command positions. I shouldn't have been surprised when he suggested Cain
be promoted to Second with Issbeck as Prime and CeeChi as
their leading Tech. Danlon agreed immediately for the first
Phantom launch.

Simal would then be promoted to Prime on the Aries with
Kiv as Second and Melo as leading Tech. Eventually, they would
be promoted to the next Phantom III, but we needed a good lead
crew on the Aries to work with the Phoenix. With their warrior
abilities, being intelligent, and unfailingly loyal, they were all
perfect choices. It was vital to have people we could trust
running these ships for the missions they'd be handling.

As we finished figuring out who we'd approach and their
positions, Danlon brought up Katie. I was surprised as I
assumed she'd be moving with the team. "I'd like to use Katie

here on Terra Moonbase. She would work officially with you and be designated to the Guardians program, but her skills in advancing the tech on the ships are needed."

I looked at Zersus and knew he had mentioned Katie's involvement in the new system functions on the Aries. Considering they had been key to how they located me and how we managed to get back to Moonbase with the Peaceship attached, it's no wonder that Danlon wanted to have her working on all of the Guardian tech. I just wasn't sure how she would feel about it.

"I'll ask her. I know she doesn't like to be separated from her family too long. The only thing that made this space trip bearable for her was my presence, but I could be overthinking it. I tend to be a bit overprotective when it comes to Katie." I looked at Danlon and knew he understood.

Katie suffered lasting effects from our short incarceration when we were young. Even though we were rescued shortly after she awoke, she still had nightmares. I knew they weren't nearly as bad as they had been when we were young, but I had no idea how she would feel about the idea.

Danlon assured me that he only wanted her to travel to Moonbase a few times a week but she could live on Terra One, where Zersus and I would be, mostly working with us from Snowden Valley.

I nodded and said, "That would probably work. It would definitely make it more appealing to her."

As we ended the meeting, Zersus turned to the chief and asked, "Would you like to come and see the Aries? Maybe chat with everyone yourself?"

"That's not a bad idea." The chief nodded and turned to Danlon. "Maybe you should join us?"

Danlon was about to answer us as the doors slid open, and Magistrate Eton stepped through with Rushim. "Ah, just in time, I see you are finished up here. Returning to the Aries?" the magistrate asked.

We affirmed that we'd discussed what we could for now and

were ready to head there. The future of the Guardians depended on how things would go with the crew. Danlon and the chief agreed to come with us, and it turned out that Magistrate Eton and Rushim also wanted to join us. The six of us returned to the transport bay. On the ride back to the Aries, Danlon asked the transport pilot to take us on a quick tour of the new Phantom III, the Phoenix.

I was curious about the name and asked Danlon. He said that one of the head engineers named it. The name suited the ship; it looked like a bird in flight. It was a black base with various deep red strokes of colour down the side of the ship, over the winged sections, and moving to the back of it. Reminded me a bit of the new Eros transport's colouring. It would be a fantastic sight against the blackness of space. The crimson markings looked almost fluid, like fire. The pilot moved us around it and even Zersus was impressed. The ship's sheer size was larger than the Aries with a broader and less bulky design. It appeared to have a more aerodynamic shape that would easily cut through space.

Zersus asked, "What sort of speed are we looking at? I'm assuming it can outperform the Phantom IIs?"

Danlon nodded and pointed to the rear section slightly higher than the side wings. "That's where the engine room is. The ship's movement is centred along the wings, so it has incredible manoeuvrability despite its size. Compared to the Aries, it's fifteen percent faster, along with being better with energy usage. It is also twenty percent larger, even though it has fewer floors. It's spread out. It can carry a crew of 600. We will be ready to run some tests in about a week so having the Aries back in the dock will give us the perfect opportunity. I believe the hole in its side section should be repaired by then, " he teased.

I laughed, and Zersus said, "Sorry about that. And just so you know, that was Katie's idea."

I jabbed Zersus in the ribs for telling on Katie.

Danlon shook his head and joked back, "Of course it was."

After we made the last pass around the other side of the

Phoenix, I couldn't help but be overwhelmed by the ship's size. It was breathtaking. It was built for power. It was meant to intimidate.

We pulled away from the Phoenix, and I saw us heading for the Aries bays. In a short time, we were inside and the pilot touched us down. When the force field was back in place, I saw Cain, Issbeck, and Sid walk into the bay. I was happy to see them again. Cain gave me one of his huge hugs which I was getting used to. I heard a throat clear behind me and turned to find Danlon and the chief watching.

"Damn, is it obvious you two are related," said the chief.

I pulled Cain forward and introduced him to both men. Magistrate Eton also stepped forward, and Cain was speechless when the man wanted to meet him.

Zersus gave Issbeck a list of people and asked him to arrange for everyone to meet in the War Room in an hour. I could see Issbeck was curious about what was happening, especially considering the people who accompanied us back to the Aries. Still, he nodded and immediately went off to take care of it.

Sid shook hands with the chief, and there was a bunch of back-slapping. I rolled my eyes and introduced Sid to the magistrate as my second-in-command. The magistrate asked if Cain would give the chief and him a tour of the ship. Cain, of course, was honoured to do so. Danlon said he'd join them, while Sid decided to head back to the bridge to assist Issbeck and ensure the team was gathered. Rushim excused himself to go and find his daughter.

That left Zersus and me alone. We needed it. We were both overwhelmed. As if on cue, my stomach growled.

He looked at me and then down at my stomach. "I think that means I need to feed you," he laughed.

"I guess so. It has been a while since we ate."

"Come on *AmKee*, let's go grab a bite. I don't think we will get much opportunity for quite a while once we get to the War Room."

I agreed, and we headed towards the Common Room. I knew there were many things we needed to discuss. Everything was moving quickly, and I was worried. He didn't appear upset about the developments and being in charge of the new Guardian teams but I needed to hear that from him.

I wasn't worried about where we would live because I had a home that would do just fine, but would he be okay with that? Christ, and then there was King to think about. Zersus had appeared to be comfortable with him when we first met at the TechStar base, but it wasn't common for Kreans to have pets. There were so many things to consider.

When we arrived at the Common Room, it was reasonably quiet. Only a few people were sitting around, enjoying their meals. They greeted Zersus and me. The news of us being together had made its way around the ship. We grabbed our plates and, for the first time, I noted the chef working in the kitchen.

"Excuse me," I said, getting her attention, "I just wanted to let you know that I have enjoyed all the meals. I am unfamiliar with Krean dishes but everything has been delicious."

She came over and smiled. "Thank you so much. I love to cook. You are probably finding the meals to your taste because I use a lot of human spices, and we grow many Terra vegetables on the ship, so they are fresh."

"That's amazing. What about the meat?" They had a variety that I knew was familiar.

She replied, "When we return to Moonbase, we restock our flash frozen meat selection. It makes it much easier to keep many meats without worrying about it going bad."

"That makes sense." I found everything fascinating. I asked her where she picked up the habit of using human spices.

She smiled. "I grew up on Terra Two, and my parents owned a restaurant in Upper Tuscan, so we adapted all of our dishes to work for both species."

This caught Zersus by surprise. "I had no idea you grew up

there, Liska. My parents settled not far from there in the Pisa-Florence Meld. When I take Jesse to meet my parents, I'd love to visit the restaurant, so you must let us know the name of it. I'd even bet my parents already know of it."

I could see she was very honoured — I forgot that Zersus' position as prime made him almost royalty to his crew. She gave us the restaurant's name and encouraged us to let her parents know who we were if we made it there. I'll admit I had known I'd have to meet Zersus' parents eventually, but his mention of them caught me a bit off guard. I looked at him, probably with my mouth hanging open and speechless. He laughed at me, touched my chin to close my mouth, leaned over for a quick kiss, and shook his head. The chef chuckled and recommended the items she thought I would enjoy.

We filled our plates, and Zersus led us to a quiet little corner where we could sit beside each other. We were both hungry, so we spent the first few minutes just eating. And I did enjoy the chef's recommendations. She had given me what appeared to be a pie with an abundance of tasty vegetables and meat in gravy. I'm not sure what the contents were, but it tasted similar to squash, turnip or something of that nature with corn, and the meat tasted like a mix between beef or pork and super tender.

I suddenly felt like I was being watched. Sure enough, Zersus was leaning back in his seat and watching me eat.

"You're going to just stare at me as I eat?"

"I'm enjoying watching you." He smiled and nodded to the chef, who clapped her hands, clearly pleased that we enjoyed her recommendations.

I rolled my eyes at him. He chuckled and raised what looked like a soft bun to take a bite. I grabbed it, split off a piece and ran it through the gravy. Damn, that was so good. It reminded me a bit of the buns on the Obsidi ship. I should mention those to Liska and get her to ask Surly about them because while these were very good, those sweet and soft buns were sheer heaven.

I went to dip the bun again, and as I was going to take a bite,

Zersus grabbed my hand, directed it to his mouth and ate it. I gave him a pout.

He hummed in agreement. "Mmm Good."

"That was the last piece," I complained.

"You stole it from me. It was only fair I should have some, *AmKee*," he cheekily commented.

I laughed. We stole the remainder of food from each other's plates like a game. It didn't take us long to finish, and I was stuffed.

I asked him something I had been meaning to for a while, "What does *Amkee* mean? You've used that expression quite a bit."

He frowned and looked confused. "Your communicator doesn't translate that?"

I shook my head. He thought for a bit before he spoke again.

"I am not sure what it would mean in your language, but it expresses great affection. My father says it to my mother all the time." He smiled when he mentioned them.

He was about to lean over and kiss me when he looked at his communicator.

"Time to go?" I asked.

He nodded. We placed our empty plates in the area to be washed and headed out. He put his arm around me and pulled me close. I could see many warriors we passed along the way, watching us with a smile. Seeing they were so happy for him was beautiful, and nobody seemed to question that I wasn't Krean.

We reached our destination: the War Room. It was packed to the brim. Along with the magistrate, Danlon, and the chief, was my team. They were all seated to the right, with Danlon between Katie and Harley.

To the left were Cain, Annie, Kiv, Melo, CeeChi, Simal, and another Krean female I didn't recognize.

Zersus bent down and whispered, "That's our head medic, Divi. You haven't had a chance to meet her yet."

Seated at the far end of the table were Rushim, Surly, Haso, and Chim. Zersus and I were the last to arrive. We took the last couple of seats at the top of the table. Magistrate Eton took the floor first. Everyone was curious about what was happening, especially having a magistrate on board.

"You have all been called here to usher in a new era of protection for our Terra planets."

Zersus and I watched that sink in.

The magistrate continued, "As we know, the Nomad has plans for us. We have also learned that many of our people are spread out all over space, some in bad situations and some in hiding, thanks to the Obsidi. What we need is a dedicated group that will be trained to protect both our people. One where we all work together — the priority being to eliminate the threat of the Nomad and to find all of our people, humans and Krean. We want to bring them home where they belong."

There was a low rumble around the room. Magistrate Eton indicated that the chief had the floor to continue. I could see him gather his thoughts and look around. He announced, "All of you have been selected as the first people we want to work with to develop the new Guardians program. Zersus, Jesse, Supreme Commander Danlon, Commandant Ed Foster, and I will head up this division.

"It will be considered a high-level ghost operation. No one outside of us and the Coalition Magistrates, when necessary, will know exactly who is in the group or the details of our missions. We have become aware that a group within our high-ranking officials, even some at TechStar, are assisting the Nomad."

I heard the gasps and the pissed-off looks that passed across everyone's faces. It was going to make our jobs more complex and risky. The chief waited for the room to die down before he continued, "Because of this, we're leaving it optional to all of you as to whether or not you wish to be part of this. We'll also be asking TS-4 if they'd like to join. Zersus and Jesse already have your general job descriptions if you should decide to accept. If you don't, you will not lose your current positions."

Danlon stood up as the chief finished. "Rushim, Surly, Haso, Chim, and the remaining Peacekeepers will stay on Terra One — temporarily. The Guardians will protect them, and Terra One's climate is closest to what they are used to. Eventually, some Peacekeepers will be distributed over the new Phantoms as they launch. We can test using their communication methods.

"Rushim will assist in retrieving the people taken that the Obsidi managed to get to safety. His intelligence has led us to one of the main traitors working for the Nomad. And we will be able to retrieve the hidden Obsidi through our missions.

"Lastly, as Jesse suggested, we will use the Obsidi ship as a holding area for prisoners we wish to interrogate. We will outfit it for our interrogation methods with Rushim's approval, per her suggestion. That will take some time, but we still feel it will work well to hide anyone we capture from being eliminated before we interrogate them. This has been a problem, with the Chatoch being the last victims."

I watched Danlon look down and take a moment before continuing, "Only a few people in this room know what I went through with the Nomad. Curalim was the person that killed my family." His voice was thick with emotion.

I could see everyone sit up to attention. I watched as Katie grabbed Danlon's hand. I think it was just instinct that made her do it. To my surprise, he looked down at her and didn't try to pull his hand away.

"My family were prime targets of the Nomad. The same as when they arrived on earth originally, the first people they killed were your leaders. That is always their plan. They did the same with our people on Allora, they did the same with the Obsidi; Rushim lost his wife and son."

Suddenly, I got it. His parents were important. I had felt Danlon wasn't an ordinary Krean, but I wasn't prepared for what he would tell us.

"My parents were the supreme leaders of the Krean people. Based on human history, you would call them royalty. When the Nomad struck, I was away on my first training retreat led by Magistrate Eton. He got me away and hid me. The Nomad don't know I exist. The time has come for them to realise that no matter what they do, WE WILL WIN!" He slammed his fist on the table, still holding Katie's in his other hand. "We won't stop until we rid space of the Nomad and along with that, we will free any other people they have enslaved. We need to make more allies and friends."

I could see everyone nodding and agreeing. Almost as if planned, everyone in that room said, "*I'm in.*"

It was music to my ears. Now, the fun starts.

CHAPTER
TWENTY-FOUR
ZERSUS

IT HAD BEEN several weeks since the formation of the Guardians. Jesse and I slowly moved into our roles as the leads. There were still many things to work through, but the first round of assignments and bringing people on board had occurred. We hit a few bumps in the road, but we met everything head-on.

We had lists of numerous potential candidates but for now, we were trying to figure out the logistics of how everything would work. Currently, we were holding our meetings via video with the chief from our home on Terra One. Chief Cole was moving into position as director of the unit but it was important to keep things quiet. There were still a lot of obvious signs that Cummings was not working alone and had to have had other upper-level people helping him. We also had a large abduction off of Terra Three that we believed was associated with recruitment for the Guardians. Very few people knew about our operation, so we were trying to figure out where the leak started, along with sending off our first mission with a couple of operatives.

Cummings was being held on the Obsidi ship, as per Jesse's idea to use it as a prisoner holding area. So far, it had kept him alive. Katie and Danlon were working on finding a format on the

Obsidi ship for the interrogation thiobarb but until they do, we assumed Cummings' information to be untrustworthy, not that it's been much.

Based on the knowledge we had gathered from the mission on Terra Four along with the information collected by the Aries during the capture of the Nomad freighter and data taken from the Nomad fighter ships, we knew that there were a lot of allies working with the Nomad.

What we didn't know was who was getting them in and out of Terra.

We hoped Cummings was involved, but Jesse felt it wasn't him. She was sure he was just a figurehead and he didn't have the technical knowledge to make all that happen. Danlon and I were inclined to agree. So that left us with nothing again on who was responsible. I was confident we'd figure it out.

I had also thought transitioning to working on a planet, and not in space, would be more of a challenge for me. I spent my teen years growing up on Terra Two, but I'd never formed a permanent attachment to it. Terra Two was a beautiful planet with fields of rolling hills, trees, plentiful fruits, and vegetables. It was the agricultural planet of the Terras, but no matter how beautiful it was, it never felt like home.

One week was all it took — one week of being with Jesse in her home on Terra One. And, of course, I couldn't forget King. I'd never had a pet. It wasn't common for Kreans to have pets at all. Probably because we spent a lot of time in space, but even back on Allora, we didn't have them. King, as a trained K-9, was more than just a pet; having him around made our home feel complete.

Jesse was teaching me how to command him. Because we used communicators and I couldn't speak the English language, she taught me the hand signals first. I found it all fascinating, and she encouraged me to speak to him in my language simultaneously so he'd get used to the verbal commands when I spoke — damn intelligent dog.

Terra One was a beautiful planet, but Jesse made it special. Everywhere we went, she'd explain why she loved it. Things I'd have previously considered mundane, suddenly became amazing. I found I enjoyed the town's character, the beauty of the surrounding mountains, and took interest in skiing, which I'd never done but suddenly wanted to learn. I believed it was because of her enthusiasm for life here in Snowden Valley.

This morning, we woke up at our usual early hour and, after our typical run, we had to prepare for a day with family.

When we returned, Jesse began preparing a typical "american" style breakfast. I still wasn't clear what that meant, but my mouth watered when I looked at the table filled with food she called omelettes, bacon, sausage, homemade pancakes, and biscuits. The smell was a combination of salty and sweet. I picked up one of the biscuits and brought it to my nose. The scent made my mouth water. She said the biscuits were her mom's recipe which she called butter-based with a touch of brown sugar for a caramel flavour. I had no idea what that meant, but I couldn't resist breaking one open and popping a piece in my mouth. Holy shit, it was incredible. The flavour exploded, and melted on my tongue. I quickly demolished the rest of it and was reaching for a second when she smacked my hand.

"Don't spoil your appetite by eating all the biscuits. Leave some for everyone else."

We were expecting a lot of company for what she called "Freedom Day." It was a celebration for all the Terras to commemorate surviving the Nomad war; the day my people showed up to assist the humans. She said it was similar to what they used to call Thanksgiving Day which no longer existed. She joked they needed another day and an excuse to eat.

I looked down at King, who whined as he watched her set out the food. The dog was a bottomless pit, practically drooling.

I laughed at her, grabbed her waist and pulled her to me. "I'd rather eat you."

She shook her head, as she wiggled out of my grip and returned to the kitchen area just as the doorbell rang. "Can you get that, please? I still have to finish here."

I headed to the door. When I opened it, our first arrival was my brother, who enveloped me in a huge hug. I hadn't seen Issbeck in several weeks and knew he was busy getting his new ship, the Phoenix, ready for its inaugural launch. Cain, who had taken the position as Issbeck's second in command, was with him. I knew Cain was a touch nervous about accepting, but both Jesse and I were confident he'd do great.

Cain stepped forward and shook my hand. Behind him was a man who, while I didn't know him, I recognized immediately. He had the same dark hair as Cain; square-shaped face, albeit with a beard, same height and build, and the same eyes. They were a dead giveaway that he was related to Cain and Jesse. The only difference was that he wore glasses, which I found odd. With our medical intervention, most general vision issues were easily repaired. I couldn't help but be curious.

Sure enough, Cain introduced him as his brother, Nate Badawi. Ah, yes, one of the critical engineers responsible for the design of the new Phantoms. I knew he existed, as we had recently discussed moving him to the Guardians.

I heard Jesse call from the kitchen, "Who is here?"

"It's our brothers and another guest." I didn't want to say anything. I wanted Cain to be the one to introduce them. Jesse hadn't forgotten about Nate. She was waiting for the right opportunity to meet him. We would have eventually met with him about moving to the Guardian program.

Nate's focus was on the voice coming from the kitchen. We all turned just as Jesse was making her way to the table with her focus on King and the bowl in her hand filled with more pancakes. She glanced over and froze as she sat the dish on the table. Nate was the first one to move. He rushed over quickly and grabbed her, hugging her tightly.

"Oh my god — are you Nate? Oh my god," she repeated while I could see the emotion and glistening of tears in her eyes.

"It's me, sis. Damn. Damn. I can't believe it." The poor guy was just as emotional as she was.

King danced around the two of them and tried to pry them apart.

I watched Nate pull back and laugh at the dog. He gave a questioning look at Jesse.

Her smile was one of the most beautiful expressions I've ever seen. "This is my SPAR partner, King."

Nate just shook his head, and with a grin bent down and gave King the rub he was craving. When he stood up, he turned to look at us over his shoulder. "You didn't tell me she was gorgeous. She looks so much like mom."

You could feel the emotion and tears in his voice. It was thick and deep, with a slight tremble. Not what you would expect from a guy the size of Nate, but the years of not knowing if your family was alive or dead would do that to a person.

I moved over to Jesse's side and put my arms around her waist. "Welcome, Nate." I turned to Jesse. "I'd say we have more than enough food for him to join us." I laughed, looking at the full table. And on cue, the door went off again.

Issbeck, being the closest, opened it to a sea of people. Another huge group slowly flooded into our home.

First was Jesse's team members, Sid, Neil, Harley, and Joe, then came Jesse's family. Maverick dashed through quickly and headed straight for the kitchen while Katie, Matt, and Alice laughed. He yelled out, "Hey, what's left to do?"

Jesse rolled her eyes and joined him to keep some semblance of control.

No sooner did they arrive and the door went off again. The last of our guests walked through — Danlon, Magistrate Eton, Rushim, Surly, Haso and Chim, and my parents, Risa and Sinto. They had been staying in Snowden Valley since Jesse and I had returned. As soon as they heard I'd met my Kindred, they showed up. I had a feeling it would become a regular occurrence for them. Jesse had won them over. Not to mention, they got along well with Matt and Alice.

I told them, "Everyone please grab a seat. It's all fresh, and there is more than enough."

Jesse's table was large and could seat twenty, which happened regularly when the two teams came over. She had just taken delivery of the custom table and was excited to see it full of all the people we cared about. Jesse and Maverick came out of the kitchen and added more plates of food. I helped her with some, including a fresh pot of coffee — another typical Terra drink that I had learned to greatly appreciate, especially in the early morning hours.

We all sat to enjoy the food that would be the day's first meal. Matt and Alice were going to host a larger group at their bar this evening — people who couldn't be here this morning, specifically TS-4, and several of the Aries crew.

I watched as everyone passed around each dish and loaded their plates. Jesse put a small bowl together and placed it on the floor for King. The dog would stay under the table waiting for the droppings. He was faster than anyone could bend over and pick it up.

All of the guys acted like it was their last meal. The men had at least two plates full. The pancakes seemed to be Issbeck's favourite. He had a mouthful of them and was moaning about how good they were. We couldn't help but laugh at him. I knew exactly how he felt. I had the same reaction the first time I ate them.

It was impossible to follow all of the conversations around the table. Everyone scattered and just sat wherever there was a chair. Anyone who didn't know the one next to them introduced themselves. I smiled because it was apparent that nobody had an issue conversing with someone they perhaps didn't know well.

Matt and Alice made Rushim, Surly and the two Peacekeepers, Haso and Chim, feel very welcome. They had taken them under their wing. I also noticed that Harley had made sure to sit beside Surly. Again, his interest wasn't unnoticed — by me or Jesse.

On the other side of Jesse was her mom, Alice. I watched Jesse lean over and have a short whispered conversation with her. I'm guessing it was about Rosie. We had asked Jesse's parents to look out for a friend's dog; she was currently unavailable. Alice said that Henry, their bartender, was going to look after her for the morning and assured her Rosie was doing fine. She was a sweet angel of a dog and, while missing her owner, never made a fuss. I think Jesse's parents were enjoying her company.

Nate sat across from Jesse and peppered her with questions. He was impressed with how far she had come in the TechStar, even a little shocked that she had been the top team lead until recently.

Jesse and I asked about his life. We knew he was a head engineer, but Jesse wanted to know how he grew up. It was difficult for her to hear that he had essentially been one of the many orphans of Terra Four. At least most of the orphanages were well monitored because of the divergence of the planets, but it was still a hard way to grow up. Luckily, Nate was brilliant and had taken advantage of the free education system. The rest was history. Nate also confirmed that he had placed his name on the list for Terra Four, but again, we knew he was missing from it. Another confirmation that something was seriously wrong.

We gave Nate a quick rundown of what we had been working on that had put her SPAR team and the Aries crew together and how the outcome had put us where we were today.

I could see the wheels turning in Nate's mind. "Can I ask — I'm assuming that we are stepping up our space program then?"

Jesse looked around, noting that my parents, Matt, Alice and Maverick had moved towards the other end of the table. They were not part of the program and couldn't know the details due to the nature of the Guardians.

They were far enough away. I nodded for her to go ahead.

She lowered her voice and told him, "Yes, Supreme Commander Danlon, Commandant Foster and all of the magistrates have made that a priority. We have to build the new Guardians facility here in Snowden Valley, which won't happen until the winter is over. They can't break ground with it being so cold right now. So, in the meantime, we are working surreptitiously from here. I have a good-sized office, and this place is large enough for meetings. It's easier to concentrate more on the space program without too many people knowing for now."

I asked Nate, "Are you on board?"

He nodded.

"Then I'll just mention that our operations are on a need-to-know basis. You can't discuss what happens within the Guardian missions with anyone. Not even the people you worked with before. We will add a few tech people from both the SPAR teams, from my ship, the Aries, and you are the only design crew engineer for now."

Nate had no reservations. He nodded again. "I won't let you down. I imagine my role isn't clearly defined, but whatever you need from me, I'm there."

I shook his hand, and Jesse smiled at him. I could see the approval on Issbeck and Cain's faces as well. With his cup of coffee, Cain stood up and said, "A toast?"

I had no idea what that was, but Jesse and Nate nodded.

I watched everyone around the table hold up their cups like Cain.

"A toast to family, great friends, and to letting the bad guys know they are in deep shit."

There was a loud round of agreement and laughter from everyone.

When the meal was over, everyone helped Jesse clear the table. Danlon and the magistrate said they had to leave but would return along with Ed Foster tonight. Rushim joined them. Matt and Alice left to go and do the prep for the evening. My parents asked if they could join them and help out. Alice threaded her arm through my mom's and agreed with a huge smile. Matt grinned, while he and my dad followed the ladies. Maverick let them know he'd join them shortly.

Jesse turned to everyone else and asked, "You guys want to join us for movie time?"

I could see the curiosity in Issbeck's eyes because, like me, we weren't familiar with the practice, but everyone else was looking forward to it.

Harley turned to Surly, who looked confused. "You'll love it, and if I know Jesse, she will have a good one planned." He looked over at Jesse for confirmation.

"We're watching the Trilogy," Jesse told them.

"No way, you have those? How the hell did you get those? They're classics." Nate was like a kid and seemed to love these so-called "movies."

Jesse's team laughed and nodded while heading for the couch's comfort.

Jesse shrugged. "If you'd seen the damn outfit that Curalim made me wear on the Obsidi ship — well, let's just say I was channelling a certain Princess."

Everyone looked at her questioningly. Then, all of a sudden caught on, wide-eyed and started laughing.

Surly was even trying hard to keep a straight face. She admitted, "I thought she was talking about a real princess when she said that. It was an *interesting* outfit."

That set everyone off. There was back slapping and "holy shits," and then Sid asked, "Damn it, and you didn't get a permanent record of that?"

I watched Jesse cringe. "No way. It's bad enough that it's etched into the brains of the poor Obsidi that saw me wearing the damn thing."

Haso and Chim grinned, and I scowled at them. They grinned more. I needed to have a chat with those guys.

Jesse turned to head to the living room area. Jesse's house

was designed so the first floor had all the rooms in one space. She called it an open concept. Outside of a few areas off the far side of the main door, including our office and bedroom, everything else was in this one area with high ceilings. A row of counters separated the kitchen.

A large L-shaped, deep-cushioned sofa that was a dream to sit on was the main piece, with matching lounge seats distributed around the square area of what she referred to as the living room. At the far end was a massive fireplace with a large monitor screen mounted above it.

On either side were floor-to-ceiling windows and sliding doors that led out to the back area. There was a perfect view of mountains and fresh snow. I saw a few animals that Jesse called deer hanging out in the yard. How could I have ever thought that I'd hate this? I couldn't have been more wrong.

I watched Jesse walk over to the monitor and turn everything on. Everyone got comfortable and was about to sit down when many communicators went off. I glanced at mine. Damn it, this wasn't good. I looked up at Jesse and saw she was watching Cain.

He was not a happy man. The communication — we had lost track of a supply ship. Which wasn't entirely true. The ship in question had a few crew members we deliberately sent out on it. Based on some Obsidi information, we suspected the ship was part of the slave scheme. But that wasn't what put the clear frown and scowl on Cain's face.

It wasn't the fact that the ship was missing, but who was on it. Annie was on that ship, which he was just learning, and we had some explaining to do.

Everyone started talking at the same time.

I held up my hand and shouted, "Quiet. Alright, here's what we do. Issbeck, you and Cain head to the Phoenix and get her ready. I will contact Danlon, and we will get permission to launch. I'm unsure how this will go, so I'll let you know as soon as we discuss the details." I turned to Nate. "Why don't you head back with them as well? I'm unsure if you'll be needed, but you might as well be there just in case."

Nate nodded, turned to Jesse and hugged her, as did Cain, and they left, along with everyone else. Jesse and I headed to the office. We needed to make that call to Danlon and Magistrate Eton. It's too bad they left. I looked over at Jesse, whose eyes were already on me, and asked, "You're thinking the same thing, right?"

She slowly nodded and said, "Annie and Melo completed their mission."

CHAPTER
TWENTY-FIVE
ANNIE

"WHO THE HELL ARE THESE GUYS?" I turned to our pilot, Ari, and hoped I was pulling off *not* knowing who the Niri were. I had only seen their ship in images, but I knew them. We weren't here by accident.

Melo answered, "They are the Niri. Captain, I thought you said they would leave us alone and let us travel through their space?"

Captain Marshall looked at Melo and me, trying to pull off the panicky look. We weren't buying it.

Ari was trying his best to avoid the Niri and not doing a bad job. Vance had headed into the back a while ago, so we sent him a message to let him know what was happening.

"Roger. Keep me posted on what you need us to do back here," Vance replied.

I had to admit there was a bit of panic in his voice.

The captain asked, "Any suggestions?"

Knowing we couldn't outrun them, I felt it was logical to suggest something else just to make things look legit on my end. I nodded. "I'm assuming you have smuggling holds?"

The captain reluctantly nodded. It was common knowledge

that these ships had those holds, but he seemed hesitant. *Asshole, got ya on that one.* I knew he didn't have a valid reason to say no.

"We need to get the crew in them." I turned back to Melo and asked, "Would they be able to know how many of us were on the ship?"

He shook his head. "Not as far as I know, they have no scanning tech. They just invade and salvage what they find."

Of course, I knew that already, but we had to make this look good. We believed the Niri probably knew precisely how many of us were on the ship.

Captain Marshall gave the command for everyone to head to the smuggling holds.

I contacted Vance again and he informed us the cargo crew were heading to the holds. I also took the opportunity, while making a show of contacting Vance, to activate the beacon Katie had given us. It would signal the Guardians that the mission was a success, and they would prepare to send the warships to rescue us from the Niri.

Everyone was worried about handling the Niri once we were boarded, but we would figure it out as it happened. Captain Marshall planned to "sacrifice" himself and let them think there was no crew. He wanted to stay out of the smuggling holds, alone, to tell the Niri he had permission to travel through their space.

What a bunch of bullshit. I moved to the smuggling hold just off the bridge, and we instructed everyone else to follow us. I wanted to hear everything that went on between Marshall and the Niri. Melo and Ari moved to the opening beside me. There were some 30 crew on this ship and while we knew everything would be fine, they didn't. They had to be worried.

It felt like we waited forever. In reality, it was only about 15 minutes. Based on the clanking, banging, and the last jolt we endured, it sounded like our ship had been loaded onto another.

Marshall could contact us via an open comms channel, but

we also had cracked a small edge to our cargo hold. Marshall sat comfortably and waited, attempting to act nervous. His demeanour did not match his acting. Just a few minutes later, we noticed several Niri entering the bridge. The voice speaking to Marshall was robotic and clipped.

"Where-Is-Your-Crew?" There was no beating around the bush for these guys.

"I'm alone," Marshall said. His tone was just a bit too casual and unworried. I looked over at Melo and he rolled his eyes. That made me want to laugh. I noticed Ari appeared pissed off. He was catching on.

"You-Are-Not-Alone…We-Sense-Additional-Organics."

Melo shook his head. He had said they didn't have those capabilities, but I guess they weren't above lying.

I heard Marshall answer, "There is organic food on the ship. I have a lot of it in the cargo holds."

"We-Do-Not-Believe-You…If-You-Do-Not-Tell-Us-Where-The-Crew-Is-We-Will-Jettison-This-Ship-And-Destroy-It."

Ari looked at us and sent us a comm message."Is it just me or is this bullshit?"

I sent him back a reply. "Definitely bullshit." The Niri would never destroy tech. They need it to survive.

He scowled, and I knew he realised the position we were in.

Melo and I both looked at him and nodded.

Ari's gaze moved between us, and I could see the realisation dawn on him. The tension in his shoulders left, and he nodded back.

We sent a quick note to Vance to see if he had perhaps been listening. I had specifically left the comms open so that anything said on the bridge was heard in the cargo bay. We received a message instantaneously: "Damn right, I heard that shit."

I told him that we were going to leave the cargo hold.

Vance's question surprised me. "I'm assuming you two Tech-Star peeps have a plan?"

I showed Melo the message, and we returned a simple "yes" before coordinating a 10 second countdown.

We all moved at the same time, leaving our hiding spaces. For now, the Niri had us, but it wouldn't be for long — we hoped.

CHAPTER
TWENTY-SIX
CAIN

AFTER WE RUSHED BACK to Terra Moonbase, Issbeck and I received another communication from Zersus to inform us that Danlon had approved the Phoenix to be prepped for launch. Nate headed for engineering while we took a transport over to our warship.

I'd taken the position of second in command at the request of Zersus, my sister, and Issbeck. While I was more than a competent pilot, I was still unsure if I could fulfil the role. I'd try, not just for my sister and the guys, but for the rest of the people still out there.

And now Annie. She was out there. We had to find her. Damn, she was supposed to be safe on Terra Three visiting her family.

We were launching a little ahead of schedule alongside the Aries with Simal as Prime.

Issbeck was my prime, with CeeChi taking the tech position. We still didn't have a full crew complement on either ship, but I guess they figured we'd be okay together.

My feelings were all over the place right now. I cared for Annie but hadn't allowed myself the luxury of thinking about it much. I'd expressed my need to move things further with her, and she'd shut me down. I was trying to come to terms with that.

While all of the possibilities were cycling through my head, I heard the doors to the bridge open. Issbeck, Zersus, my sister, and Supreme Commander Danlon walked in. Surprisingly, Nate was also with them. I was unsure why, but sure I'd find out soon enough. It was then that I realised there were two dogs. King, of course, and a golden retriever. Wait, what the fuck? Was that Rosie? What were they doing with her?

Issbeck headed towards me. "Have we gone through all of the checks for launch?"

I nodded. "Yes, Prime, we have them all confirmed. Everything reads positive, and the engines are ready."

Danlon said, "We are having Nate accompany you on this trip. It's not normal, but we don't want surprises because it's a deep space mission and the first for the Phoenix. He's the best qualified to deal with anything that could go wrong. Plus, he's an extra Guardian for the mission. Harley is joining Simal's team."

That made perfect sense. Nate was the lead engineer behind the design of these new Phantoms, and Harley was one of the best techs next to Katie.

"We managed to get a hold of CeeChi, who was visiting her family on Terra Four. She will be here shortly. While we prefer a launch with some fanfare and a more complete crew, there is no time. The Aries is also ready."

I replied, "We hope to pick up a trace of them once we get to their last known position or find the ship has lost contact for a technical reason." I had my fingers crossed that the latter explanation was what had happened, but I couldn't help the bad feeling in my gut. I had to ask, "Is that Rosie?"

I watched Zersus and Jesse look at each other before my sister stepped forward. As she hugged me, she said, "We need to tell you both something."

Issbeck and I looked at them. We were both confused.

Zersus was the first to break the uncomfortable silence. "They didn't go out there for the reasons you think."

Issbeck frowned. "What do you mean?"

"Zersus means that Annie and Melo were given a specific mission," my sister answered.

They were on a mission? But what did that have to do with them having Annie's sister's dog?

Issbeck asked, "Wait, you mean they were out there on purpose?"

Jesse moved to me and took my hand, while addressing us both. "We will send you the encrypted details for their mission. Katie designed a tracking system similar to what she had installed in the Wraiths. Melo loaded it on the Cobra supply ship. Annie and Melo are the only two that know it's there. It's been leaving a trail to follow. They were ordered to get captured."

To say that both Issbeck and I were in shock would be an understatement but once the surprise wore off, I couldn't help feeling pissed off. "Why Annie?" I asked. "Does it have anything to do with why you have Kelley's dog?"

Jesse, still holding my hand, replied, "Yes." She was upset.

What the hell was going on?

"Annie's parents, along with a large group of people, were abducted a few weeks ago. Kelley happened to be visiting when it happened. The authorities found Rosie in the house slightly injured. Annie collected her and left her with us. Of course, we hope this mission leads to where those people were taken because it appears this supply ship was involved in removing the group from the island. You will find the full details in the file."

I was stunned for a second. I looked at everyone and saw that it wasn't an easy subject. I knew Annie had lost her original family, so she'd do anything to get this one back. And I'd do anything I could to help. So would everyone else on this ship.

I was also pissed. I was mad that Annie left and never told

me. I was angry that my sister didn't tell me, even though logically I get why she didn't, and I was mostly mad that Annie felt she had no choice but to do this. "As much as I don't like it, I understand. I even understand why you asked her. We will find them. I won't let anyone down," I said as my gaze swept over everyone.

CeeChi walked onto the bridge right at that moment. "Prime and Second, reporting for duty aboard the Phoenix, permission to take third position," she formally requested.

Issbeck gave her the clearance, and she moved beside me. We had a hell of a crew, I trusted them all with my life and I'd give mine for them.

I felt King's nose hit my hand. I looked down and found him on one side of me and Rosie on the other side, clearly trying to comfort me. Jesse gave me a final quick hug. She commanded the dogs to follow her. She, Zersus and Danlon left for the transport bay. They told us they would watch the launch from the moon-based observation decks.

If I was being honest, I would have loved to watch the launch that way. The Phoenix was an impressive warship. It was larger than the Aries, and the design was gorgeous. The Phoenix was built like a bird in flight. With winged sides, it held many of the primary operations on one main floor, giving accessible access to all of the critical areas of the ship quickly.

The mid-section wasn't as tall as the Aries; it was wider. When looking at the two ships together, they looked like they belonged to the same fleet, with the only creative difference being that the Phoenix had flames in different shades of crimson going down the sides from its nose to tail and over the wings.

It indeed resembled what you might envision as a Phoenix bird. I assumed my brother Nate had something to do with the name and design because, even as a kid, I remembered him being obsessed with the legend of the Phoenix.

We took our positions and ran through the final sequences. Nate sat off to the left, covering the system that monitors the ship's tech. CeeChi was also familiar with all the tech but was to concentrate on the new cloaking systems that Katie designed and installed for us. CeeChi was also taking on a bit of navigation on this run which would have been Annie's job had she been here. It will be — we were going to find her and bring her home.

About 30 minutes later, we were ready to go. The engines activated, and we received clearance from the construction bays as they moved away from us. The Aries pulled alongside. We were heading out in the opposite direction towards the sun. We would shoot around it and end on the other side, travelling towards the next solar system.

CeeChi, Issbeck, and I could watch the Aries moving in tandem with us since the Phoenix had side-angled windows to allow a better overall view of space. The Aries didn't have the advantage of a peripheral view like ours.

As we slowly passed between Terras Two and Three, we could see the large spread of space ahead of us. We noted several Wraith fighters escorting us out; a formal salute for the Phoenix's first launch. I knew it wasn't as big a deal as it should've been. I turned to Issbeck with an inquiring look.

He nodded. "I'm assuming the Supreme Commander arranged the send-off."

As we reached the edge of the two Terra planets, the Wraiths flew in a pattern across our bow and headed back towards Moonbase. Our ship and the Aries communicated affirmative-to-go, and we engaged. We couldn't move at our top speed because the Aries wouldn't be able to keep up, but we settled into a comfortable, quick pace alongside it.

And now, I had time for my thoughts to turn to Annie.

Hang in there, Annie. We're coming.

GLOSSARY OF THE GUARDIANS

Allora - once the home planet of the Kreans, destroyed by the Nomad.

AmKee - a Krean word that expresses great affection for a Kindred.

Aries Phantom II Warship - one of Space Corp's warships. The ship carries a crew of 450, 50 two-person Wraith fighters, and 25 Wraith transports that carries 20.

Biosuits - protective suits with cloaks that SPAR teams wear on missions. Warships have a version as well, but the cloaks will be a later addition.

Cell Chamber - prisoner holding area on a warship.

Chatoch - a bug alien species allied with the Nomad and involved in the slave trade.

Coalition - the group voted to be in charge of the each Terra, Space Corp, TechStar and the Kreans.

Command Central - main building structure of Terra Moonbase.

Commandant - head of Space Corp human military.

Common Room - the dining and kitchen area on a warship.

Communicator - a device worn on missions, similar to a watch, enabling communication among team members.

Creepy Blue Guy - Curalim, a particularly nasty Nomad, a humanoid-reptilian species, named by six year old Jesse and based on how he looked to her at that age.

Divergence - the term used when discussing the cataclysmic event that occurred in 2036 when the earth exploded because of the Nomad and was brought back together by the Krean's counter-weapon to form the four Terras surrounding the Moon as a fifth planet; it was an accident that created chaos, separated families, and billions disappeared into thin air.

Eros Hover Transport - new space planet travel; Eros I is a small transport that carries six, Eros II can carry 12 and are meant to be used by SPAR teams for interplanetary missions; both can hover like Earth's helicopters.

Etion Power - a stable Krean power option that saved humans after the divergence. It is easily generated on the moon and transmitted to large devices on each planet. It powers everything. It is a clean power and an endless supply. Warships are also powered with Etion generators and so are all Krean pulse weapons.

Feranth - a benevolent species that has partnered with the Nomad and involved in the slave trade. Their physiology is unknown as they wear full armour, however, they walk upright and look like they could be humanoid.

Freedom Day - the day the Kreans showed up to assist Earth in their war against the Nomad, turning things around and eventually leading to their defeat.

Guardians - the group formed by the humans and Kreans to ally with other species and put a stop to the Nomad's slave trade.

Kindred - a Krean's one and only soul partner.

Krean - a humanoid space faring species that showed up when the human's needed them. They helped defeat the Nomad, and chose to stay after the divergence. Humans and Kreans are visually almost identical with only minor differences.

Laser Weapons - traditional weapons for TechStar, each rifle or pistol carries a cartridge that provides quick reloads and holds approximately 100 rounds. The weapon has three strike settings.

Latch Wielder - device designed by the Kreans that can be used to tunnel through two ships, and create a secure barrier to pass through. Typically used on Wraith transports, which then have the ability to close the hole once a mission is completed.

Niri - a robotic species involved with the Nomad in the slave trade. They trade humanoids for tech parts they need to survive.

Nomad - the alien humanoid-reptilian species that attempted to invade Earth in 2032, was at war with humans for just over three years when the Kreans showed up and finally helped get rid of them, or so it was believed. It is discovered in 2064 that they are now behind multiple disappearances on the Terras, among other things.

Magistrates - the voted leaders of each planet in the Terras

Magnetosphere - keeping the five planets of the Terras together as a group as they circle the sun. Also used as a protective barrier that has been enhanced by the Kreans for security.

Maintenance Docking Bays - a set of docks that hang in space, surrounding Terra Moonbase where warships come in for repair. Also used for the building of new ships.

Monitor Bags - devices used in the gym for combat training. They register hit counts, speed and force.

Moonbase Residence - a structure built to house the members of Space Corp, especially if they work on Moonbase, but also crews that are in transition. It is protected and fairly well hidden from view. It can only be reached via a train transit system from the moonbase.

Obsidi - a humanoid species that appears to be helping the Nomad, however, things are not always as they seem.

Obsidi Peaceship - one of a large number of spaceships carrying approximately 150 Obsidi per ship. They have no weapons, but they do have a unique communication method.

Pashon - the room where the head of the Obsidi resides on his spaceship.

Phoenix Phantom III Warship - the newest design of the Space

Corp warships. Holding a crew of 600, 100 Wraith four-person fighters and 50 Wraith transports that carry 30.

Prime - leader of a warship.

Pulse Weapons - Krean rifles, of varying sizes, using Etion power. They are not typically able to be used by humans as they require the user to imprint on them. They do not require reloading or charging and have six levels of impact settings.

Stonehedges - restaurant and bar owned by Matt and Alice Williams, Jesse's adoptive parents, in Snowden Valley.

Supreme Commander - head of Krean Space Corp.

TechStar - organisation formed to lead all of the technical, security and Space Corp needs to help the Terras develop and also their continued protection, particularly on each planet.

TechStar Head Director - each TechStar base has a Director that heads up their specific section. There are two bases on each of the four planets surrounding the moon.

Terra Alliance - the term used to describe the five planets that now have replaced Earth.

Terra Four TechStar Lazarus Base - the base used to hold the majority of TechStar prisoners on the harshest of the four planets. It is only accessible by interplanetary transport.

Terra Moonbase - where Space Corp operates its space military, both humans and Kreans.

Terra One TechStar Snowden Valley Base (SPAR Operations) - the key location all SPAR teams are housed, trained and deployed from.

Terra's Missing Lists - lists created on each planet that everyone could put their original names on in an attempt to find their lost family members after the divergence.

Thiobarb - an interrogation mist from the Kreans that is used to force the truth from prisoners. Only used at Space Corp's moonbase and on warships.

TOTS (Terra One Transport System) - a public transportation system that allows people to travel from one side of the planet to the other. It allows individuals to easily travel anywhere for work.

Training Arena - the areas designated on a warship for warrior training.

Translator - a Krean device that is planted inside the ear to allow for effective communication between species. It can be easily turned off with a quick touch behind the earlobe.

Space Corp - the military designation for anyone working on the moon or a warship.

SPAR (TS-4 and TS-5) - stands for Security, Protection and Reconnaissance. Highly trained special forces. Currently there are five teams with six members each.

War Room - the conference area for meetings on a warship.

Wraith Transports - a larger transport used for rescue missions on a warship. The Phantom II versions hold 20 people, the new Phantom III will hold 30. They are also the only ships that use the Latch Wielders.

Wraith Fighters - quick, highly manoeuvrable, short range ships with weapons capabilities. Used primarily for space confrontations. The current versions carry two people, a pilot and a navigator. The new versions will carry a crew of four, pilot, navigator, weapons specialist and a tech.

AUTHOR'S NOTE

I'm so thrilled that you have decided to embark on the Terra Alliance journey beginning with The Guardians, my first story in this ongoing Space Opera series.

In the first book, you will be introduced to new worlds, many amazing characters, and storylines that will curl your toes. Books 1-6 in the series invite you into the history of the Beaudreau family tragedy. I believe you will be captivated by Jesse's journey, the only Beaudreau daughter, as she fills in the holes of her history while learning to love as she pursues a shared enemy.

As a science fiction based series, you may find that you'll need some help with the terms. For that reason, I've created a Glossary that will be provided as bonus content in the printed book.

I would also like to mention my editors. These two amazing ladies, Ashleigh and AL, have been a godsend. They are the reason the story makes sense. Honestly, I'd have been lost without their direction, suggestions, and proofreading skills. Thank you ladies, from the bottom of my heart to the pages this book is printed on.

It's my hope that you will welcome my characters and embrace the adventure with an eagerness urging you to continue with Book Two, planned to launch at the end of 2024, and Book Three in Summer 2025.

And lastly, to check out my visuals for this book, be sure to visit my Instagram: @judyc_elementz_mj

AUTHOR'S BIO

J.A.M Cormier, professional photographer of 25 years, authors her debut novel, *The Guardians*. When she isn't writing, she currently spends her days in front of the computer retouching other photographer's images to perfection or outside in the city of Hamilton, Ontario where she lives, also known as the "City of Waterfalls."

Art is clearly in Cormier's blood, but writing is a brand new path she has begun travelling. After some much needed encouragement and help from a few friends, she has decided to delve into her Spicy Space Opera series, *The Terra Alliance*. J.A.M. Cormier is hoping her own journey of becoming an author is as fulfilling to her as it will be for her characters.

As the series evolves, you may enjoy bonus content accessible to those on my mailing list. To join, please email magicjudy2019@gmail.com with the Subject: Bonus Content. As a debut author, I am thrilled to put together my main ARC team! If you are interested in joining the ARC team, include that in your email for the Bonus Content, or if you would prefer to be an ARC reader only, please use the Subject: ARC.

Follow along on Instagram: @judyc_elementz_mj